PARA HANDY ALL AT SEA

Para Handy All At Sea

MORE CONTINUED VOYAGES OF THE VITAL SPARK

Chronicled with affection, acknowledgement and apology to Neil Munro
by

STUART DONALD

Neil Wilson Publishing Ltd • Glasgow • Scotland

First published in 1996 by Neil Wilson Publishing Ltd
303a The Pentagon Centre
36 Washington Street
GLASGOW
G3 8AZ
Tel: 0141-221 1117
Fax: 0141-221 5363

The moral right of the author has been asserted.
A catalogue record for this book is available from the British Library.
ISBN 1-897784-54-6

1 3 5 7 9 10 8 6 4 2

All photographs courtesy of Argyll and Bute Libraries.

Typeset in 11/12pt Caslon 224 Book by The Write Stuff, Glasgow.
Printed by The Cromwell Press, Melksham.

BY THE SAME AUTHOR

NON-FICTION
In the Wake of the Vital Spark, Johnston & Bacon Ltd (1994)
New edition published by Neil Wilson Publishing Ltd 1996
A topographical, historical and literary companion to
Para Handy and his world

FICTION
Para Handy Sails Again
First published by Neil Wilson Publishing Ltd 1995
Reprinted 1996

Dedication

For our next generation
ANDREW and SUSAN
with love

Doon the Watter for the Fair — *Rothesay Pier's turreted clock tower and arcaded pier buildings have long gone — but this is six minutes to three o'clock on an Edwardian summer's afternoon at the zenith of the popularity of the capital of Bute. The handsome paddler pulling away from the pier is the Glasgow and South Western Railway Company's* Glen Sannox, *only an occasional visitor to Rothesay for she was the mainstay of the Ardrossan to Brodick service. Still berthed ahead of her is another G&SWR vessel, the* Glen Rosa.

CONTENTS

	Introduction and Acknowledgments	ix
1	Pushing the Boat Out	1
2	The Umburella Men	9
3	A Naval Occasion	16
4	The Centenarian	23
5	High Teas on the High Seas	30
6	A Stranger in a Foreign Land	37
7	Cavalcade to Camelon	44
8	Scotch and Water	52
9	Many Happy Returns	60
10	Here be Monsters	67
11	The Tight White Collar	74
12	That Sinking Feeling	81
13	A Boatman's Holiday	89
14	Santa's Little Helpers	96
15	The Black Sheep	103
16	On His Majesty's Service	110
17	All the Fun of the Fair	117
18	Cafe Society	124
19	The Sound of Silence	132
20	Twixt Heaven and Hell	139
21	A Matter of Men and Machinery	146
22	May the Best Man Win	153
23	The Appliance of Science	161
24	The Gunpowder Plot	168
25	Nor any Drop to Drink	175
26	Para Handy's Ark	183
27	Follow My Leader	190
28	The Rickshaw and the Pram	198
29	Sublime Tobacco	206
30	Hurricane Jack, Entrepreneur	213

Introduction and Acknowledgements

When my first collection of 30 new Para Handy stories was published last year I confessed, in my introduction to it, that I realised that in 'borrowing' Neil Munro's marvellously-drawn characters I was tampering with a national institution and had only myself to blame if aficionados of the Vital Spark demanded my head on a platter. I went to some length to explain how and why I was taking that risk.

The only introduction I need to make on this occasion, and the greatest acknowledgement as well, is to place on record my debt to readers — and reviewers — for the generous reception which that first collection was accorded. *Para Handy Sails Again* had to be reprinted earlier this year, which encouraged me to write this second set of new stories — and my publisher to accept them! Indeed, we hope to offer a third collection in 1997.

I said in that first introduction that writing the stories had been great fun. It still is!

I just hope that Para Handy enthusiasts will derive as much pleasure from reading the tales as their author had in writing them.

My thanks, again, to Argyll and Bute Libraries for allowing me to use another selection of Victorian and Edwardian photographs from their priceless MacGrory archive collection. Far more effectively than words could ever do, they help to establish the atmosphere of Para Handy's times and places.

My greatest debt, as with the previous volume, is to Neil Munro himself, the originator of what I hold to be the most memorable cast of humorous characters ever created, whose appeal is both timeless and universal. I am just grateful for being allowed to borrow them.

Sandhaven, Argyll
July 1996

1

Pushing the Boat Out

The possession of a sturdy, seaworthy dinghy of one sort or another is an essential prerequisite on board a steam-lighter. There are occasions when the vessel must anchor off outlying communities where either there is no jetty at all, or else such facility as does exist is too small and in waters too shallow to allow the parent puffer to berth: thus if the crew are in need of provisions, or a refreshment, the puffer's dinghy is their sole means of communication with the shore.

I am sorry to have to place on record, though, that in the case of the *Vital Spark* the role of its dinghy is frequently a more nefarious one, for no other vessel in the coasting trade on the west coast has a more infamous reputation for the poaching activities of its crew.

Neither her Captain nor any of his shipmates have yet featured in the case-lists at any of the District or Sheriff Courts in the West Highlands, nor have their misdeeds been recounted in the columns of the *Oban Times*, *Campbeltown Courier* or *Argyllshire Standard*. But nobody who knows the *Vital Spark* can be under any misapprehension about the nature or purpose of the night-time excursions of her crew when salmon and sea-trout are running in the mouths of the Aray or the Shira, the Ruel or the Eachaig, or any other of a dozen rivers in reach of wherever the puffer happens to be lying overnight.

I previously recounted an earlier incident in which Para Handy was forced to abandon the puffer's dinghy to the water bailiffs in order to make his escape back to the ship and I am afraid that this was not an isolated occurrence. On two further occasions the Captain has had to make this ultimate sacrifice in order to preserve (at least in official quarters) his own reputation, and that of the *Vital Spark* as well.

While not exactly condoning the activity which has led to such avoiding action being required, I admit to a certain sneaking sympathy with the Captain, for surely there are more salmon in their waters than the Duke or the Marquess or the Earl and their households could ever consume, and many Scotsmen would regard their freedom to take a stag from the hill or a fish from the river as an inviolable, inherited right.

The whole subject was brought to mind again last month. I was in St Catherines, bound for Inveraray, having come through Cowal on the 'overland' route by way of Loch Eck, and had an hour to pass before the next posted passage of the sturdy skiff which provides a periodic ferry service across Loch Fyne to the Campbell capital from that village. A poster advertising a displenishing sale at an adjacent farm caught my eye and when I wandered into the yard where various items for auction were on display, I was surprised to encounter Para Handy himself.

"Boats," said that mariner in answer to my enquiry as to what he might have his eye on at the sale. "Chust boats. I am afraid we had a bit of a calamity last weekend at Loch Gair, and the shup iss withoot a dinghy again."

"Not *another* poaching debacle, Captain!" I exclaimed. "Surely you have learned your lesson on that score by now."

Para Handy winced.

"I do not like your lenguage, Mr Munro," he protested, "who said onything aboot poaching? We wass chust looking for a fush for our teas, ass iss the right of any man, when here and does the Asknish gamekeeper and his cronies no' come burstin' through the undergrowth and into the shallows, wi' torches and dugs and cheneral aggravation. There wass nothing else we could do but abandon shup so to speak for the dinghy iss a heavy boat and slow under the oars, and make the best of our way three miles over the hill to Loch Gilp, where we had left the vessel.

"This is the first opportunity that I have had since then to do something aboot replacing the lost boat."

There was a choice of two small craft lying in the yard — one a heavily built, broad-beamed, flat-bottomed rowing-boat of the traditional type, about 16 feet in length: the other was a very narrow, shallow, delicately-constructed skiff which gave every indication that she would be a very fast boat under oars, light and easily manoeuvrable.

"Not that I in any way approve your nefarious nocturnal doings you must understand, Captain," I said, pointing towards this craft, "but I would suggest that this is the boat for you. Look at the lines of her! I don't think any water bailiff would have much chance of catching you in a flier like that!"

Para Handy shook his head sadly.

"I am afraid she chust would not do, Mr Munro," said he. "You are quite right, of course, she would be chust the chob for the poachin', but I am afraid that we need a boat on the shup that can do more than chust make a getaway from the gamekeepers of Argyll.

"Blame the owner for that! If he wass using the shup the way she should be used, caairyin' excursionists or shootin' perties or nice clean cairgos like whusky or firkins o' butter aal the time, then it would be a dufferent matter. But wi' some of the terrible contracts he makes the shup work to, we need a dinghy that can carry a cairgo chust ass readily as it could carry a fushin' expedition.

"That iss a bonnie wee skiff, sure enough. But she would neffer do for the *Vital Spark*."

Ten minutes later, the two boats came up for sale. The skiff went for £4-10s to a sharp-faced man who announced his bids loudly and almost threateningly in the unmistakeable vernacular of the East End of Glasgow. ("A professional!" whispered Para Handy sadly, "That iss the kind of man who iss spoilin' aal the fushin's for us amateurs!") The stout dinghy was knocked down to the Captain for £2-12s, a price with which he seemed quite content.

Since the *Vital Spark* was berthed at Inveraray (from whence the Captain had come by the same ferry service which I had intended to take in reverse) he would of course row his new acquisition over and, in accepting his invitation to cross with him, I responded by inviting him to join me at the St Catherines Inn for a refreshment before we set off.

"What did you mean a few minutes ago," I asked as we carried our glasses to a corner table, "when you said the *Vital Spark* had to have a dinghy that was capable of carrying a cargo? I thought you were always able to beach or berth the puffer for loading or unloading?"

3

"It iss neffer loading that iss the problem," said Para Handy, "but there iss times — not many, you understand, but we have to be able to cope wi' aal emerchencies — there iss times when we have to unload the shup usin' the dinghy, and a right fouter it is too, ass well ass a beck-breakin' business."

And, lifting his dram, he gave me good health in the Gaelic and disposed of the contents in one gulp, optimistically shaking the empty glass upside-down over the tumbler of pale ale with which I had complemented its purchase, lest even one solitary drop of the precious golden liquid should be carelessly lost.

"What sort of cargos are those, then?" I prompted. "I mean the ones that give you the trouble of needing a big dinghy like the one you've just bought?"

"It iss not so much the cairgo ass its destination that iss the problem," replied Para Handy. "For instance, wance a year we have a contract to tak' the winter coals to a wheen o' the west coast lighthooses, and there are some of them that have no sort of a jetty at aal, nor any sandy ground where you can beach the shup, and that means that effery drop o' their coals hass to be manhandled ashore usin' the dinghy.

"That chob is a richt scunner, I can tell you. No problem at Oban, of course, where we load the coal wi' a sling: but the coal iss all bagged, no' loose like the way we usually cairry it, and at lighthooses like Eilean Musdile off the sooth end o' Lismore, or Rhudagan Gall on Mull, we have to lie off the rocks, load the secks into the dinghy wi' the winch, row her in to a convenient flet rock — and then unload effery demned seck one by one by hand.

"It iss a nightmare, for we are not funished even then, for the contract iss to deliver the coal to the keeper's hooses or to the light tower itself. Sometimes, if we are lucky, there iss a sort of a path up to the station and mebbe the keepers will have a barrow or a sort of a truck. But maist o' the time we chust have to carry the secks on our becks, one at a time.

"It's no way to be treatin' a fine shup like the *Vital Spark*, or her crew come to that. What I say iss, if the owner wants to do business o' that kind then he should have bought himself a coal gabbart for it in the furst place, no' a vessel that wass aalways meant for better things.

"It is demeanin' and a disgrace, and I am bleck-affrontit

that we have to do work like that. But we canna avoid it if we want to keep oor chobs, so I canna think to buy ony-thing other than a strong wee boat like the one I bought today."

The Captain cheered up considerably when he saw me signal to the barman for another gill of whisky.

"Could you not think to have another, smaller dinghy as well then," I suggested, "so that you have the best of both worlds with a boat for work and a boat for, er, the fishing too?"

"It would be an expense," said the Captain, "but I could make the second boat pay for itself, right enough" — I did not press Para Handy for more detail on this point — "but the problem iss there iss no space on deck. The shup is a fine, smert boat but she iss no' awful big, and what wi' the hetches and the steam winch and the capstans and the ven-tilators and aal, there chust would not be the room for two boats on board her."

"Well," I suggested, "have you considered one of these new folding boats. I understand they are..."

Para Handy nearly choked on his beer, and broke into a paroxysm of coughing from which I was only able to release him by dint of several hefty smacks on the back.

"Folding boats!" he declared with some vehemence once he was able to articulate again. "Do not speak to me aboot folding boats. They're nothin' but a snare and delusion for the unwary: if Dougie wass here he would tell you himself. Chust ask Wullie Jardine on the *Saxon*. The poor duvvle wass near drooned, thanks to one o' your precious folding boats, and it's purely thanks to it too that his name iss now on the Court records at Dunoon.

"Wullie had the same idea ass yourself, he went and bought one o' these new-fangled Berthon dinghies. She packed up flet, the sides kind of tucked in and there wass hinges on her keel and gunwales so that she folded up in half and back on herself like you wass closin' the blades of a scissors. The first moonless night — they were in the Holy Loch at the time — Wullie and his Mate opened her oot and put her together, slupped her ower the side o' the *Saxon*, took a wee bit o' a splash net wi' them, and off to the mooth of the Eachaig like hey-ma-nanny.

"Efferything wass going chust dandy at first, and Wullie had a half-a-dozen wee salmons in the boat in no time at aal, they belonged to nobody, they didna have ony labels on them, when suddenly there's a bellowin' from the bank chust below Ardbeg, and out shoots wan o' the Benmore Estate boats wi' Mr Younger's gamekeeper and a wheen o' his men.

"It wass a mile to where the *Saxon* was anchored off Kilmun pier but there wass several other puffers there and Wullie reckoned that if they could get a lead on the keeper's boat, then they could lose her in the derk and Mr Younger's men wouldna be able to tell which shup the poaching-perty had come from.

"So Wullie and his Mate fair threw themselves at the oars, and a good speed they made too, till efter aboot a half-a-mile or so there wass an awful crackin' sound like wud spluttin' in two and the boat chust folded up on itself in less than a second, the bows came oot the watter and the stern came oot at the same time and they snapped together in the air like the chaws o' a sherk, and trapped Wullie and his Mate inside the hull.

"It wass a mercy they didna droon! She toppled over, but then floated chust long enough for the keeper and his men to come alongside and open her up and take poor Wullie and his Mate oot, and then it wass off to the polis for them, and up to the Sheriff in the mornin'.

" 'I'm gled I didna droon, Peter,' Wullie said the next time I met him. 'And I kinda ken noo whit Jonah must have felt like yon time he wass in thon whale. But I think it wass a luberty o' the *Argyllshire Standard* to carry the story under the headline SKEDADDLING SKIPPER SCUTTLES SKIFF.

" 'It made me a laughing-stock on the river for weeks!' "

FACTNOTE

The puffers did indeed undertake contracts which involved their crews in some truly back-breaking labour, and the delivery of coal to the more isolated lighthouses was one of the most hated of these. I had a first-hand account of a Ross and Marshall puffer which supplied coal to the cliff and rock stations in and around Mull in the 1940s: even listening to the tale made the muscles ache at the mere thought of the physical hardships.

Folding or collapsible boats are no myth, either.

The 'Berthon' boats were possibly the best known of these. They were the invention of Edward Lyon Berthon, a

A New Lifeboat — The MacGrorys captured every detail of Campbeltown's 'great day' in the summer of 1912 when the town's first powered lifeboat the William Macpherson *was handed over. It is shown being manoeuvred out of the builder's (onshore) yard, carted through the streets of the town amidst a great throng of people, formally named down at the harbour, and then finally launched — as shown here — with considerable aplomb. I wonder who the lady was?*

man who deserves to be better known if only for the bizarre circumstances of his life and career. Born in 1813, he died in 1899 and in the years between charted, with mixed success, a strangely diverse and various voyage through life. He originally studied Medicine but in his mid-30s he returned to University to read Theology and served as a Curate in several Parishes in the South of England.

Throughout all these years however, invention, and specifically marine invention, seems to have been his great interest though it was pursued with scant success — and even less luck. For in 1835, and a full year before Pettit-Smith registered the first patent for a screw propellor for ships, Berthon submitted plans for just such a device to the British Admiralty — who rejected them.

His next invention, a nautical log, was also thrown out by the Admiralty. A trier, if nothing else, he then developed a design for a folding boat and this, too, was submitted to the powers-that-be in Whitehall. Once again (and with a regular monotony which hints at a lack of imagination somewhere within official circles) the Navy did not want to know — though in this case they did at least give a prototype a 'trial run'.

It says much for Mr Berthon's perseverance that he returned to the fray some years later and this time his improved design for a folding boat was accepted and endorsed by the Admiralty.

The boats which were finally manufactured were usually of small size and were popular for some years with yacht-owners, as when not in use they stowed more easily and occupied less space. But they could — and sometimes did — fold up on themselves without warning when in use!

More serious attempts to develop larger versions of what were now being intended as collapsible ship's lifeboats were made early this century: the Englehardt design was the best known. There were four boats of this type on the *Titanic* though only two were assembled in time to launch before the ship sank.

2

The Umburella Men

Para Handy pushed open the brightly-coloured stained-glass door of MacGrory's double-fronted drapery store on Campbeltown Main Street and shut it smartly behind him against the biting cold south-easterly March wind. In response to the tinkle from the bell set above the door, the curtain at the rear of the shop which led to the fitting rooms was swept aside, and one of the two brothers who owned the business appeared, a tape-measure round his neck and a pair of serrated cutting-scissors in his right hand.

"Ah, Captain MacFarlane," he said jovially when he saw who his customer was. " Pleased to see you as always. What may we do for you today?"

"No' much to be worth your trouble, Mr MacGrory," said Para Handy. "But I am after a new woollen comforter. I lost my auld wan overboard yestreen, what wi' the wund, and it no' properly tucked in, and it's a cauld spell o' weather to be withoot."

The draper pulled down a glass-fronted drawer from the wall of such drawers behind the counter and in a matter of moments Para Handy had selected a bright red scarf and wrapped it securely round his neck.

"There iss no need to be makin' a parcel of it. I will chust wear it straight aff", he said, and bringing a handful of coins from his pocket he paid for his purchase and moved towards the door.

"Before you go, Peter," called MacGrory, "could I ask a favour of you? I hear you're off to Glasgow tomorrow morning with a load of whisky and then straight back in a couple of days with a cargo of barley. Is that right?"

"Chust so," said the Captain.

"Well," said MacGrory. "It's like this…"

His tale was soon told.

Campbeltown, standing in splendid isolation at the foot of the Kintyre peninsula a hundred miles or so from Glasgow, has too small a population to make possible the provision within the town of all the services which modern life expects. Thus it is that the MacGrory brothers, though *purveyors* of umbrellas, are unable to offer a repair service for broken ribs or torn panels from their own resources.

Umbrellas brought in for repair are kept within the premises and then at regular intervals conveyed to Glasgow to the workshops of the reputed wholesale house of Messrs Campbell and MacDonald, courtesy of their representative Mr James Swan, when he visits Campbeltown on one of his regular journeys in the West. They are returned, once repaired, courtesy of that same gentleman, who sees this service as being the very least he can do for one of the most valued and valuable customers on his entire circuit.

"Mr Swan was here just three weeks ago, Peter, and took a stack of umbrellas to Glasgow with him. I've now had a telegram from Campbell and MacDonald to tell me they are repaired and ready for my customers, but Mr Swan has broke a leg wi' a fall on icy cobbles, and won't be back to Campbeltown for at least another month.

"I was wondering if you would be good enough to collect them for me when you're in Glasgow and fetch them back doon later this week…?"

~

The *Vital Spark* edged in to the private quay at the distiller's Partick bottling plant late the following afternoon and for the next three hours the puffer's steam-winch spluttered and coughed as the precious cargo of finest Campbeltown Malt Whisky was swung ashore under the watchful scrutiny of the plant's own security men, a pair of bleak-eyed Customs Officers — and Para Handy and his frustrated crew.

"Chust imagine," said the Captain with some rancour later the same evening as he grudgingly slapped his sixpence onto the bar counter at the nearby Auld Toll Vaults and picked up the glass containing his diminutive dram, "chust imagine here and we've been and delivered enough whusky to keep the whole o' Partick in drams for a twelve-month and we are expected to pay for chust the wan wee taste o' the cratur.

"There's nae justice at aal in this world."

Dougie, Sunny Jim and MacPhail could only shake their heads sadly in silent, sympathetic agreement.

~

Next morning the puffer made the short crossing over to the southern shores of the river and tied up at the jetty serving a Govan grain-merchant's yard. Once the loading process was under way with MacPhail on the winch, and Sunny Jim — and a couple of the merchant's warehouse-men — ready to stack the sacks as they came juddering down into the hold in netting bags, Captain and Mate headed ashore.

"Dougie and I will away into the town and collect Mr MacGrory's umburellas, boys," said Para Handy as he scrambled up the iron ladder bolted to the quayside: "and we'll see that you have a share of the bottle the man has promised us for the favour."

And the two set out to walk to Govan Cross Subway Station from whence one of the much-admired new underground trains would whisk them, in just a matter of minutes, to St Enoch Square and the warehouse of Messrs Campbell and MacDonald.

They had only walked a couple of hundred yards, however, when there was a sudden flash of lightning followed by a crashing peal of thunder, and in a matter of seconds raindrops the size of pan-drops were bouncing violently off the cobbled street. In even fewer seconds Captain and Mate instinctively searched for, identified, and raced towards, the nearest public house.

"My Chove, Dougie," said the Captain as they supped a glass of pale ale in the snug bar. "That iss some cloudburst to be sure. We will chust sit here and let it aal roll by before we go any further. Indeed we could be doing with having Mr McGrory's umburellas with us right now, for here we are without so much ass a coat or a kep between us."

However, the rainstorm showed no sign of moving on. An hour later it was as heavy as ever, and Para Handy pulled his watch out to check the time.

"The boys will be wondering what has become of us,

Dougie," he said. "We should have been there and back before this and I do not want them to be thinking we iss malingering on them or that we have maybe bumped into Hurricane Jeck and gone off on a spree and forgotten them. I am thinking we must chust face the rain and make a dash for it to Govan Cross. What do you think yourself, Dougie?"

For answer, Dougie tugged on Para Handy's sleeve and pointed surreptitiously in the direction of the outer door of the snug bar. Beside it, there stood a battered umbrella-stand which had seen better days. Resting within it, however, was one solitary umbrella — shinily new, neatly rolled up, and quite bone-dry. A quick glance round the other occupants of the bar revealed nobody who looked even remotely like the possible owner of such a fine and expensive accoutrement.

"Some toff must have set it there and forgotten aboot it days ago, Peter," whispered the Mate. "For sure and it has not been out in the rain today. Aal I am suggesting is that we *borrow* it. We wull can put it back on our way back to the shup..."

Para Handy again looked round the company. Nobody was looking in their direction. The other occupants were variously grouped in animated conversation. The Landlord had his back to them as he reached up to a high shelf for a bottle of port.

As the two sailors reached the door Para Handy casually reached across and quickly — too quickly — tried to scoop the umbrella out of the stand. It was bad enough that it rattled on the side of the stand: much worse that it caught on it, tipped it over, and sent it crashing to the floor.

"Hoy! You pair! Where the blazes d'ye think ye're aff to wi' my best brolly?"

Para Handy, the umbrella clutched guiltily in his hand, turned to see the Landlord leaning halfway across the mahogany counter of the bar, gesticulating furiously with the bottle of port and being restrained with some difficulty (by two of his customers) from hurling it in the Captain's direction.

"My mistake, my mistake," gabbled Para Handy. "I thought it wass my own umburella, for it iss the very spit of it, but you are right, I completely forgot that I left mine on the shup."

"A likely story," howled the Landlord. "Thieves! That's whit ye are! And me wi' a funeral to go to up in toon this afternoon. A richt clown I'd ha'e looked wi'oot my brolly! Get oot, the pair o' ye. And never let me see either wan o' ye in this pub ever again. This is an honest hoose!"

∼

It was a shamefaced pair who, all thoughts of the promise to the MacGrory emporium temporarily forgotten, scuttled through the teeming rain to the nearby quayside — and the comparative haven of the *Vital Spark*.

"We will wait on board, Dougie," said Para Handy, "and go up to the toon when the rain is past."

It was almost four o'clock before the downpour finally fizzled out as suddenly as it had begun, and the chastened mariners headed again for the Govan Cross Subway. This time they reached it without incident.

Less than half-an-hour later they emerged from Campbell and MacDonald's capacious St Enoch's Square premises, each of them clutching, with both arms in front of their chests, the awkward burden of a substantial bundle of umbrellas of every size and description, ladies' and gentlemen's alike, secured with a couple of rope ties.

At the ticket office Para Handy fumbled in his pocket with some difficulty to extract the coppers for their fares, and the two clattered down the stone steps onto the subway platform.

In a minute or so the two bright red carriages of the train came looming out of the tunnel mouth and into the station with a distinctive whoosh of disturbed air — and an unmistakable but indescribable, warm smell: an aroma of mystery and of quite unfathomable depths which — when once first encountered — would never be forgotten by succeeding generations of patrons of the Glasgow Underground.

Para Handy and Dougie took their seats on one of the slatted wooden banquettes which ran down each side of the carriage.

Opposite them, someone was hidden behind an opened copy of the Evening Times and Para Handy leaned forward curiously to read the day's headlines.

As he did so, the paper was lowered — and the Captain found himself looking into the eyes of the Landlord of the Govan pub, dressed now in a dark suit, wearing a black tie, a mourning band on his arm, and with his rolled-up umbrella across his knees. The two men stared at each other for some moments in silence. Finally the Landlord, having glanced several times in bewildered disbelief from the strangely-assorted bundle on Para Handy's knee to that on Dougie's and back again, leaned forward and said with heavy sarcasm and in a penetrating stage-whisper:

"Well, I'm glad to see that you've had a good day..."

FACTNOTE

The MacGrory Brothers, as well as owning Campbeltown's leading drapers at the turn of the century, were enthusiastic amateur photographers and the illustrations in this book are taken from the substantial archive of their original glass plate negatives which is now in the safe hands of Argyll and Bute Libraries.

Campbeltown was probably the most prosperous community on the outer edges of the Firth at the time, and certainly one which had founded its wealth on industry rather than tourism.

As well as a substantial fishing fleet, with its ancillary boat building yards, net and rope factories and — of course — curing stations, the town had a rich agricultural hinterland. Within the burgh there were more than twenty whisky distilleries and other industrial activity included coal-mining, salt-pans, shipyards, cooperages and shipping companies.

Glasgow's underground railway is a 6-mile circular route with clockwise and anti-clockwise tracks sharing a common, central platform at each of 15 stations. The line twice passes under the Clyde, linking the city centre north and south. First cable-driven, it opened in 1896: and ran virtually unchanged for 80 years, though it was electrified in the mid-1930s. Some of the original rolling stock was still in use when the system closed down in 1977 for a three-year modernisation programme from which it emerged with the scarlet Victorian passenger carriages replaced by equipment of a gaudier hue, which quickly earned the facility its new sobriquet of *The Clockwork Orange*.

Known to generations of commuters as the Subway (never the Underground — London terminology eschewed by Glaswegians) there have been proposals down the years for extending the network but these have come to nothing. The simple circle has served efficiently, effectively and economically as a mover of people for exactly one hundred years.

The old Subway did indeed have an odoriferous atmosphere all its own, lost for ever in the process of modernisation. Warm, damp, musty, primeval (yet not unpleasant) it was pushed in front of the carriages as they threaded the dark tunnels: spilt out into the stations as the trains arrived: and percolated up the escalators to the streets above. Nobody knew what caused or created it but it was unique to the Glasgow system — and sadly missed by those who remember it with affectionate nostalgia.

Devotees of Neil Munro's tales of the adventures of 'Jimmy Swan the Joy Traveller' will recognise in this episode the shadowy figures both of Mr Swan himself, and of the Glasgow Wholesale House whose kenspeckle representative he so successfully was.

RING A RING OF ROSES — One of the most appealing features of the MacGrory archive is that so many of its pictures are natural and spontaneous though most other surviving photographs of the age were carefully and predictably posed. This lively picture of schoolgirls at play is a delight and, given the ponderous equipment and the slow shutter-speeds of the time, a remarkably crisp action shot.

3

A Naval Occasion

The puffer had spent the last two days at Salen, on the island of Mull, unloading the mixed parapher-nalia of a farm flitting and was now bound for Oban where a cargo of whisky in cask from one of the local distilleries awaited her on the town's North Pier, scheduled for delivery to a blending and bottling plant in Dumbarton.

It was ten o'clock on a glorious July morning as the *Vital Spark* passed out of the Sound of Mull, leaving Duart Castle on the starboard beam, and the panorama of the Lynn of Lorne and the sheltered stretch of water between the islands of Lismore and Kerrera came into view.

At least a dozen navy vessels ranging in size from dread-noughts to torpedo-boat destroyers were at anchor outside Oban harbour to the west of Ganavan Bay. Furthest from the shore, towering over the other ships of the flotilla, lay the giant dreadnought battleship *Bellerophon* and inshore from her a scattering of smaller vessels including the ven-erable cruisers *Theseus* and *Grafton*, several light cruisers, and two modern destroyers, the *Cossack* and the four-fun-nelled *Teviot*.

Para Handy, at the wheel, guided the puffer to pass as closely as commonsense dictated beneath the soaring grey bows of the *Bellerophon* and gazed admiringly at her tow-ering upperworks and huge twelve-inch guns.

"Brutain's hardy sons," he said with some emotion, watching the ratings drilling on the quarterdeck as the *Vital Spark* crawled the length of the battleship's hull.

The squadron, part of Britain's Atlantic fleet, was in Scottish waters on an inshore training excercise and had anchored just a matter of three hours previously, having entered the Firth of Lorne after negotiating the sound between the Torran Rocks off the south-west corner of Mull, and the island of Colonsay.

The signal halyards were busy as the fleet exchanged messages and instructions, and a number of cutters and motor launches manned by immaculate ratings sped between ships carrying men and materials.

Very conscious of the uncomfortable contrast between his own command and the naval elegance so openly on display, Para Handy rounded the northernmost point of Kerrera with — almost — some sense of relief and some recognition of the shortcomings of his beloved *Vital Spark*. Even here, though, he could not escape the presence of naval supremacy for one ship had been deployed into Oban Bay itself and was now the centre of attraction for the summer holiday crowds thronging the esplanades and the piers of the popular summer resort.

Moored some 300 yards off-shore and approximately equi-distant from the South and North Steamer Piers was the cruiser *Shannon*, the equal of the *Bellerophon* in overall length though not, of course, in bulk or armament. Ratings were swarming over her decks erecting white sun-awnings, and a mahogany companionway ladder was being deployed from the midships entry port on her starboard side (facing the South Pier) onto a floating pontoon against which two motor pinnaces were tied up. On the port side of the cruiser a more modest Jacob's Ladder hung from the rails of the quarter-deck.

The *Vital Spark* bumped gently against the timber uprights of the cargo berth on the North Pier and Sunny Jim leapt ashore with the bight of the bow mooring rope in his hand.

Ten minutes later, with the puffer safely secured and the crew now perched up on her main hatch watching the passing show as a veritable fleet of dinghies and small yachts circled the anchored cruiser, Para Handy presented himself at the dingy dockside office — little more, in truth, than a small wooden hut — of his owner's local agent.

"I'm afraid I have to tell you that your cargo is still up at the distillery, Captain," said that worthy, somewhat shame-faced and flustered. "What with the fleet coming in and all, the town has declared an unoffical holiday and there is just no way that I can get even one carter today, never mind a squad.

"Why don't you just regard it as a holiday for yourselves

and take the day off? I can promise you a top-notch team to fetch your cargo at first light tomorrow."

~

"Well, at least we couldna get a better day for it," conceded the Captain as he, Dougie and Macphail settled down on a bench outside the Lorne Arms with a glass of ale apiece. Sunny Jim had gone to take a stroll about the town, no doubt — as his somewhat envious older colleagues correctly surmised — to see what young ladies in their summer finery had been attracted onto the Oban esplanade by the fine weather and by the occasion.

"Better day for what?" snapped Macphail ill-temperedly. "Better day for drummin' wir heels in this back-o'-beyond towerist trap for near enough twenty fower hours? Ah can think of mony places Ah'd raither be and mony things Ah'd raither be daeing."

Para Handy shrugged but maintained diplomatic silence while Dougie went off in search of one of the Bar's sets of dominos in the hope that a test of skill and chance at a half-penny each game might help to pass the time in a pleasanter atmosphere.

Macphail, however, was in no frame of mind to be fobbed off with such an inadequate palliative as a game of 'the bones', as he disparagingly described it, and tensions were again mounting when Sunny Jim rejoined the party, just before one o'clock, and in a state of some excitement.

"Ah've been roond on the Sooth Pier," he announced breathlessly and without preamble, "and it's fair hotching wi' folk. The Navy's openin' the shup to the public-at-large this afternoon and layin' on twa pinnaces to tak' them oot and back."

"Bully for the Navy," said Macphail caustically. "What's that tae us?"

"Simple," said Jim. "There's money to be made on it."

The recollection of some of Sunny Jim's previous money-making schemes, from the successful but nearly catastrophic affair of the Tobermory Whale to the totally unrewarding scam involving a purported marathon swim the length of Kilbrannan Sound, lurched uncomfortably through the memories of his audience.

Para Handy was the first to recover his composure.

"How?" he asked bluntly.

"Easy!" said Jim. "The pinnaces is runnin' to the shup from the Sooth Pier only. There's nothin' to prevent us takin' oot a hired rowing-boat for the afternoon and ferryin' the towerists oot to the shup from the *North* Pier at saxpence a time, and landin' them onto the Jacob's Ladder on the port side where the Officers and that'll no' see them, for they'll be too busy on the starboard helpin' the young lasses aboard and then tryin' to tempt them wi' the offer of a tour of the shup's engines."

There was a moment's silence, until:

"Capital, Jum, capital!" cried Para Handy. "You aalways have the eye for a bit of business wheneffer the opportunity arises and you have excelled yourself this time. The towerists from the North Esplanade hotels will be chust delighted that they do not have to walk aal the way to the Sooth Pier, and how are they to know that the service there iss for free?"

Even Macphail was grudgingly, cautiously welcoming of the idea and it was Dougie who spotted a possible flaw in the management of the operation.

"There iss chust wan wee thing," he pointed out. "How are we to bring them back again? It's one thing to slup them on board on the quiet side of the shup but another thing entirely if they start queueing at the head of the ladder and looking for us."

That had not been thought of, and for some time the four sat wordlessly, exploring the possibilities of overcoming what now seemed an intransigent problem.

"Got it!" Sunny Jim cried excitedly after some minutes. "We jist dinna tak' them back at all! We tell them it's a roond trup and they're to go back to the Sooth Pier in the pinnaces.

"Once they're on board, we can forget all aboot them. They're no' oor problem then, they're someone else's. The Navy's, and they'll jist huv tae tak' care of it."

~

The afternoon, even by the most exacting standards, could only be judged an outstanding financial success.

Such was the popularity of the passage by rowing-boat from the North Pier that the crew — who had intended to take it in turns to row as pairs (Para Handy teamed with Sunny Jim, Dougie with Macphail) — found themselves forced to hire a second boat from McGrouther's slip, and provide a non-stop shuttle service to the unsuspecting *Shannon* for more than two solid hours.

Sunny Jim's surmise — that the Officers and crew would be much too busy appraising the young ladies attracted to the *official* point-of-entry on the starboard side — proved to be perfectly accurate and the crew of the *Vital Spark* landed their own contraband consignments throughout the afternoon without any trouble whatsoever.

By half-past-four the crowd on the North Pier had thinned to an unrewarding trickle and, in any case, the crew by that time were exhausted by their unbroken exertions in the heat of the day. Sending the last handful of their prospective passengers, some of them protesting querulously, to walk their way to the South Pier, Para Handy and his crew returned their hired boats and settled with their owner.

After meeting all expenses (which had had to include recruiting a local youth to marshal the queues on the Pier while the boats were on the water) a substantial surplus remained. Sunny Jim was despatched to the nearest butcher's shop to buy steaks: the Mate went in search of a green-grocer's from which he returned burdened with punnets of wild mushrooms and fresh strawberries: Macphail staggered back from the Argyll Arms bearing two very large canisters of ale: and Para Handy negotiated a 'favoured friend' price for two bottles of finest malt whisky from the Manager of the distillery whose wares they were to load the next morning.

As the sun sank slowly towards the mountain ridges of Mull the crew sprawled across the main hatch in the cooler, evening glow and sighed with satisfaction. They had been fed and watered in such luxury as could, all too easily, have become a habit — but for the fact that the opportunity of raising the cash to fund such an epicurean existence came their way but once in a blue moon.

Para Handy lit his pipe (a fresh supply of finest tobacco had also been a part of their shopping-list) and surveyed the world about him with the greatest contentment. He had no quarrels to make with anyone. Not even Macphail.

~

Aboard the *Shannon*, the wardroom was hazy with cigar-smoke as her officers relaxed with coffee and brandy after a sumptuous dinner which for them was more or less a matter of routine.

Her captain, however, had one lingering doubt as he leaned back in his chair at the head of the long, highly-polished table and studied his fingernails with a puzzled frown.

"All involved in today's operation deserve our congratulations and thanks," he said at length: "and I will ensure that the men enjoy some well-earned shore leave tomorrow.

"There is, though, just one thing that puzzles me greatly and I wonder if any of you can shed any light on it.

"Why is it, I ask myself, that the head-counts taken by the officers on the pinnaces show — beyond all doubt — that while we landed exactly 317 visitors onto the *ship*, we then managed to return no fewer than 453 to the *shore*?

"Has anyone any idea how this could happen?"

FACTNOTE

Ships of the Royal Navy were indeed frequent visitors to Oban and to the waters of the west coast in the early years of this century and of course the numerical strength of that Edwardian Navy was measured in the hundreds. Nowadays in all probability the entire British fleet could be very comfortably accommodated within the area of the Firth of Lorne — and with room to spare.

Para Handy and his crew were going about their business in and around the Clyde at the time of what was probably the greatest period of change in naval history. The turbine engine, first tested in a Clyde steamer, was but a part of that revolution.

Underwater the submarine was coming into its own as a practical and very lethal piece of military machinery. Indeed there were arguments about the very ethics of deploying such an invisible aggressor possessed of such a deadly strike-rate, and against which current defensive and offensive strategy by surface ships was virtually impotent.

Surface strategy itself had been revolutionised by Britain's development of the Dreadnought class of battleship. These ships were not necessarily any larger in their dimensions than their predecessors had been: but their armaments and construction heralded and belonged to a new generation of naval technology.

First of them all was the eponymous *Dreadnought*, which came into service in February 1906. She was swiftly followed by more vessels of the new specifications so that at the outbreak of the First World War the British Navy had

RULING THE WAVES — Here is one of the nine 15,000 ton, 400ft battleships of the Majestic class (it is not possible to identify precisely which one) at anchor in Campbeltown Loch. They were completed between December 1894 and November 1896 which says something both about the naval finances and the shipyard capacity of the age: but by the time this picture was taken they had been outgunned and outperformed by the new Dreadnought class.

more than twenty ships of this category in service. The *Bellerophon* was one of these, launched from the Admiralty's Portsmouth yard in 1907 but engined and boilered from the Clyde by Fairfield and Babcock respectively.

The four-funnelled cruiser *Shannon*, which came into service in March 1908, was of almost identical *size* to the dreadnoughts of the *Bellerophon* class, but of a much lighter construction and with a much less potent ordnance. With a top speed of 23 knots she was one of three sisters which were designed to post a significant improvement over their immediate predecessors — the four vessels of the *Warrior* class commissioned in 1905.

Sadly, despite their enhanced design speed they never delivered what they promised and were therefore generally regarded as something of a disappointment on most counts in comparison to the *Warrior* and her kin.

This class was among the last to be built for the British Navy with a distinctive and steeply-angled ramming prow.

4

The Centenarian

On this occasion there was no doubt. The mishap could not in any way have been perpetrated or contributed to by the *Vital Spark*, her Captain or her crew. The puffer, as she had every right to be, lay moored alongside the Albert Harbour basin in Greenock. Para Handy and his crew were sound asleep in their bunks, having had an early night and retired to rest before midnight. First thing next morning they were due to begin loading the cargo of bricks (consigned to a Rothesay builder) which awaited them on the quayside.

The night was cloudy, but calm: and the clock on Greenock Town Hall had not long struck two when a small coaster began to pick her way with hesitant manoeuvres through the narrow entrance to the Harbour. The *Glen Affric* was heavily-laden with slates from the Eisdale Island quarries, and she was very late in arriving at her destination. From the moment she left the Crinan Canal she had suffered intermittent engine-failure and her passage down Loch Fyne, through the Kyles, and up-river to Greenock had been erratic, spasmodic and painfully slow. Her long-suffering crew were irritable, irritated — and very tired.

That, probably, was what caused the accident. But for whatever reason the coaster, as she swung into the basin with plenty of space for her length to be comfortably accommodated immediately for'ard of the *Vital Spark*, failed to nudge her way into that waiting berth but, instead, cannoned fiercely against the hull of the puffer with a crunching noise and a reverberating shock which echoed through its stubby hull and awakened instantly all the sleepers in the fo'c'sle.

Para Handy was the first to scramble into trousers and guernsey and stumble bleary-eyed onto the deck to see what had happened.

The bulk of the coaster loomed large across the puffer's bow and her navigation lights cast a faint illumination upon the scene. From her bridge at the stern came sounds of angry altercation, abuse and accusation, and finally a gruff voice which commanded that 'Wullie' should get ready to leap for the quay with the bow rope readied to moor her, while 'Callum' was ordered ashore to see if there was any immediately apparent damage done to the coaster, or to whichever vessel it was that she had struck.

Ten minutes later the crews of both vessels had made as full an inspection as circumstances — and the darkness — would allow and at that point had found nothing obviously amiss. It was then agreed by the two skippers that no further progress could be made that night, and that a detailed and more searching examination would be made at first light.

All concerned then retired to their bunks, and peace fell again across the Albert Harbour.

Next morning Para Handy and the Mate opened the main-hatch to inspect the puffer's empty hold, and found more than a foot of water in it.

"Bless me!" said the Captain. "I certainly thought that that was one terrible dunt we took last night, and sure enough, here and we have gone and sprung a plate, by the look of her, chust see the watter that she's takin' in! A plate gone, I am sure"

This was also the diagnosis of the diver employed by the owner of the *Vital Spark* (as soon as he was advised by telegraph of the events of the previous night) to carry out a thorough underwater examination of her hull.

By lunchtime the owner himself was at the quayside and — while the lawyer he had brought with him from Glasgow went off with a bulging briefcase and a grim expression to open the preliminary parley with the skipper of the *Glen Affric* — he took Para Handy up to the nearest chop-house.

"You have nothing to reproach yourself with, Peter" he said firmly, to the Captain's considerable relief, "and the pump is coping with the leak. But she will have to go into dry-dock for repair before you can think of sailing. Now, I cannot get her a berth anywhere in Greenock: the nearest available space is at Ferguson's Graving-Dock in Port

Glasgow, but you'll be able to sail her there with no problems, just keep the pump running and don't be tempted to look for too much speed from her and you will be all right. What I must ask you to do is stay aboard to keep an eye on operations but the crew can take some leave if they want it: this job is going to take a week at the least."

And, pushing away his plate of lamb cutlets, reduced now to but a collection of well-picked bones, he signalled to one of the pot-men to replenish their tankards of beer.

~

Para Handy and Macphail brought the *Vital Spark* up-river to the Port Glasgow Yard of the Ferguson Brothers later that same afternoon, having seen Dougie and Sunny Jim safely aboard a Glasgow train and off on an unexpected (and, it must be said, unpaid) week of leave.

"There surely iss no point in keeping the boys, Dan," he had suggested to the Engineer with some apprehension, lest that worthy had thrown a tirravee at the very idea of being delayed in harness while others holidayed. "I need an enchineer, but it only takes the one man on deck to run her to Port Gleska."

Dwarfed by the mighty ocean vessels under construction in the Greenock and Port Glasgow Yards as she hugged the shore on her way upstream, the puffer finally reached Ferguson's, the last yard on that stretch of the Renfrewshire coast of the river between Port Glasgow and the Cart at Paisley.

The graving-dock had been excavated on the open fore-shore beyond the high brick walls of the yard, to the east-wards of and parallel to the builder's construction slips, and it was entered by way of a lock gate very similar to those with which Para Handy was familiar on the canals. Guided by one of the yard's foremen, and with three of his men operating the gates, the puffer was directed into the dry-dock and, as the water was drained off, settled onto the massive blocks on its floor.

Macphail, once he had damped down the fire, came up on the deck wiping his hands on a piece of rag and stared about him in some awe. The dry-dock had been designed to accommodate the largest cargo-vessels using the Clyde and the *Vital Spark* lay within it as insignificant as a child's toy boat. From the dock floor the surrounding walls soared above them, cranes to either hand soaring even higher. A flight of concrete steps was let into the walls to right and left and down one of these came a gang of men, two carrying a long wooden ladder which they propped up against the hull of the puffer so that the Captain and Engineer could disembark.

As the docks squad swarmed round the *Vital Spark* and began to construct a scaffolding frame around her hull, Para Handy and Macphail climbed the stairway and headed for the town centre.

Port Glasgow was in festive mood. Everywhere bunting was draped across the streets and flags and banners hung from windows. The sound of a distant brass band could be heard even above the din of the riveters' hammers and the screech of a passing tram.

Para Handy and Macphail made their way to the railway station where the Engineer established the time of the next train to Glasgow and bought a single ticket. With half-an-hour to pass the pair went into the bar of the Station Hotel.

"The toon is fairly hotchin' today," Macphail observed to the barman as he ordered two beers. "Whit's up? Is't a wedding?"

"Naw", replied the barman, "it's jist pairt o' the celebrations for the *Comet* — the auld shup, ye ken, it is just exactly wan hundred years since she wis launched at Woods's yerd and the Cooncil is havin' all sorts of hootenannies to mark the occasion. This is party-time at the Port. I hear there's even to be a replica o' the shup herself arriving on the river tomorrow!"

∼

"Well," said Macphail as he boarded his train and leaned out of the carriage window to take farewell of Para Handy, "at least ye'll no' want for company or cheer by the look o' Port Glesga, but Ah'm vexed ye have to be watchman on your own shup!"

"No problem at aal," said the Captain: "there iss plenty I can do to pass my time. She could be doing do with a lick or two of paint for a stert."

And on his way back to the ship. after waving the Engineer's train out of the station, Para Handy called into a conveniently placed ship chandler's and bought a tin of black paint, a tin of white paint, and two brushes. That evening, after the dockyard squad had packed up for the day and gone home, he climbed onto the planked scaffolding surrounding the ship and began to apply a fresh coat of black paint to her bulwarks.

That job of refurbishment took longer than expected as it had to be abandoned during working hours, when the dockyard gang was busy about the puffer, and therefore it was the following evening before it was finished. At seven o'clock Para Handy put the paint and brush away and climbed the dock stairway, heading towards town for a deserved refreshment. At the top of the stairs he paused to look down on his handywork, admiring with some satisfaction the gleaming band of black which encircled the hull. Tomorrow he would use the white paint to restore the puffer's name at bow and stern, which had of necessity been overpainted as he applied the fresh coats of black and then — if there was time — he promised himself that he would give her just a touch of gold beading to set her off to perfection.

～

Half-an-hour in the Clune Bar was more than enough for the Captain. The saloon was crowded and noisy, and the talk was of nothing but the *Comet* celebrations, and the expected arrival of the replica, which was discussed at considerable length with excited anticipation.

As the Captain made his way back to the foreshore in the bright evening sunshine he was aware of greater-than-expected numbers on the street ahead of him, and of a constant stream of people hurrying past in the direction of the river.

There was an air of excitement about, and he caught frequent references to the *Comet* and cries of "She's here!" and "She's arrived!" and "Come on, let's have a look at her!"

He was quite astonished to find, as he came round the corner of the high brick wall surrounding the shipyard and within sight of the graving-dock in which the puffer was lying, to see a huge crowd lining it on all sides, men, women and children leaning over the parapet and pointing excitedly into the depths of the dock.

"My Chove," he said to himself, "they must have put the *Comet* in beside the shup! I wonder chust what she looks like? Well, her crew will be company for me." And he quickened his steps.

There were complaints as he pushed his way through the press of people but when he protested indignantly: "My shup iss in there, you must let me through!" a respectful hush fell on the assembled crowd and they drew back to leave a passage for him.

Para Handy reached the parapet and leaned over in anticipation, eager to see this fabled replica of the world's first successful steamship.

There was nothing in the dry dock — nothing except the *Vital Spark*. Not of course that anyone else would have known that that was her name — not since her Captain had overpainted it with gleaming black.

Para Handy was dimly aware of the cries and questions from the crowds around him.

"My Lord, imagine anyone having the courage to sail in *that!*"

"Where's her nameboard?"

"They're probably fitting it in the morning."

"She's even smaller than I would have believed!"

"Did you ever see anything like that in your life! It's come straight out of the Ark!"

Drawing himself up with dignity, Para Handy paused at the top of the stairway leading down to the dock-floor.

"Ye're a bunch of ignorant gowks," he shouted, "that issna able to recognise wan o' the finest examples o' modern shup-building on the whole river! And when the *Vital Spark* celebrates *her* centenary, you'll no' need to build a replica to celebrate. She will still be aroond herself."

And with his back ramrod-straight and his chest puffed out with determined pride, he made his way down the stairway and clambered aboard the smartest vessel in the coasting trade.

Factnote

The incident in the Albert Harbour was suggested by the more serious accident which befell the three-man estuary puffer *Craigielea* in 1952. She was side-swiped in the hours of darkness by an incoming, heavily-laden coaster and was in fact sunk (though later refloated). Fortunately, her crew were all asleep at home in Greenock.

Henry Bell's *Comet* was the first succesful attempt to

provide a regular passenger service by steamer in Europe and, like so many other great Scottish 'firsts' it came about in spite of and not because of the attitudes of the Government and established commercial interests of the day. Bell had been an apprentice in a shipyard on the Forth, worked in a London engineering workshop, and studied both theory and practice when he tried, in the early years of the 19th century, to obtain government backing for experimental work to develop the application of practical steam-power to shipping.

The government was totally uninterested. Bell moved on to other things, and ten years later was owner of a large and prosperous hotel business in Helensburgh. The difficulties he experienced in finding comfortable and reliable transportation from Glasgow for his customers provided the incentive for a return to his earlier experimentation with steam. The result was the *Comet*. Bell designed not just her hull, but her engine as well. She was 50ft overall, with a 4 h.p. engine driving two tiny paddle wheels on either side of the hull and steering was by tiller.

This very first of the 'Clyde Steamers' had a top speed of just 5 knots — reduced to almost nothing against wind or tide. She offered accommodation in two classes — 'Best Cabin' at 4/- and Second at 3/-. These were astonishingly high fares at that time and there was indeed a small cabin for passengers paying the higher fare, shoe-horned in astern of the engines. The tiny vessel was built at the Port Glasgow yard of John Wood, and launched in July 1812. She gave eight years of generally reliable service before being stranded at Crinan in mid-winter 1820. Just what she was doing up there I do not know. The boat was broken up but her engine was rescued and today sits in the South Kensington Science Museum. Why *there* instead of Glasgow's superb Transport Museum I do not know either.

I have cheated shamelessly over the question of the replica for although one *was* built (by Lithgows Port Glasgow) for the 150th anniversary of 1962, the only manifestation of the little ship which was featured in the otherwise lavish and extensive centenary celebrations in 1912 was the 'conversion' into the *Comet* of one of the town's electric trams, which ran as an illuminated replica.

5

High Teas on the High Seas

Macphail squeezed into his place at the apex of the triangular table in the forepeak of the fo'c'sle and studied with quite unconcealed disgust the plate which had just been placed before him.

On it a couple of rashers of half-raw streaky bacon sat in a pool of fat next to three black, smoking objects which could with some difficulty be identified as sausages. At the side of the plate two eggs demonstrated their cook's ability to achieve what most would have deemed impossible: the yolks were startlingly hued in a bilious green and of the consistency of an india-rubber, while the whites were transparent, glutinous and virtually uncooked save for their ragged edges which were charred to an intense black.

With a heavy sigh, the Engineer slowly raised his face from its contemplation of this culinary feast and, with a shake of the head and a prolonged sigh, stared with narrowed and unfriendly eyes at its perpetrator.

The Mate — for he it was — shuffled uncomfortably and avoided the Engineer's steely stare.

"I'm sorry, Dan," he said apologetically: "I chust havna got the knack of the stove yet, it's aalways either too hot or too cold wi' me: but I wull can only get better."

"Which is mair than I can say is likely for ony of the rest of us," said the Engineer unfeelingly. "Whaur the bleezes did *you* learn tae haundle a frying-pan? The try-hoose on a whaler?"

"Now, Dan," said Para Handy in a placatory tone, "Poor Dougie iss makin' the best chob of it he canm in the conditions, for he signed on ass the Mate of the vessel remember,

30

no' as its heid cook and bottle-washer. He iss chust ass much a victim of the circumstances ass we are."

~

The circumstances, in a nutshell, were that the *Vital Spark*'s cheerful resident *chef de cuisine*, Sunny Jim, had taken a few days leave of absence to attend a wedding in Kirkcudbright — "a notorious toon for jollification and high-jinks," he had warned Para Handy: "no weddin' ever lasts less than three days there so Ah'm likely to be gone a week." Para Handy's dismay at this pronouncement was only slightly mollified when Jim added that he had arranged, as replacement, that his cousin Colin Turner, the Tar (he of mixed memory for the crew of the puffer) would officiate as relief deckhand and cook during the week of his absence.

Given the Tar's past reputation, it was perhaps not altogether surprising (though nonetheless annoying) that, on the morning of the vessel's scheduled departure from Bowling, he simply failed to appear as promised.

"Whit else wud ye expect frae Colin Turner?" was Macphail's unsurprised comment: but the patient Captain gave the missing crewman the benefit of the doubt until early afternoon before he accepted that the Tar just was not going to turn up, and gave orders for the puffer to slip her moorings and set off for her destination which, on this occasion, was a forestry pier on the Sound of Mull.

Though the Tar would be sorely missed on their arrival at that pier to take on a cargo of sawn timber — a backbreaking job loading this at any time, but most especially when three-handed instead of fully crewed, and with little help expected from the forestry men — there was a more immediate problem, namely the question of the catering arrangements on board, which must be resolved.

The larder was well-stocked for the outward jorney — Sunny Jim had seen to that before he left: but it would have to be fully replenished, probably at Oban, for the return trip. But even a well-stocked larder requires somebody to prepare its contents for the table and this was the subject of a great debate as the *Vital Spark* sailed slowly down-river in the late afternoon.

Nobody on board wanted the responsibilities of acting-cook.

Though the argument was debated loud and long for an hour or more, there was really no doubt in the mind of any of the three protagonists, from the very outset, as to what the outcome of it would be.

Para Handy would be able to argue that, as Captain with overall responsibility for the navigation and the general maritime integrity of the vessel, he could not possibly be distracted from those duties by the mundane requirements of making cups of tea or frying sausages — particularly in a location from which he would have no view whatsoever of the outside world and the circumstances and whereabouts of his command.

Macphail would advance similar pleading for his role in the hierarchy of the running and management of the ship, pointing out also that where the Captain and Mate could to a degree be interchangeable in respect of their duties as navigators and helmsmen, *nobody* on board could deputise for the engineer of the vessel, who must plainly be sidelined totally when it came to a decision on responsibilities for the commisariat.

The engineer also had the distinct advantage of knowing that however much the other two were anxious to avoid the role of ship's cook for themselves, neither would view with equanimity the prospects of food-preparation being (quite literally) in the hands of somebody who had just finished shovelling a load of nutty slack into the furnace and then topped that activity off with an application of the oil-can and its accompanying oil-rag to a tangle of greasy engine parts.

The unfortunate Mate realised from the very first that he was a doomed man, placed by fate in circumstances over which he could have no control. Though it was with ill-grace, when the debate was at last concluded, that he made his way to the fo'c'sle to study the contents of the larder and plan his menus, it was also with a condemned man's recognition of the inevitable.

His offering that first evening was mince and tatties.

Unhappily, he was unaware of the important role played in such a delicacy by the introduction of finely-chopped onions to the mince: nor that the best way to cook mince was not to *boil* it fiercely in a large pan of seawater: nor that potatos required more time to cook through than the few moments it took to bring to boil the pan of water in which *they* had been placed. Nor did condiments play any part in his cuisine.

Most of what was served to his shipmates on the enamelled metal plates of the puffer's only dinner-service finished up over the side of the vessel, and Para Handy and Macphail made the best of a meal they could from bread, cheese, and (eaten raw) the onions which the Mate had ommitted from the mince.

The three retired to their bunks, with the *Vital Spark* moored at Kilchattan Bay, in a frosty silence.

The Mate slept but fitfully: dreams of the acclaim of his shipmates as he served them five-star meals and basked in their warm compliments were interrupted by nightmares in which they rose in horror against the culinary disasters placed before them, and threw their perpetrator over the side of the ship.

He awoke the next morning red-eyed and ill-tempered and began to set out his breakfast ingredients with grim determination.

◇

The results of his early morning endeavours, which have already been described, again finished up overboard and, with no cheese left to quieten the pangs of hunger, Captain and Engineer did what they could with a loaf of bread, a pack of butter and a tin of orange marmalade.

For the next two days (as the *Vital Spark* made her passage to the forestry pier, loaded up such a quantity of cut timber that her deck was so heaped with it that the puffer's rowing-boat had to be unshipped and towed astern, and headed down the Sound of Mull to Oban to replenish food-stocks) a succession of quite appalling meals were served in the fo'c'sle and — more often than not — hurled angrily over the side a few moments later.

When the stocks of bread ran out, and the company was reduced to staving of their growing hunger pains with months-old ship's biscuit, the Mate began to fear for his safety.

At four o'clock in the afternoon, the *Vital Spark* tied up at the North Pier in Oban's capacious harbour. The Captain handed the Mate the ship's mess-money for the purchase of provisions for the return voyage to Bowling and announced that he and the Engineer were going ashore for a refreshment "to waash the taste of your cookin' oot" as he very kindly put it: and that when they returned at six o'clock they would expect that the Mate would have spent the money on food that he *could* cook, and would have an appetising meal on the table for them.

The Mate stood disconsolate on the deck as his shipmates made off, and stared miserably round the harbour. The *Vital Spark* had the North Pier to herself. Over on the South Pier MacBrayne steamers were loading passengers for the evening services to Tobermory to the west, Fort William to the north.

In that moment, Dougie saw a solution to all his problems.

~

Para Handy and Macphail returned from the Lorne Bar with heavy hearts, each imagining what horrors might be waiting for them on the mess-table.

To their astonishment, it was neatly laid out with plates of sliced and buttered bread and teacake, pancakes and a selection of fancies — there was even a single rose in a small vase as a centre-piece.

As they seated themselves, the Mate went to the stove and with pride took from its oven three plates of delicious, crisply-battered haddock fillets with golden chips and tastily-minted peas.

Wordlessly, the crew fell to and demolished the delicious food set before them.

"Well, Dougie," said the Captain, finishing the last morsel of currant-cake and pouring himself another cup of tea, "I don't know whether to thank the Oban proveesions, or the improvement in your cooking, but that's the best meal I've had for months!"

And even the Engineer grudgingly concurred.

The miracle continued all the way to Glasgow. Breakfast before leaving Oban was a revelation — crisp bacon, golden-yoked eggs and sausages of a spicey perfection. Indeed the Mate insisted on buying fresh provisions that morning, and sent his shipmates for an early constitutional towards Ganavan while he did so.

Lunch at Crinan (where they shared passage through the Canal with MacBrayne's *Cygnet*), served after the Captain and Engineer, at Dougie's insistence, had stepped ashore for a refreshment to set their appetites up, comprised roast leg of lamb with mint sauce, new potatos and carrots followed by jam roly-poly with a delicious custard sauce.

They arrived to berth overnight at Tarbert just twenty minutes before MacBrayne's *Iona* left for Ardrishaig, there to berth for the night herself. Tea, when Captain and Engineer returned from the Harbour Inn, consisted of cold roast beef with a delicious salad and another fine selection of cakes and pastries.

Breakfast (again at Tarbert) and then lunch at Rothesay, where the Mate insisted on berthing to replenish his supplies, and sent his shipmates up to the Argyll Arms for a drink at his own expense, were again a revelation of their temporary cook's new-found culinary skills and there was even talk of readjusting the whole duty rota of the *Vital Spark* on Sunny Jim's return.

But late supper at Bowling, where they berthed at ten o'clock, was a repeat of the stomach-churning disasters of the outward trip. Greasy bacon, half-raw Lorne sausage, cold tinned beans.

"My Cot, Dougie," said Para Handy in disgust, pushing his plate away, the food on it virtually untouched. "What on earth went wrong tonight?"

"Simple," said the Mate, "there's no MacBrayne shups here."

"What in bleezes d'you mean?" asked the mystified Captain.

"What d'you think?" replied the Mate: "You surely didna think ony of that good cooking wass *mine*?

"Wi' our skiff handy in the watter astern, I've been rowing to the MacBrayne boats in Oban and Crinan and Tarbert and Rothesay and *buying* meals ready-made from the passenger-galley cooks.

"It cost me money oot of my ain pocket, what wi' the extra for the food, and givin' you two beer-money to get you oot the way whiles I did ma 'shopping': but at least it wass worth it no' to have your abuse aal the way from Mull to Gleska the way I had it aal the way from Gleska to Mull!"

FACTNOTE

I am not sure what the good folk of Kirkcudbright did to merit Sunny Jim's observations about the town's notorious abilities for celebrating a wedding in style!

Shipboard catering — at least in the context of provisions

for ocean-going passengers — must always have been fraught with problems in the days before the invention and general use of stabilisers. Early (and not so early) accounts of Transatlantic liner passages tell tales of woe in all classes, for of course sea-sickness is no respecter of persons.

Most poignant perhaps are the stories of society ladies in the first-class acommodations in the luxurious days of White Star and CGT, both expecially renowned for their cuisine, who spent the entire week of the crossing prostrate in their cabins, with the double frustration of failing to make their mark on their fellow-passengers at the elegant functions and soirees, and unable to keep down so much as a cup of bouillon, never mind the caviar and lobster and tournedos and out-of-season fruits.

And of course, for all of this irretrievably lost opportunity and gone-for-ever delights, they had paid handsomely — very handsomely. More than one purser recounts being importuned on arrival at New York for just one jar of caviar to compensate in some way for the outlay which had been lost — overboard.

Catering on the Clyde steamers rarely encountered weather problems and was surprisingly good, most particularly on MacBrayne's vessels: and even allowing for the horrendous inflation in the generations since, it seems to have offered remarkable value as well. In 1911 MacBrayne's first class fare from Glasgow to Ardrishaig and return was 6/- or just 30p: while for a mere 4/6 (22p) more, the excursionist could enjoy a package of breakfast, lunch and tea.

In *The Victorian Summer of the Clyde Steamers* Alan Paterson reprints the day's menus on one sailing of MacBrayne's *Lord of the Isles*. Breakfast offered (among other choices) Salmon, Fresh Herring, Steaks, Ham and Eggs, and a whole range of breads, rolls and trimmings. Dinner included Salmon again, plus Roast Beef, Boiled Mutton, Roast Lamb, Fowl, Tongue, Assorted Sweets, Cheeses. High Tea was a simpler repast of just Fish, Cold Meats, Boiled Eggs, Fancy Breads and Preserves.

And the costs? Breakfast was 2/- (10p) as was High Tea. Dinner was 3/- (15p).

I reckon Dougie did pretty well by his shipmates if that was the kind of fare he was putting on the table!

6

A Stranger in a Foreign Land

Para Handy's blinkered devotion to the West Coast and its islands is legendary. "Have you never regretted that you didn't decide to go foreign yourself, Captain?" I asked him one evening as we sat on the pier at Gourock watching the Anchor liner *Columbia* pass the Tail o' the Bank at the start of her passage to New York.

"No, not really," said Para Handy without hesitation. "I would neffer have had the dignity of my own command if I had, for wan o' the qualifications for bein' Captain wi' the likes of the Anchor Line or the Blue Funnel is that you have to pass a wheen o' examinations in seamanshup and navigation and the like, and I wass neffer a man for examinations.

"Forbye, you canna learn seamanshup oot of a book, whateffer they say, it iss something you either have or you have not, and ass for navigation, weel, my idea o' navigatin' is doon to the Garrioch Heid, first right for Tighnabruaich, second right for Ardrishaig, straight on for Brodick, left for Saltcoats — that kind o' thing. Aal this business wi' sextants and chairts and compasses and the rest is way beyond me. It iss wan thing for the men who have the agility for them, like Hurricane Jeck for example — he has a heid for figures and he passed for his Master's Certificate the fastest effer in the merchant marine.

"It wass a peety he lost it chust aboot ass quick, but ass Jeck himself would say, what's for you wullna go by you, and what you're no meant to have you wullna keep.

"The wan thing I disagree wi' him aboot in sayin' that iss when it comes to the matter o' money, for I'm sure that there wass neffer anybody better suited to *have* it than

Jeck. Money could have been invented for him, he spends it wi' such dignity and style that it is a privilege simply to waatch him doin' it. But then at the same time, you see, it iss exactly because of that that he can neffer *keep* it. It chust runs through his hands like watter from a tap."

I felt it best to offer no opinion on the question of Hurricane Jack's suitability to be a member of the moneyed classes.

"But I wass abroad myself, chust the wan time" continued the Captain, "and I decided then and there that wance wass enough for me."

I stared in surprise. "I had no idea," I said. "When was this, and where to?"

"Luverpool," said the Captain. "Chust before I got the command o' the *Vital Spark*."

"But Liverpool isn't *abroad*, Captain," I protested. "Liverpool is in England."

"Weel, if England issna abroad then I would be very pleased if you wud tell me what it iss," said Para Handy scathingly and with considerable conviction. "They are a very strange sort of a people indeed doon there. They aal taalk a lenguage that you simply canna understand, they dinna drink whusky, their beer iss like watter, not wan o' them hass so mich as a single word o' the Gaelic, they canna mak' a daicent bleck pudding or bit of breid, nor cure bacon, nor catch fush, they've neffer even heard o' Hurricane Jeck, they dinna like the pipes, and instead of amusing themselves wi' something ceevilised like shinty, they play some sissy game caalled cricket."

Before an attack set on so broad a front, and one so vehemently delivered, I was for a moment speechless.

"Well, Captain," I said after a moment, "that is a different way of life to ours, perhaps, but it does not make England a foreign country. I am sure that many English people who come to Scotland would be just as entitled to describe *us* and *our* ways as foreign if they applied the same criteria as you have."

"I am sure I have neffer applied a criteria in my naitural Mr Munro," said the Captain indignantly, "and I would be grateful if you wud chust bear that in mind."

I decided that this was neither the time nor the place to embark on a short lesson in semantics.

"And in any case," Para Handy continued, "any Englishman trying to miscaall *us* as foreigners wud be in serious trouble. I am a peaceable man, myself, and wud simply try to persuade him of the error of his ways in a chentlemanly fashion, but the likes of Hurricane Jeck wud have a mair immediate and violent means of debating hiss misconceptions wi' him."

"Tell me more about your visit to Liverpool…" I prompted.

"I wass between chobs at the time, ass I said a while back. I wass waiting for the *Vital Spark* to be laaunched, and I had signed aff a gabbart I'd been crewing oot of Ardrossan, I chust couldna stand her skipper, he wassna a chentleman at aal.

"So I wass lookin' for a berth for two weeks or thereby, and when I made an enquiry at the Ardrossan Docks Office they telt me that there wass a shup o' the Burns Line on a charter cairgo run to Luverpool that wass short of a deck-hand, and I got the chob the same mornin'.

"The shup wass the *Lamprey*, she wass usually on the regular Belfast service but she had been chartered to tak' a load of steel plate from Harland and Wolff's to wan o' the shipyerds in Luverpool.

"We wass two days in Belfast takin' the cairgo on board. I have a lot of time for the Irish, they could be chust ass good ass the Scots if it wassna for those few miles of sea cuttin' them aff from us. I ken that their whusky is different, but then you dinna really notice that after the third gless or thereby, for you get kind of used wi' it.

"We had a very rough passage across the Irish Sea to Luverpool and wi' the load of steel plate the shup took a fair pounding. I wass the happy man when we cam' safe to the docks.

"Efter the steel had been unloaded the owners wass trying to find a cargo of some sort for either Belfast or Ardrossan so they could mak' somethin' oot of the home trup — I can tell you there iss nobody near ass greedy ass a man that owns a shup, he canna stand sein' it no' makin' money wi' effery turn o' the propellor.

"So for two days we wass coolin' our heels in Luverpool. There wassna mich to do, and we wass runnin' desperate low on coin, we didna have ass much ass would pay for even chust the wan wee quiet dram. I had got friendly wi' wan o' the stokers, a laad caaled Danny, frae Stornoway: Danny had wance been a piper wi' the Bleck Watch and he still had his pipes aboot him — he practiced oot on the poop deck when he wass aff duty — so I put a proposeetion to him.

"I telt him that they wudna often ha'e the chance to hear a daicent piper in Luverpool, and if we went into the toon and he played and I went roond wi' the hat, we wud surely mak' enough to put oorselves in funds for a refreshment.

"Danny chumped at the idea, dashed doon below to get his pipes and aff we went.

"We picked a spot where two o' the main streets crossed, and there wass a big public hoose at each corner.

" 'This'll do fine and dandy,' says I. 'The chentlemen comin' in and oot o' the Inns wull be pleased enough to hear a cheery tune. Wait you and you'll see. We wull do weel here!'

"Danny sterted to tune up his pipes, and wud you credit it, he hadna been blawin' for mair than a hauf a meenit when a big fella wi' a long white apron, and a bleck waist-coat on him same ass he wis a meenister, came rushin' oot o' wan o' the public hooses.

" 'Whit sort o' racket d'ye caal this,' he shouted, very red in the face. 'Are you tryin' to scare my customers away? Whit the bleezes is yon man daeing?'

" 'It iss aal right,' said I: 'stop you and you wull see some-thing worth listening to in a meenit. For the moment he iss simply tuning his pipes.'

" 'Tuning them is it, for peety's sakes.' howls the man. *'Tuning* them indeed! And wull you tell me chust how the bleezes he's meant to know when he *has*?'

"And he disappeared into the public hoose. Twa meenits later, when Danny wass chust gettin' warmed up wi' *The Glendaruel Highlanders*, he cam' oot again, wi' a smaall cairdboard box in his haunds, and went across the street and into the ither three public hooses, wan efter another.

"When he cam' oot o' the last Inns, he walked over and tipped a wee pile of sulver oot o' the cairdboard box into the kep I was holding.

" 'Now,' he shouted, purple wi' rage by this time, 'That's frae me and my fellow publicans. Wull you please now be reasonable for we are aal trying to run a business here. Wull you and your frien' now *please go away!*'

"Well, we wassna weel content at the way we got the money, but at least we had enough for a few refreshments. 'We'd better no' go near wan o' these hooses, Danny' said I, 'we shall look for a likely-looking Inns close by.'

"We foond this wee public hoose doon an alley and in we went and I ordered up two drams. 'Drams?' says the barman, 'What in tarnation is *drams*? We dinna sell drams in here.'

"So we ordered beer, and I can tell you it wass chust like drinking coloured watter. Mr Younger would neffer get awa' wi' foisting rubbish like that on your average thirsty Gleska man. But we had paid for it, and we would drink it if it killed us. Danny had his pipes under his airm, of course, and after a meenit the barman leaned over the coonter and said, quite jocco, 'We dinna get mony bagpipers in here.'

" 'Wi' coloured watter at saxpence the pint, I'm not at aal surprised aboot that,' said Danny. And we never got to feen-ish the beer, they threw us oot.

"By this time the public hooses wass aal shutting for the efternoon. Danny stopped a man in the street and asked him where we could get a refreshment. 'The only place iss the cricket metch,' says the man. 'The Inns there iss open aal day.'

" 'I havna the faintest notion what a cricket metch is,' says Danny. 'But if the public hooses are open, who cares?'

"We paid oor sixpences to get in the gate, and made for the refreshment rooms. There wass a whole wheen o' chaps in white shirts and troosers standin' in the middle of a field throwing a red ball at a man haudin' some sort of club. Personally I dinna think this cricket is a game at aal, it's some kind of a magic ritual, for ass soon ass the wan that wass throwin' the ball hit the man wi' the club on the legs, aal the ithers threw their arms up in the air and shouted 'Howzat!' — and wud you credit it, at that very instant the rain came *pourin'* doon!

"The Inns kept open, but efter an hour or thereby they wudna serve ony more to Danny and me. We'd been blethering awa' in the Gaelic and they thought that we wass the worse for drink and said it wassna a lenguage at aal, it wass chust us so fu' we couldna speak. 'If Hurricane Jeck wass here,' says I quite angry, 'You wouldna get awa' wi' refusing *him*.'

'Hurricane *who*?' says the man behind the bar.

"We sailed for Ardrossan the next morning wi' a half cairgo of pit props, so it wassna a total loss for the owners.

"But the food on the way hame wass deplorable. They'd stocked up the galley in Luverpool, and aal we got wass bleck pudding filled wi' lumps of fet, rubbery breid, taste-less streaky bacon wi' nae cure to it, and fush that aromatic you wouldna put it doon to a cat.

"Don't talk to me aboot England no' being a foreign country. I wass there — I've seen it for myself!"

And I thought it best not to argue with the Captain, but
to take him for a quiet glass of something with which to
wash away the taste of such an unhappy — if misinter-
preted — memory.

FACTNOTE

The Anchor Line was established by two brothers —
Nicol and Robert Handyside — in Glasgow in 1856 and lasted for exactly a century. The name 'Anchor Line' was only
adopted in 1899.

Though usually thought of as a Clyde-based transatlantic
company, Anchor traded to America from a score or more
of European and Mediterranean ports, and to India and the
East.

The *Columbia* was a three-funnelled passenger and
cargo liner of just over 8000 tons, almost 500ft in length
and carrying 345 passengers in first class, 218 in second
and 740 in steerage to take advantage of the booming traffic and she sailed mostly on the Glasgow to New York run,
with a regular call in Ireland on the outward journey to take
on emigrant familes. She served as an armed merchant
cruiser (renamed the *Columbella*) in the First War, was
sold to Greek interests in 1926, and was finally broken up
in 1929.

There was a complex network of shipping links between
Scotland and Ireland in the early years of the century, and
G & J Burns of Ardrossan held a substantial share of this.
Later amalgamated to become the Burns-Laird Line, they
moved the centre of their operations to Glasgow and a gen-
eration ago their handsome vessels provided a comfortable
and reliable overnight service to ireland from the
Broomielaw, and their cargo ships criss-crossed the irish
Sea and the North Channel.

Harand and Wolff in Belfast were — with Vickers in
Barrow-in-Furness — the only serious rivals to the Clyde
Yards on the western seaboard. The Belfast builders are
probably best remembered nowadays for the *Olympic* and
above all for the *Titanic*, the two giants which (with the later
Britannic) were intended to set the seal on the superiority
of Ismay's White Star Line. Instead they nearly destroyed it.

There is a piece of maritime folklore associated with the

naming of the *Britannic* — as there later was with the naming of the *Queen Mary*. It is said that the original plan had been that the three huge sisters, which dwarfed anything else on the high seas at the time of their launch, were to have been named *Olympic*, *Titanic* — and finally *Gigantic*.

But legend has it that the sheer horror of the *Titanic's* loss convinced the company that to call their third ship by such an arrogant and boastful name would simply be to tempt providence (particularly after the bitterly-regretted claims about the unsinkability of her sister) and the plan was shelved, with the patriotic and uncontroversial *Britannic* being chosen instead.

7

Cavalcade to Camelon

t was just past two o'clock of the afternoon of a fine
Saturday in early May. The *Vital Spark* lay against the
stone facing of the passenger quay on the east side of
Craigmarloch bridge on the Forth and Clyde Canal.

A welcome, idle weekend was in prospect for her crew.
She was scheduled, first thing on Monday morning, to load
a cargo of cask whisky from the Rosebank distillery at
Camelon, on the western fringes of the historic Burgh of
Falkirk. Until then a long and lazy meander across central
Scotland was in prospect, a passage no longer plagued by
the taunts of the urchins of the towns and villages which
fringed the Canal. The manner in which a previous generation of those youthful predators on the inland voyages of
the vessel was devastatingly dealt with — thanks to the
ingenuity of Sunny Jim — has already been set out in one
of my earlier accounts of the travels and travails of the *Vital
Spark*, and is now firmly entrenched in the folklore of
today's towpath tearaways who therefore give to the puffer
a wide (and respectful) berth.

Para Handy and Macphail were seated on the main hatch
in a most companionable silence, replete with fried
sausages and potatos and in lazy contemplation of the tranquil canal. To their right hand the silver ribbon of its waters
curved out of sight along a gentle bend towards
Kirkintilloch with, on the nearer bank, the towpath: and on
the farther, a long phalanx of mature trees at their freshest
springtime green.

The Captain stretched luxuriously and reached into the
flap of his trouser pocket for his oilskin tobacco pouch and
his safety matches.

"I tell you, Dan, on a day like this I think that there iss a lot to be said for a landlocked life. There iss not the lochs and the bens, to be sure, and the view iss not what it iss when you are comin' doon Loch Fyne, but then neither iss the weather either. A peaceful existence!"

The Engineer nodded.

"True enough, Peter," he said. "But wud ye no' get awfu' bored wi' it, aye jist the same places and the same faces year in and year oot, the same cairgos and the same carnaptious duvvles to deal wi' at the locks? At least we get some sort of deeversity on the ruver, and a lot o' different harbour-masters yellin' at us for no good reason, no' the identical yins a' the time."

"You are probably right," conceded Para Handy. "And for sure neither iss there the same opportunity for cheneral high-jinks or entertainment to be had. I mean to say, chust look at Dougie and Jum!"

The Mate, ever the optimist whether confronted with the lively tidal waters off the pier at Brodick or, as here, with the dark depths of a sluggish canal, could be seen a couple of hundred yards away seated on the bank with his legs dangling over its edge. In his hands was the *Vital Spark*'s acknowledgement of the tenets of Izaac Walton — a ten-foot bamboo pole: from its tip there dangled a length of tarry twine terminating in a rusting hook baited with a worm whose luck had run out when Dougie had spotted it, sunning itself on the grassy bank, at precisely the right time for him — but very much the wrong time for it.

Sunny Jim was more strenuously employed on the broad swathe of grass beside the imposing but at present unopened Craigmarloch Refreshment Rooms, widely patronised in summer by excursionists and day-trippers on the Canal. He was playing kick-about with a handful of local youths with a battered football which had been spied floating, forgotten and abandoned in one of the locks at Kirkintilloch on their passage through them that morning: and commandeered enthusiastically by their young deck-hand.

The Captain viewed with mixed emotions the prowess demonstrated by his young shipmate as he showed quite remarkable skill with an impressive display of the traditional game of 'keepie-uppie' with boot and knee which had the Craigmarloch youths staring open-mouthed in amazement.

"Nimble enough wi' his feet, right enough," he said. "But for why? What good does it do the laad? It is chust the same as chumpin' through girrs, that iss aal it iss, fine enough for a penny street-show but I am sure and you could neffer be making a livin' from it.

"And as for Dougie...! Has he effer, I ask you, caught a fush in his naitural? I am telling you, Dan, if we had to depend on Dougie Campbell's skills for the proveeshuns on the vessel then we would aal surely sterve."

"Hairmless enough, Peter," replied the Engineer, on whom the peace and beauty of his surroundings had wrought an unexpected and most unusual air of goodwill. "For surely you need to enjoy some divershun in this world, as weel as work? Life iss no jist aboot the daily grind, as it says in the Scruptures, there has tae be a chance for relaxation." But he surreptitiously and shamefacedly hid the copy of his newest penny novelette under a fold of hatch tarpaulin as he spoke.

Para Handy snorted. "That's ass may be," said he: "but the day that Dougie brings us in any sort of catch, or the day that we get ony good out of Jum's fancy tricks wi' a foot-baal, iss the day I'll take and treat you aal in the nearest Inns at my expense!"

"Weel," said Macphail darkly, "Ah heard you say that, Peter, so be sure Ah'll keep you to it."

"Chance would be a fine thing," said the Captain, undismayed and unperturbed, and set about filling his pipe.

A few minutes later the two men stretched out across the main hatch and dozed fitfully in the warm sunshine.

Time passed.

On the towpath Dougie fished — but caught nothing. On the grassy bank the football hopefuls set up goals marked by folded jackets and played five-a-side and, when an ill-judged shot sent the ball spinning into the canal, pushed its perpetrator into the water (despite his protests) to retrieve it.

Time passed.

At three o'clock the peace was shattered. A horse-drawn wagon came clattering down the narrow, winding road from Kilsyth and pulled into the forecourt of the Refreshment Rooms. Three young women in the black dresses and white pinafores of waitresses or parlour-maids jumped from the bench behind the driver's raised seat and moved towards the building: two men began to unload boxes and crates from the dray.

The driver, a smartly-dressed individual in a brass-button navy blazer and with a jaunty straw boater, took one glance at the panorama of angler, footballers and puffer and came rushing over to the quayside against which the *Vital Spark* was lying.

"Get this eyesore out of here this minute!" he yelled with such ferocity that Para Handy was wide awake in a moment. "Are you crazy? In thirty minutes the *Gipsy Queen* will be here with the first excursion party of the year from Glasgow, and I've got little enough time to get their teas ready as it is. This is a berth for the gentry and their ladies, not a dumping-ground for a filthy coal-boat. Get it shifted this very minute!

"And you lot," he added, rounding on the footballers without pausing to draw breath, "away to Hampden Park if football's all your brains can cope with. Don't waste my time with it here!"

"And you," turning to Dougie — for he was obviously determined to leave nobody out, "have you got a fishing licence?"

Para Handy got to his feet and drew himself up with dignity. "I am sure and there iss no need to take that attitude," he said, "for we have effery right to be here same ass you. But ass it happens we were chust on the point of leaving anyway so I will not put you to any further trouble…"

~

"Why wass he tellin' you to go to Hampden Perk?" the Captain enquired of Sunny Jim shortly afterwards as the *Vital Spark* negotiated one of the locks between Castlecary and Bonnybridge.

"Jist bein' clever by his way o' it," said Jim. "It's the Cup Final today. Wush I *could* have been there, Raith Rovers and the Bairns."

"Bairns?" asked Para Handy in a puzzled tone. "Whit the bleezes iss the Bairns?"

"Falkirk, of course," said Jim. "They cry them that frae the toon's slogan: 'Better meddle wi' the de'il than wi' the bairns o' Falkirk.' A spunky team."

"Falkirk!" shouted a contemptuous voice from the depths of the engine-room. "They couldna play cat's-cradle, never mind fitba'. The Rovers wull eat them alive."

Before Jim could take up the challenge, Para Handy

remembered something more important than an argument about football.

"We've nothin' for oor teas," he cried, "what wi' Dougie's usual success wi' the fushing, and the shops'll be shut by the time we get to Rosebank. Wheneffer we get to Bonnybridge Jum will have to make a wee excursion to get some bacon and eggs from the grocer's."

Nobody paid too much attention, when they moored by the towpath at the village, to an abandoned, empty chara-banc slewed across the road at the Wellstood Foundry, its front wheels splayed out like the flippers of a seal. It was obvious that the axle had broken and the vehicle was hope-lessly immovable.

"Poor duvvles," said the Captain. "And a Sunday School trup or the like by the look of it — see the bunting and the flegs on her! I chust hope that they dinna have much fur-ther to go."

~

He had the answer to both those questions a few minutes later when Jim returned (with Dougie, who had chummed him on it) from his shopping excursion — with a bizarre following.

Behind them came some 15 or so young men, smartly turned out in matching blazers and grey trousers, each car-rying brown canvas holdalls. At the van of this party were half-a-dozen older and distinguished-looking gentlemen, one carrying with exagerrated care a large silver cup, its handles pennanted with navy-blue and white ribbons.

A large crowd — half the population of Bonnybridge, by the look and sound of them — followed this group, whoop-ing, cheering and cavorting exuberantly.

Both Jim and the Mate were grinning with delight as they came up beside the puffer. The frock-coated gentleman car-rying the silver trophy held up his hand to the cheering crowds behind him. Their noise died away and he turned towards the vessel.

"Captain," he said to Para Handy. "I would deem it the most enormous favour, since I understand that you are headed for the Rosebank Distillery, if you could give my fellow-directors and our boys passage. Our charabanc, as you can see, has met with an accident, and I do not want to disappoint the crowds waiting us in the town, nor the horse-carriages awaiting our arrival at the road-end to drive our boys into their home-town in their hour of triumph."

Para Handy was non-plussed. "What boys? What hour of triumph?"

"Why," said the gentleman: "here is the Falkirk football team and here we are on our way home with the Scottish Cup. You surely will not deny the boys their glory? Nor yours, either, for I am sure that your kindness will be well rewarded..."

The puffer's passage those last four miles to Rosebank on the western outskirts of the team's home town remains among the very happiest moments of Para Handy's maritime life. On either bank, cheering crowds raced along beside them: the team stood on the main-hatch, the silver cup held aloft in pride. At masthead and from the stern jackstaff flags and bunting, recovered from the charabanc, fluttered proudly in the evening sunlight.

At the Rosebank basin the waiting crowd had to be numbered in thousands and the rapturous reception for the team and its directors split the heavens. But all good things must come to an end, and within minutes the triumphant 'Bairns' had climbed aboard the brightly-decked open coaches which awaited them, and driven off towards the town centre and a gala civic banquet.

Heroes of the moment in their own more modest way the crew were hailed ashore, taken to the Rosebank Inn, and enthusiastically 'treated' by a large party of Falkirk supporters.

"Let this show you," said Dougie to Para Handy good-naturedly, "that I can fetch home mair than fush — and that Jum's football skills are not aal in vain, for it wass he that recognised the team at the roadside at Bonnybridge."

"And don't forget," chipped in the Engineer, "that means *you're* due to treat us now as weel — for I telt ye I wuddna forget whit ye said on the canal! Mine's a dram!"

FACTNOTE

The earliest passenger traffic on the Forth and Clyde Canal was not leisure travel, but workaday journeys or, at least, travel with a purpose. And since the boat service offered was not only faster but also much more comfortable than the coach-and-horses which were the only alternatives in the Canal's early years, it prospered and grew. In time, though, the convenience and comfort of the waterborne transport was overtaken in every respect by the development of firstly the rail network and then the motor-car and charabanc.

By the early 1900s the Canal boat companies almost exclusively provided pleasure cruises in purpose-built vessels which ran afternoon, evening or full-day excursions from Port Dundas in the centre of Glasgow. The *Gipsy Queen* was almost the last and probably the most capacious and luxurious of them all. Although restricted in size (like the working puffers) to an overall length of under 70' by the dimensions of the locks she had to navigate, she had three decks, the lowest (fully enclosed) having a tea-room capable of seating 60: and a lounge as well.

Craigmarloch, in a sheltered and handsomely wooded valley, was the most popular destination for charter parties and scheduled excursions alike, and the Restaurant and Tea Rooms were opened in 1905 to provide a necessary service (and indeed a *purpose* to the whole outing, namely a couple of hours ashore) in what was otherwise a remote and inaccessible corner.

Though I was born and brought up in the West, both my father's and mother's forebears had connections with Falkirk and the surrounding district and from an age when indeed I knew no better I was therefore inducted as a supporter of Falkirk Football Club and I have never regretted that despite the vicissitudes of the last 40 years. The Club is something of a Cinderella in Scottish football and a glorious uncertainty as to likely performance goes as they say 'with the territory'. Not for nothing is 'Expect the Unexpected' an unofficial rallying-cry for many Falkirk fans. All teams have their ups-and-downs, but ours are often particularly dramatic: and traumatic. A team which can travel to Parkhead as hopeless underdogs and come away with the points can also host a home game against a minor Division minnow in the Cup — and lose.

But we *did* win the Cup in 1913 against Raith Rovers: and again (and I own to being old enough to have actually been there) in 1957 against Kilmarnock. A modest gap of 44 years between these landmarks seems somehow appropriate in all the circumstances. Pragmatic and superstitious Falkirk fans the world over — and there *are* Falkirk fans the world over, and great is their kind camaraderie — therefore have high hopes for 2001.

PADDLE POWER — *In a cavalcade of another category, half-a-dozen sail-powered fishing vessels get the benefit of a steam-driven tow out of Campbeltown Loch, presumably on a day of adverse wind or tide: or both. The high freeboard of the fishing boats is as striking as the astonishing beam displayed by the tug, although this may simply be exaggerated by the camera angle. However, at least the procession would mean a brief respite for the hard-driven fishing crews.*

8

Scotch and Water

As the *Vital Spark* passed the end of Meadowhill Quay on her way down river, at that point where the river Kelvin debouched into the Clyde, Para Handy leaned from the wheelhouse to watch with particular interest the delicate manoeuvres of the crane-man who was busily occupied in lowering, with a quite impressive precision, a gleaming and curiously shaped copper tank into the fore-hold of a small three-island steamer.

"A still," he said enviously to the Mate, who was seated below him, cross-legged on the main-hatch. "A *still*! I wonder where it's bound for? Campbeltown, I wouldna wonder. My chove though, it iss a real whopper! If you had wan o' them at the foot of your drying green you would be set up for life!"

"Or *daein'* life mair likely," remarked Macphail, easing himself out of the engine-room, "and wi' little chance of ony remission for guid behaviour neither."

Para Handy ignored the comment. "I am chust aawful vexed that Jeck is no' with us, for he'd be maist interested in her," he continued. "It has aalways been his ambition to go in for what you might caall serious commercial production, raither than chust pickin' awa' at the business wi' a pocket-size version that canna do much more than turn oot the odd bottle or two for frien's or family.

"He wass very disappointed that we neffer once had a contract to cairry a still whiles he wass on the vessel. I told him the hold chust wassna big enough to tak' wan, but he wass aalways hopeful that we would get the chance of wan as deck cairgo. His idea wass that we could say that we had lost it overboard in heavy weather and have the dustillery

chust claim off their unsurance, for he aye had the notion
to land a still on Eilean Loain, at the head of Loch Sween,
and set up in business on his own account.

" 'Loain iss well-wooded and we could hide the operation
withoot ony trouble," he would point out: 'forbye, there iss
no a hoose within a mile of the island and anyway they are
aal Highland chentlemen in that part of Argyll, they would
be well pleased to have a local enterprise such ass a smaall,
privately-owned whusky still on the doorstep and would
neffer even think to let the Customs people know that there
wass something there for them to investigate. Indeed it
would be fine and handy for the Loch Sween men: maist o'
them are carryin' on their own private operations in the
same line o' business and when we wass buying grain in
bulk for our dustillery we would look efter their needs at
the same time, and shup barley in for them at cost.' "

Macphail snorted. "The man should be locked up!" he said.
"He iss nothin' but a one-man crime wave, if you ask me."

"But I didna ask you," said the Captain brusquely, "so awa'
back doon and play wi' your enchines and leave us in peace."

The engineer climbed back into his cubby and slammed
the metal hatch angrily behind him.

"That's put his gas at a peep," said Para Handy firmly.
"There iss only wan way to treat a man like Macphail and
that iss to let him know who iss master on the shup!"

Sunny Jim, who had been perched up in the bows as the
puffer made her way down river, came aft and sat down
beside Dougie on the hatch.

"So Hurricane Jack never got his still, eh?" said he.

"Not while he wass with the *Vital Spark* he didna, no,"
said the Captain: "but he did when he was working one
summer ass a deck hand on the *Ivanhoe*."

"How on earth did a steamer come to be cairrying
cargo?" asked Sunny Jim incredulously: "and whit way
could a deckie manage to steal it?"

"I didna say it was cargo, Jum," said Para Handy patiently.
"It wassna like that at aal. What happened wass that Jeck
installed a spurit still on the vessel. As he said to me when
he wass makin' his plans, a moving target iss that much
more difficult to hit, it iss neffer in the same place two days
running and if a bottle or two of the white spirits wass to
come on the market in, say, Tarbert on a Thursday mornin'
and be intercepted by the chentlemen from the Excise
Offices, who would effer think that the source of it might be

moored at Bridge Wharf on Friday afternoon?

" 'The point is, Peter,' said Jeck, 'the powers that be aalways expect a stull to be a kind of a fixed asset, ass they say in financial circles, no' something that's aye on the move.'

"Putting her on a steamer wass a brulliant notion, but the real stroke of genius, which you would expect from a man of Jeck's natural agility, was to put her onto the *Ivanhoe* of aal the vessels on the Clyde. I mean, even if a whisper effer came to the ears of the Customs men that there was a shup on the river traipsing aboot wi' a portable still on board, which offeecial would effer jalouse that onybody would have the sheer effrontery to put it on the wan and only temperance steamer on the Firth? They would be ass likely to expect to find the Grand Master o' the Ancient Order of Rechabites calling for a round in the snug bar of the Saracen's Heid at the Gallowgate.

"Of course, it wass chust a wee machine, but it wass perfectly capable of distilling two bottles of spurits each trup that the *Ivanhoe* made, and Jeck wass neffer effer an over-ambitious man, what he couldna either sell or swallow himself he wassna interested in.

"The Golden Goose he chrustened it, and each evening he came off the vessel at the Broomielaw wi' two bottles under his shirt, wan to tak' home and the other to sell discreetly at the pier-head. He wassna greedy neither, three shullings the bottle wass aal he asked."

Sunny Jim burst in with the question he had been desperate to ask for some minutes. "Where on earth," he enquired, "did Jack put the stull on the shup, and how did he hide it?"

"One of Jeck's responsibilities," continued the Captain, "was the regular inspection and maintenance of the lifeboats. Aal their equipment — oars, water-bottles, flares, biscuit-boxes, signal lamps and the like — wass aal protected from the weather and the depredations of ony passing stevedores or light-fingered passengers by a heavy tarpaulin cover.

"There wass one boat chust abaft the paddle wheel at each side of the shup but they were far too much in sight of the Officers on the brudge: but there wass a third one at the stern, lying inboard on a cradle chust immediately above the shup's galley.

"It wass ideal. That piece of deck wass out-of-bounds to the passengers, it wass hidden from the brudge by the line of the upper deck which formed the roof of the aft saloon, and since aal the ventilation shafts and chumneys from the stoves in the galley came up aal aboot it, nobody wass going to notice one more wee vent pipe in among aal that lot, and nobody would think it at aal oot of the ordinary if there wass an occasional smell o' barley aboot the place.

"Jeck stayed aboard late one night till aal the crew was ashore and then he removed a couple of the thwarts from the boat to give him room and bolted doon a wee copper stull wi' a paraffin burner and a funnel vent that he'd bought from an acquaintance.

"It was plain sailing from then on. Each mornin' he'd sneak on board really early wi' a big jar o' home-made fermented barley wash, tip it into the still, prime and light the burner, and away to his duties. At denner-time he would dump the lees of the wash in the river and set up the second distillation. Each evening he would decant the day's production out of the jar below the condenser and into a couple of empty bottles, cork them firmly, and head off.

"From the start of the summer season in May efferything went as smooth as silk for Jeck. He had to take a couple o' the other deck hands into his confudence. There wass occasions when there wass towerists leaning on the after rail o' the promenade deck watchin' what Jeck wass up to on the stern deck below them, and someone official-lookin' wass needed to go up to the promenade deck and clear them awa' from the after end o' it till he had finished his business. But that wass no problem.

"Jeck made his fatal error of chudgement at the time of Gleska Fair. The shup wass absolutely packed wi' truppers day on day.

"Till now, Jeck had neffer been tempted to sell at retail, ass you might say: he wass quite happy to dispose of the output of the Golden Goose at wholesale price, and by the bottle. But during the Fair he suddenly realised that, what wi' the demand for a place on the boats, there was many truppers takin' the *Ivanhoe* not *because* she wass a teetotal boat (as wass aalways the case in other months), but *despite* it, and because they wass chust gled to get passage on *any* doon-the-watter steamer.

"The result wass that Jeck and his shipmates wass constantly being importuned by very thursty-looking Gleska chentlemen as to whereaboots the Bar wass and where refreshments wass being sold. Their language on being told that the shup wass teetotal would have shamed the Trongate on a Saturday night, neffer mind the driest shup on the river!

"Jeck wass sorely tempted. When he did his sums he realised that the bottles he wass selling at chust three shullings would bring in three times as much if he wass to sell the contents by the gless, and he had a stockpile of spurits at home to top up the two bottles a day that the Golden Goose wass producing. It could be a very profitable Fair Fortnight if he wass careful.

"What decided him wass that he found an old unused paint-locker let into the paddle-box casing on the starboard side of the shup, across the passageway from the viewing platform for the enchines. It had wan o' these splut-doors that let you open the upper part of it and keep the bottom half shut. And though it wass a busy spot, efferybody wass watching the big pistons on the enchines, they wass the most popular sight on the shup, and nobody was lookin' at the casing wall at aal.

"First thing the next morning Jeck shut himself into the cubby wi' half-a-dozen bottles of spurits, a stack o' paper cups, and a wee wudden box for the money. His shupmates were on commission at a penny a gless and it was their chob to identify ony chentlemen that looked in need of a refreshment. They wass told that if they went to Jeck's locker and knocked on the door once and then three times — rat: tat-tat-tat — then it would be Open Sesame, and the whisky wass sixpence a gless.

"For five solid days the money chust poured in, and Jeck wass so delighted with the way things was going that he volunteered for a Sunday shift, a thing he'd neffer done before aal his time on the vessel. He wass busier than effer that day, for what with it being the Sabbath there wass double pleasure for the chentlemen in being able to get a dram, and the news o' Jeck's shebeen spread like wildfire through the shup.

"Tragedy struck at chust past mid-day. Jeck had been pouring almost non-stop since the *Ivanhoe* had left Brudge Wharf at nine o'clock, and when there wass a sudden wee lull in the knockin' at the cubby door, he thought nothing of it and was quite glad of the chance to draw breath. Though ass a rule Jeck neffer, effer drank while he wass on duty he thought he would treat himself to chust the wan wee dram. He wass enchoying the first smack of it when there was a kind of a scratching at the door. Jeck opened the upper-half wi' one hand, the gless of spirits held tight in the other, and asked cheerily and politely (for he wass aalways the perfect chentlemen) 'How many wull it be boys, speak up and dinna be feart, we're aal Jock Tamson's bairns on the good shup *Ivanhoe*' — and found himself staring into the horror-struck faces of the shup's Captain and First Officer.

"Nobody had thought to warn Jeck that the Sabbath run wass the occasion for the Captain to make his weekly inspection of the shup, and that no corner or compartment wass effer likely to be overlooked. Indeed, Jeck found oot later that the Captain had even been in under the tarpaulin o' the stern lifeboat and the only reason the still had survived wass that the Captain had neffer seen wan in hiss life, wouldna have recognised wan if it wass comin' doon Renfield Street on a Number Three caur, and thought that Jeck's Golden Goose wass some new piece of equipment for purifying watter that the lifeboat suppliers had installed during the annual overhaul o' the boat.

"But he had no difficulty in recognising wan o' his own crew wi' a gless in his hand, and a stack of bottles at his feet, and they didna even wait till *Ivanhoe* got back to Gleska, Jeck wass thrown aff at the next stop, Kilcreggan, and since the shup refused him passage on the return leg he wass stuck till next day with only the clothes he stood up in. Mercifully, the local polis wass a kind of a second cousin, and Jeck got the use of wan o' the cells for the night."

"What did Ah tell ye," Macphail shouted from the engine-room at this point. "Justice at last! The man's nothing but a natural jailburd! He shouldna even be allowed oot loose."

"You're just jealous, Macphail," said Para Handy wearily, "and not chust of Jeck's popularity, but because you're no' on the *Ivanhoe* and nobody effer wants to look at *your* engines!"

FACTNOTE

Bootleg liquor didn't start with Prohibition in America: indeed it could well have been earlier Scottish immigrants who brought the traditions of illicit stills to the Land of the Free! From the 18th century onwards there was a constant running battle across Scotland between the government enforcers on the one hand and the do-it-yourself distillers on the other.

Nor (to scotch another myth, and I apologise for the verb) were illicit stills confined to rural locations. There was probably as much home-made whisky circulating in Glasgow as in the rest of the country put together at the height of the traffic.

The other side of the coin were the temperance movements which crop up elsewhere in these tales. *Ivanhoe*, the Clyde's first and only teetotal steamer, was however the product of a response to general public demand rather than the direct result of temperance campaigning. The plain fact was that by the late 1870s more and more families and excursion parties were being dissuaded from traditional Clyde cruising because of the anti-social behaviour of a small minority of travellers, and the mismanagement of a handful of steamers, which became floating shebeens of the worst sort, and whose reputation undeservedly sullied that of other operators as well and got the whole Clyde steamer industry what we would call 'a bad press'.

The *Ivanhoe* was a most handsome ship, and a resounding success in her early years: as the drink problem elsewhere was better managed, and a degree of discipline was restored across the fleets, demand for a strictly teetotal ship fell away and in 1897 she was purchased from her original owners and operators the Frith of Clyde Steam Packet Company by the Caledonian SPC for the sum of £9,000, and sailed fully licensed from then on.

Incidentally, I have taken at least one liberty with the facts in presenting this story. The *Ivanhoe* never sailed down river on Sundays during her temperance years. There was something of a moratorium on Sunday sailings from about 1880 to 1895 as a direct result of the horrific problems of the Sabbath-breaking booze-boats (there is no other word which can satisfactorily describe them) of the 1870s.

The sight, sound and smell of the magnificent engines which drove the blades was *the* great spectacle, and memory, of a day spent on the paddle-steamers. And since the real bars aboard were usually on the same deck level as the observation areas at which the public in general (and small boys in particular) could spend hours gawping at such raw power in action, the adult male's euphemism for a trip to the bar was 'let's go and look at the engines, shall we?' And, on the *Waverley*, it still is today!

COASTAL COMMERCE — *I have been unsuccessful in tracing the history or ownership of the* Planet Mercury *but she is seen here, riding very light indeed, at an unidentified pier. She is very typical of the small 'three-island' coastal steamers of the early years of the century, so called from the raised fore, main and poop decks rising like islands above the well-decks fore and aft. She was certainly large enough to carry Para Handy's copper pot-still!*

9

Many Happy Returns

I was striding purposefully along Sauchiehall Street towards Charing Cross railway station, intent on catching the earliest possible train home to Helensburgh, but my progress was slower than I could have wished, for the pavements were thronged with shoppers — and sightseers — on this, the first Monday of the traditional Glasgow Trades Fortnight.

As I dodged round yet another family group rooted like a rock in the surging flow of pedestrian traffic, quite transfixed by one of the stunning window-displays in Messrs Treron's elegant emporium, there was a touch on my shoulder and, turning, I was surprised to see the mate of the *Vital Spark* behind me, with a large brown paper parcel tucked under one arm.

"How are you yourself, then, Mr Munro?" asked Dougie. "You seem in a terrible hurry, to be sure. Wull ye no' tak' time to come up to Spiers' Wharf and see the Captain, for we iss there chust waiting for a cairgo o' cement which shows no sign at aal of arrivin' and he would be very pleased to see you."

I explained that, much though I would have liked to take him up on the invitation, I must decline. I was in a hurry to get home early, I added, as today was my birthday and my family, I knew, had a surprise waiting for me and it would not be wise for me to delay the meal which my wife would have lovingly prepared.

"Your birthday, indeed," said Dougie. "Well, I wush you many happy returns — on behalf of us aal on the shup. I chust hope you have a mair propeeshus day than poor Para Handy had a few years back on a sumilar occasion."

And, as we proceeded together along the street, he unfolded an extraordinary tale.

~

It had happened many years previously, when the *Vital Spark* was less than a year old, and Para Handy and his crew were relative strangers who were just beginning to get to know each other.

It was long before Sunny Jim had joined the ship. His cousin Colin Turner, the Tar, fulfilled the functions of deckhand and chef de cuisine on board. It was so long ago that Macphail was still in a state of honeymooner's euphoria with his engines — a state which did not prevail for very much longer. It was long before Para Handy's marriage and Dougie himself, still a young man, had only three children (as against the current count of eleven) and — though they had crewed a sailing-gabbart together on several occasions — had yet to acquire that intimate knowledge of his Captain's character and situation which comes with familiarity.

One April afternoon the puffer was lying alongside the cargo jetty at Tarbert on Loch Fyne. Her cargo of coal had just been discharged but there was no sign of the load of pit-props from the local sawmill which she had been contracted to convey to Ayr for inland despatch to the coalmines around Darvel. Dougie and Macphail were seated in companionable silence on the main hatch: the Tar was wiping off the coaldust besmirching the wheelhouse windows. Para Handy had retired to the fo'c'sle.

It was from that confined space that there now suddenly issued a deep groan followed by a long, protracted sigh.

Alarmed, Dougie rose from the hatch and peered down the open companionway into the crew's cramped quarters.

All he could see of the Captain was the top of his head. Para Handy was standing at the foot of the ladder, holding in his right hand the ship's solitary mirror (which was badly stained and cracked, and which normally hung on a nail on the end of the engineer's bunk) and studying his face in it, his left hand scratching at his stubbly chin. Dougie stared in some surprise, for the mirror was normally used by the Captain but once a week, on the occasion of his customary Sabbath shave, and at no other time.

Again Para Handy groaned, and shook his head at its grubby reflection.

"Man, man," the Captain muttered half under his breath, so that the Mate had to strain to catch the words. "Man, man. Tomorrow iss the bleck day indeed. Bleck, bleck. Today chust a young man at the height o' his prime, but tomorrow is the watter-shed for it iss not chust anither ordinary birthday, but the big wan. The big zero. The big 'O'. And efter that old age, and nothin' to look forward to but totterin' doon the hill to the grave."

And he put the mirror down with another heartrending sigh and vanished out of Dougie's line of sight in the direction of his own bunk. Moments later, the Mate heard the creak of wood as Para Handy climbed into it and lay down.

Dougie walked back to the main-hatch, where Macphail had now been joined by the Tar.

"Boys," said Dougie. "We must do somethin' to cheer the Captain up. Tomorrow iss his birthday, and no' chust a usual one. This is what Para Handy has caaled the 'Big Zero' and it iss getting him doon. Poor duvvle, I had neffer realised it, but this means that he must be fufty tomorrow!"

"Fufty!" exclaimed the Tar. "*Fufty*! I find that very hard to believe, Dougie."

"Me too," said the Mate, "for he iss the sort of man that seems neffer to change in the very slightest way from wan year's end to the beginnin' o' the next, chust the same aal the time."

"Ah'll no' disagree wi' that," said Macphail sharply. "He's aye struck me as a cantankerous auld fool, a dangerous combination of a man, ignorant and thrawn all at the same time."

Dougie paid no attention.

"We must gi'e him a perty tomorrow," he said, "and let him see that this birthday of his is nothing special and most certainly nothing to be depressed aboot — that it iss no different to any other except that it's an even happier one for him. Otherwise he'll be in a bleck mood for weeks, and we do not want that to happen, laads, do we?"

And with the unhappy memory of some of their Captain's previous tirravees all too fresh in their minds (such as the never-to-be-forgotten occasion when he announced that he was giving up drink and indeed did — for all of three days which felt, to his crew, more like three months) his shipmates nodded in agreement.

~

For the next few hours there was feverish but guarded activity in and around the *Vital Spark*.

A whip-round of the available resources of the crew produced the princely sum of two shillings and fourpence, but the Tar then pointed out that a figure as well-known in Tarbert as Para Handy was could surely expect some interest in (and pecuniary contributions to) such a landmark birthday as what everyone, in deference perhaps to the implications of the actual figure, now referred to simply as 'The Big Zero'. Only the Tar periodically shook his head in disbelief (which Dougie found quite touching and indicative of an admiration of his Captain and his apparent youthfulness which he had simply not realised the young man so strongly felt) and muttered "Fufty! *Fufty!* It fair makes you think!"

The funds available to celebrate the auspicious landmark in the Captain's life soon mounted up. The crew, wisely restricting their collecting-round to the local Inns, found that there was an encouraging support for their cause not only from many habitues of these establishments but from their owners as well.

"Peter Macfarlane has been a staunch supporter of mine over a lot of years," observed the Landlord of the Harbour Bar in the sort of response typical of his colleagues in the Tarbert and District Licensed Trades Association, "and it wud be churlish not to give him the encouraging word and the helping hand in his hour of need. Fifty! I find that very hard to believe."

By late afternoon Para Handy's 50th Birthday Fund stood at the very handsome total of two pounds twelve shillings, and there now began a debate as to how best to dispense this magnanimous sum for the better pleasing of its unsuspecting recipient, who dozed the day away fitfully in his berth on board the puffer.

It was decided, after some heated discussion, that two-thirds of the funds collected should be expended on the purchase of a smart new navy-blue pea-jacket for the Captain. His own had seen much better days and was sadly frayed at neck and cuff, but was, even in that state, worn with pride on the Sabbath and on other special days or circumstances, for Para Handy was a man who would have been a commodore if he could, and retained pride both in his command and his appearance.

This still left almost a pound in the kitty, ample to finance a modest refreshment the following morning, on

board the *Vital Spark*, for those who had made some contribution to it and who could be relied upon to help to cheer
the Captain up on his day of gloom. The pea-jacket would
be presented to him at the same time, by Dougie, on behalf
of the assembled company.

When the crew awoke the following morning no hint was
given to the Captain that anyone other than himself was
aware that this was a special day. When Para Handy, as
usual, went ashore after breakfast to telegraph the Glasgow
office of the owner of the *Vital Spark* (and on this occasion
to protest the delay in the arrival at the quayside of their
return cargo, and to wait for a reply) the opportunity was
taken to complete the purchases necessary for the surprise
party, and assemble the company on board the puffer to
await the Captain's return.

The publicans brought with them the beer and spirits for
which Dougie had paid the previous evening and the very
last three shillings was entrusted to the Tar, who was sent
ashore to make the last-minute purchase which was (the
pea-jacket aside) to be the centrepiece of the party.

"Go you to MacNeill's Bakery," said the Mate, "and get
the very best iced cake you can for a half-a-crown. Then go
next door into the newsagents and buy one of they gold
lettered cardboard favours you get for laying on top of the
icing, one that says 'Congratulations and Many Happy
Returns on your 50th Birthday.' And buy a wheen o' wee
cake candles at the same shop to put roond the edge."

The Tar pocketed the coins, muttering again to himself,
"Fufty! I still dinna believe it. Fufty! *Never!*" and went off
to carry out his instructions.

On his return (Para Handy thankfully still not having finished his business at the Telegraph Office) he was sent
below to the fo'c'sle where the pea-jacket lay, neatly par-
celled, on one of the top bunks.

"When I gi'e you the shout," said Dougie, "and you hear
us aal sterting to sing 'Happy Birthday to you', stick the
pea-jaicket under your arm, light the candles on the cake
and bring it up on deck."

~

Ten minutes later Para Handy appeared on the stone
quayside and stared in astonishment at the company gathered on the deck of the *Vital Spark*.

"Mercy," he exclaimed. "What iss the occasion for this, boys?"

"You're the occasion, Peter," said the Landlord of the Harbour Bar. "Dougie found out that it's your birthday, and a rather special one, and we decided we should mark the occasion. It's not every day you reach 'The Big Zero', eh, Peter?"

"Well, well," said Para Handy, delighted, and cheering up quite dramatically, "It iss at a time like this that a man finds oot who his friends are.

"It iss indeed 'The Big Zero' (though I cannot imachine chust how Dougie knew aboot it) and it iss a date that iss a reminder of time passing and a sobering thought indeed for any man when he reaches his fortieth birthday."

Dougie, at the back of the crowd and adjacent to the hatchway down to the fo'c'sle, blanched.

"Colin," he whispered urgently to his shipmate at the foot of the ladder, "Para Handy's 'Big Zero' is his *fortieth* birthday, no' his fuftieth. We're in big trouble when he sees thon cake!"

"We're in bigger trouble than you think," replied the Tar, "for I told you time and again I couldna believe it wis Para Handy's fuftieth birthday. He looks an auld man to me.

"I wis sure it wis his *sixtieth* — and that's the number on the favour I bought for the cake..."

FACTNOTE

Glasgow's highly-regarded and usually independent Department Stores are now nothing but a memory for — with the honourable exception of House of Fraser in the pedestrianised and improved Buchanan Street — they have succumbed to the changes in retail trading patterns and changes wrought (or so the retailers would have us believe) by consumer preferences.

It is passing strange though, that in London there survive such household names as Harrods, Selfridges, Army and Navy Stores, Harvey Nichols, Fortnum and Mason, Liberty — many more: while in Glasgow we have long lost the echoing galleries of Pettigrew and Stephen, Copland and Lye and, missed most of all, Treron on Sauchiehall Street, a seminal legacy of Edwardian architecture sadly gutted by a disastrous fire. The store was lost but at least the City Fathers decreed that its original fascia must be preserved and it now houses, among other residents and tenants, the respected MacLellan Art Galleries.

Spiers Wharf at Port Dundas, on the Glasgow branch of the Forth and Clyde Canal, was named for an Elderslie Tobacco baron whose influence in canal development in late 18th century Scotland was considerable. His warehouses survive, overlooking the now landlocked basin, converted into offices and town flats for the upwardly mobile.

Tarbert or Tarbet — there are at least three places in Scotland bearing the name — derives from the Gaelic for 'Isthmus' and the topography of each confirms that.

Tarbet on Loch Lomond stands just over a mile east of the Loch Long village of Arrochar while in Harris in the Outer Hebrides Tarbert on the Minch coast of the island is less than a mile from the Atlantic shoreline to the west.

Best known of the Tarberts, though, is that on Loch Fyne where once again just about a mile separates the sheltered waters of that Clyde estuary loch from the Atlantic seaboard to the west which gives access to the islands of the Hebrides and the towns and villages of western Argyll.

In every instance, tradition speaks of Norse longships hauled by brute force across the narrow isthmus between one stretch of water and the next. At Tarbert in Argyll such manoeuvres made sense — not just in the semi-mythological reports of Viking incursions, but into recent historic times. Small fishing boats could readily be moved overland from coast to coast with less difficulty than they would face in undertaking the dangerous alternative of almost 150 sea miles round the notorious Mull of Kintyre in some of the stormiest waters in the country.

10

Here be Monsters

Para Handy was more than happy to see that the puffer would be sharing the first of the long flight of locks at Banavie, at the base of that triumph of engineering ingenuity known to all mariners on the Caledonian Canal by the sobriquet of Neptune's Staircase, with two small yachts.

"It will mean more hands, and the more hands that we have, then the lighter the work for us all," he commented to the Mate as they contemplated the daunting series of locks — eight in all — which rose in front of them, tier on tier for more than quarter of a mile, and which the *Vital Spark* must now negotiate to gain access to the tranquil waters of the Canal and a lazy lock-free six mile passage to the entrance to Loch Lochy.

It was some years since Captain and crew had last negotiated the Canal. Most of their work was in and around the waters of the Clyde and the west coast lochs, but just occasionally the owner managed to secure some business which took them out of those familiar surroundings.

They were bound for Drumnadrochit on Loch Ness, in ballast, to collect a cargo of railway sleepers which had been brought down to the lochside from the big Forestry Sawmill at Cannich twelve miles inland. It promised to be a contract quite fraught with difficulties, for there was no pier at Drumnadrochit and, in a tideless inland loch, no way in which the *Vital Spark* could be brought close inshore on the flood to ground on the ebb. When Para Handy pointed out these problems to the owner, he was assured that the forestry team from Corpach had been loading such cargos successfully for many years, and that they would be perfectly capable of doing so once more.

It took four hours for the little flotilla to climb the locks to the top of Neptune's Staircase and, by the time that summit was reached, all hands were exhausted with the constant effort of manoeuvring the heavy wooden sluice-gates of each lock by muscle-power alone.

Para Handy consulted the pocket watch suspended from a nail in the wheelhouse.

"Six o'clock. I think we will chust moor here for the night and make oor way up to Drumnadrochit at furst light," he announced firmly. "We have had a long day and I think that tomorrow wull be longer. And a smaall refreshment would be very welcome after aal oor exertions at the locks and I seem to recall that there is an Inns hereaboots."

The crew's frustrations on discovering that the Banavie Inn was at the foot of the lock system rather than at its summit may be imagined.

"Well, if I had known that then I am sure we could have made good use of it while we were negotiating the first lock," said a disgruntled Captain: "aye, and carried a canister or two of refreshments to keep us cheery on the way up."

"Knowin' you lot," put in Macphail, who was more nippy-tempered even than usual after the struggles of the past few hours, "If you'd been drinkin' your way up the locks then Ah'm sure you'd have forgotten, half-way up, which way she wis meant to be goin', and then for sure you'd have taken her right back doon to the bottom and had it do all over again."

"Pay no heed, Dougie," said Para Handy with dignity. "The man iss chust in a tantrum because he has had to do a day's work for wance, instead of sittin' in yon cubby of his with his nose in wan o' they novelles. Are you comin' with us, Dan, or are you chust goin' to stay up here and worry aboot what iss likely to be happening to poor Lady Fitzgerald and her man in the next episode?"

With ill grace the Engineer went to the pump and washed himself and a few minutes thereafter the three senior members of the crew headed off towards the Inn, leaving the unfortunate Sunny Jim on unwonted and (for him at least) unwanted guard duty.

"I am truly sorry, Jum," said the Captain as they left: "but this iss unfamiliar territory to us and I dare not risk leaving the shup unprotected. Who knows what the natives might steal on us if they had the chance."

"Ah suppose you think this is Red Indian country," remarked the Engineer sarcastically. "In any case, who in their right mind would want tae steal onything aff of this auld hooker? There isnae a decent piece of marine equipment on her, and the local pawn wuddna gi'e much for yon old watch of yours."

~

The trio were in much better spirits and a more amicable frame of mind when they returned just before midnight, for they had had a good run at dominoes, playing the locals for drinks, and an ungrudging conviviality prevailed. Even the discovery that their night watchman was fast asleep in his bunk, and by the look of him had been so for some hours, and did not even so much as stir when the shore-party tumbled noisily into the fo'c'sle, did not ruffle the Captain's equanimity.

"Och, you wass probably right, Dan," he conceded. "There iss not a lot to steal from the *Vital Spark* and in any case I am sure that the locals iss aal true Highland chentlemen."

Nobody was foolish enough to remind Para Handy of that cheerily expressed opinion when, at first light, Sunny Jim staggered up on deck to look at the weather, and found two individuals in the act of jumping onto the canal bank with the oars of the puffer's dinghy over their shoulders.

~

The oars, recovered from the towpath where the thieves dropped them in their flight, were firmly lashed, upright, to the mast of the *Vital Spark* as the puffer proceeded to make passage up Loch Lochy and Loch Oich, and then came to the historic little town of Fort Augustus at the foot of Loch Ness.

"You know," confessed Para Handy from the wheelhouse window as the vessel nosed out onto the dark waters of Scotland's longest loch, "if it wassna for having to work aal those dam' locks by hand there would be a lot to be said for a command on the canal for I am sure that you would neffer have to worry aboot the weather or the wund or the fog. An easy life!"

His crew, who had back-breakingly worked their way through every single one of the locks, at each of which their Captain's only contribution to the process had been shouted (and all too often contradictory) instructions emanating from that same wheelhouse window, said nothing.

The puffer arrived at Drumnadrochit later that afternoon, too late for any work to be started that day, although the forestry men had got there ahead of the *Vital Spark* and a huge stack of sleepers lay piled up on the shore beside a tiny concrete slip.

Para Handy surveyed the scene with a marked lack of enthusiasm.

"How in bleezes do they propose to get aal of that out to the shup?" he asked querulously. "We cannot get closer in than 50 yards and I for one am no' goin' swimmin' for anyone."

∼

He had his answer in the morning.

By eight o'clock the loading process was in full swing, with two foremen from the sawmills — one ashore and one on board the *Vital Spark* — supervising and co-ordinating the operations.

A raft some twelve feet square lay alongside the concrete slip, attached by two ropes to the collar of a towering but placid Clydesdale horse which, having been led down the slip by its handlers, now stood in the loch to the front of the raft up to its hocks in the water.

Once the raft was loaded, the two handlers — who wore only canvas trousers cut off at the knee, and heavy boots with substantial, studded soles — took one rein of the bridle apiece and led the horse across the sandy bottom of the loch till they were in up to their waists and the the loch bed began to deepen rapidly. At this point the cargo was within twenty yards of the puffer, lying in the deeper water, and the forestry foreman on board the *Vital Spark* threw a light rope, lead-line for a heavy hawser which was itself coiled round the drum of the puffer's steam-winch. The handlers unloosed the patient horse, Macphail started up the winch at the foreman's signal, and the raft was reeled in to the side of the ship as an angler might reel in a fish. The men in the water, who had retained one line attached to the stern of the cargo-carrier. pulled it back once it had been unloaded and returned with it and the horse, once more set within its traces, to the shore.

The process continued all morning till the hold of the *Vital Spark* was full and a substantial deck cargo had been built up on the main hatch.

Para Handy watched the proceedings with some admiration.

"Now that iss chust astonishing," he said. "And that horse iss a wonder. Wass she no' awful hard to train, for I'm sure and she canna like the watter at aal."

"On the contrary," the foreman laughed. "She just loves it, for most horses are great swimmers. We sometimes have a job keeping her in the shallows. She'd be swimming out with the raft given a half a chance!"

Para Handy looked appraisingly at the sleepers stacked on the main hatch.

"I think that will do us," said he. "It iss not ass if we only have to take them doon the loch. We have to get back doon to Gleska and I will not overload the shup."

"Fair enough," said the foreman. "You know your own business best. But we would ask one wee favour of you, it will not be a problem I'm thinking, and that is to let me put just three new wooden mash-tubs for the distillery at Fort William on top of the lot. If you would just drop them off at the distillery pier, I know that the maltings manager will see that it is made worth your while."

Para Handy nodded his agreement and the foreman then bellowed instructions to the shore party. Three very large barrels were rolled down the slip roped together in line, and the first of them attached to one of the Clydesdale's towing ropes.

Just what happened was never too clear. Probably one of the handlers slipped on a rock and took his colleague with him, but next second the two men had let go of the horse's bridle and disappeared, briefly, under water.

By the time they surfaced, spluttering, the horse was gone. Pulling this much lighter burden behind her with ease, she splashed out into the deeper water, kicked out, and began to swim out past the *Vital Spark* with the three barrels bobbing in her wake. As she past the puffer she turned to the south and proceeded to swim along parallel with the shore.

" 'Dalmighty," exclaimed the foreman. "She's off! Please get your dinghy in the water, Captain, and I'll row after her and catch her. Otherwise she'll probably swim a couple of miles or more before she decides she's had enough and heads for the shore"

Launching the dinghy was the work of a moment — but of course it was then realised that her *oars* were firmly lashed to the puffer's mast. By the time these had been loosed, the horse was a hundred yards away and the prospects of catching her slim.

The foreman and the puffer's crew watched the horse with its attendant barrels move into the distance, silhouetted darkly against the mirror-brightness of the still surface of the loch.

"I'll tell you something," chipped in Sunny Jim after a moment, laughing delightedly. "See wi' jist the heid o' the horse oot o' the watter like that, and they three barrels like humps behind it, the whole shebang fair pits ye in mind o' a dragon: or better yet a sea-serpent, eh?"

Para Handy chuckled.

"Aye Jum, that'll be right. A monster in Loch Ness! Now that *would* be something to excite the towerists, eh?"

And, helping the foreman into the dinghy, he rowed him ashore to find a pony and trap with which to pursue his errant charge along the road which wound along the lochside.

"You and your monsters, Jum!" protested the Mate. "All I know iss that this wan has cost us the chance of a dram from the distillery, and that iss most certainly a monster inchustice, to be sure!"

FACTNOTE

Telford's Caledonian Canal was a formidable undertaking for the technology of the age. It took 18 years to complete and was opened formally in 1822. Using the natural fault of the Great Glen and the string of lochs (Lochy, Oich and Ness) which gave immediately navigable waterways over two thirds of its length from Corpach at the head of Loch Linnhe to Inverness on the Moray Firth, it is 60 miles long and vessels traversing it have to negotiate 29 locks.

The government of the day was first moved to find the funds to build it by the exigencies of the Napoleonic Wars. A sheltered passage from Scotland's East to West coasts, wide enough and deep enough to enable frigates and small merchant vessels to use it, would help the Navy to deploy ships to and from the various theatres of the maritime war more readily: and it would offer a safer passage for merchant and fishing vessels, one that would shelter them not just from the storms of the Pentland Firth but from the intrusions of the French privateers which skulked off the Scottish coasts on the lookout for unwary and defenceless prey.

The flight of eight locks at Banavie was an engineering marvel, an achievement without parallel at that early stage of canal development and still today an impressive prospect.

What can one say about the Loch Ness monster that either hasn't been said before or is palpable nonsense?

It would be very satisfying to believe in its existence and I suppose that it must be real enough in one sense, for it has spawned an immense tourist industry, and lured individuals and organisations from the patently dotty to the seriously scientific, and from all quarters of the globe, to expend years of effort and enormous sums of money in an attempt to track it down for the discomfiture of non-believers.

All this despite the fact that the first and most famous of all the Loch Ness photographs — the 'Surgeon's Picture' of 1933, the basis really for all the subsequent monster mania of the last sixty years, has now been acknowledged — by no less an authoritative voice than that of its perpetrators — as a quite deliberate hoax.

At one time there were two distilleries at Fort William though they were under the same ownership and the second one operated only for a few years at the turn of the century. Both stood on the river Nevis, and were served by a private jetty on Loch Linnhe. The water for both was drawn from a single well, high up on the slopes of Ben Nevis.

11

The Tight White Collar

From the window of the Inns at Crarae, Para Handy watched with interest the comings and goings in and around the pier of the little Lochfyneside village — a popular destination in summer for day-trippers, and a much-loved oasis of peace for those who were fortunate enough to manage to secure rooms in one of its handful of boarding-houses for the Fair Fortnight.

The steamer from Glasgow had just berthed, and was disgorging the usual motley selection of human kind. The *Vital Spark*, with Sunny Jim just visible — perched on her stern-quarter with a fishing-line — was sharing the inner wing of the wooden pier with two local fishing boats.

At that moment, the three man crew of one of these vessels came in sight, having just left the Inns by the front door and now striding across the lochside road to the pierhead. As they did so they were confronted by a group of Ministers, unmistakable in the dark frock-coats and contrasting white collars which were their badge of office, making their way up to the village from the excursion steamer. Suddenly aware of the presence of the approaching gentlemen of the cloth the fishermen hesitated momentarily and then side-stepped to the right, thus giving the clergy as wide a berth as the narrow pierhead allowed, before proceeding onwards and down towards their skiff.

Para Handy turned to his Engineer and Mate and remarked: "Well now, there iss a sign of the times and no mustake! It iss not aal that many years ago that a fisherman meetin' a Meenister on his way to his vessel would chust have turned for home again and neffer sailed that day. It wass thought to be duvvelish bad luck, and a sure sign of disaster or poor, poor fushin's at the very least, to meet with the clergy like that. Yet here is Col MacIlvain and his laads cairryin' on aboot their business quite jocco, and them efter meeting not chust the wan Meenister but a good half-a-dozen o' the species! Changed days indeed!"

Macphail nodded.

"Right enough," he said: "Ah've seen jist one English munister on his holidays turn back the hauf o' the Tarbert herring fleet at the very height o' the fushin's in the good days, by takin' a daunder alang the quay at the wrang time o' day!"

Dougie snorted.

"Chust nonsense," he protested, "superstitious nonsense. There iss no more ill-luck aboot a Meenister than there iss aboot ony o' God's creatures. The man that tells you different doesna ken ony better and that's the truth of it! It would tak' mair nor a Meenister to keep me from my shup any hour of the day, I can assure you of that."

"Mind you," Para Handy observed, "I think it must be admutted that there have been many times when it hass been the fushermen or the sailormen — Brutain's hardy sons! — that have made life difficult for the Meenisters.

"Hurricane Jeck hisself wass aalways gettin' into trouble wi' the Church for wan reason or the ither..."

"Ah'm no' surprised in the very least aboot that," interrupted Macphail caustically: "that man has the happy knack o' gettin' into trouble wi' onything that lives or breathes. Dear God, he wud pick a fight wi' a dry-stane dyke if ye were tae gi'e him the opportunity!"

The Captain paid no attention.

"There wass one time," he continued. "that Jeck was asked by wan o' his kizzins, whose wife had chust had a new bairn, if he'd be the Godfather to it" — there was an explosive spluttering as the Engineer nearly choked himself on a mouthful of beer — "and of course Jeck said yes, he'd be delighted. You know yourselves that he iss the kind of a man that would neffer willingly refuse onything to onybody, for he has aalways been the perfect chentleman.

"The chrustening wass to be at St John's in Dunoon, a fine kirk and congregation and a most handsome building. The trouble came from the fact that the wean wass to be laaunched, as you might say, ass a pert o' the evening service and no' the morning wan ass usual, because Jeck's kizzin and his wife couldna get doon to the town wi' the bairn till the afternoon, what wi' them aal livin' away oot in the muddle o' nowhere on a wee ferm that they tenanted from wan o' the MacArthurs up at the head o' Loch Striven.

" 'Don't you worry about a thing, Jamie,' said Jeck to his kizzin. 'Rely upon it that I will be there for you, and in the very best of trum! For to be sure, us Maclachlans must stick together in the hour of need! We aalways have and we aalways wull! I wull come over to Dunoon on wan o' the efternoon boats and meet you outside the Kirk at six o'clock.' He wass lodging in Gourock chust then, and had a kind of a chob loading coals onto Mr MacBrayne's shups at the Cardwell Bay bunkering pier, for he wass doon on his luck at the time.

"Well, Jeck wass early to his bed on the Saturday, and without even a single dram in him, for he wass taking the duties of the next day seriously to heart: so much so that when he woke on the Sabbath he decided that he would come over to Dunoon early to be sure of being there on time, for he wass that determined not to let his kizzin doon.

"At eleven of the clock next morning he presented himself on the pier to tak' the first shup he could get with the idea of a meat dinner at the Argyll Hotel and then a quiet stroll on the sea-front till time for the service, and what shup wass it but the *Dunoon Castle* herself, the most notorious of aal the 'Sunday Boats', on an excursion from Broomielaw to Rothesay?

"Jeck neffer paid heed, it wass chust a twenty meenit crossing and it was neither eechie nor ochie to him whit shup it was, so he boarded her without realising it.

"The bar had been open since the moment the shup had cast off from the Broomielaw but even that wouldna have mattered as Jeck wassna thinkin' aboot drink at aal that morning" — once again the Engineer seemed to encounter problems getting breath, and once again the Captain paid no attention — "but the very first person he clapped eyes on when he got aboard her wass his old shupmate Donald Baird, who'd been his Furst Mate on the clupper *Port Jackson*. The two of them hadna seen each other for near on five years.

"Donald had been two hours on the vessel, and the most of them spent in the Refreshment Saloon, so he wass feelin' no pain at aal. And he wouldna tak' *no* for an answer, neither.

" 'To bleezes, Jeck,' said he with some conviction, when

Jeck told him where he wass bound for and why, and chust why he wouldna tak' a dram in the by-going either: 'you have aal the day to get through before tonight's chrustening, and I am sure that nobody wull force you to tak' a refreshment if you are set against it. Stay on board chust for the baur! We have a lot of catchin' up to do, and since the shup wull get back to Dunoon from Rothesay at five o'clock that gives you plenty of time for you to present yourself at the Kirk.'

"Jeck aalways finds it very difficult to refuse that kind of an invitation, ass bein' a true chentleman iss aal a part of his upbringing and his cheneral agreeableness. He would neffer wullingly hurt a fly, neffer mind the feelings of his fellow human beings! So while the shup crossed over to Dunoon he stood at the rail with Donald and exchanged the news of the last five years. But then ass soon ass the vessel was away from Dunoon and past the Gantocks on course for Innellan and Rothesay, did he not allow himself to be inveigled doon to the Refreshment Saloon 'for chust the wan wee gless of ale for the sake of the heat that's in the day' ass Donald put it: and though Jeck had little enough coin with him, for he wass doon on hiss luck yet again poor duvvle, ass I have told you already, Donald had chust been paid off efter a seven month trup to the Far East wi' mair money than he knew what do do with, and he simply wouldna let Jeck refuse his hospitality for aal his protests.

"The outcome wass inevitable. By the time the *Dunoon Castle* got back to Dunoon at five o'clock Jeck wass in chust ass good trum as Donald. The dufference, of course, wass that Jeck — being a perfect chentleman in efferything he did — could carry his dram and it wass only when you were really up close that you became aware that the man was not totally in control of himself but was operating by unstinct raither than logic, and that ass a result onything might happen — and probably would.

"There wass aalways a most stumulating atmosphere of complete uncertainty aboot, wheneffer Jeck was in good trum!

"Jeck and Donald had a tearful farewell, and Jeck headed off to St John's Kirk. He had a half hour to wait before the kizzin arrived, so he sat on the wall in Hanover Street and took a few good deep breaths of the Cowal air, and sooked on a wheen of candy-striped baalls he'd had the sense to buy from a sweetie barrow on the esplanade.

"By the time the chrustening perty arrived, and they wass aal ushered into the vestry o' the Kirk, Jeck *looked* the pert right enough: but there wass still enough drams coursin' through hiss veins to float a toy yat, and his view of the proceedings wass hazy to say the least. But, ass you know, wi' aal the cheneral agility he had, only Jeck himself would have known it.

"The only wan o' the perty that jaloused that maybe efferything wass no' chust what it seemed wass the Meenister himself. But he said nothin', until they wass in the Kirk and when, half way through the chrustening, Jeck was handed the wean by the mither and telt to tak' it up to the Meenister so that it could get the watter splashed over it.

"At that point the Meenister got his furst real whuff o' Jeck's breath — and in spite o' the candy-striped baalls he'd been sookin' ye wouldna have needed to be a bloodhound to realise that there wass that much spurits to it that you could have set it alight if you'd had a match — and asked him in a piercing whisper that could be heard aal roond the Kirk: 'Are you sure you're fit enough to hold that child?'

" 'Fit enough to haud it?' cried Jeck loudly, and he grupped the bairn in both airms and held it ass high over his head ass he could stretch and waved it aboot from side to side, 'fit enough to *haud* it? Man, I'm fit enough that if you chust gi'e me the chance I'll tak' it ootside right noo and throw it over the roof of the Kirk, steeple and aal!'

"Jeck's Glenstriven kizzin has neffer spoken to him since, and the St John's Meenister iss now aawful wary of ony chrustenings which involve sailors or their femilies: so mebbe the men of the cloth should be ass superstitious noo aboot the fushermen o' Crarae as the fushermen used to be aboot the Church!"

The pierhead now being clear of crowds, and the steamer having departed for her ultimate outward destination — Inveraray, by way of Furnace — the three shipmates left the Inns and headed back towards the *Vital Spark*.

"If we get away within the half-hour," said Para Handy, pulling his watch out of his trouser pocket, "we can be in Rothesay by eight o'clock and ready to load the Marquess of Bute's potatos first thing tomorrow."

There was a sudden, protesting croak from the Mate.

"Peter," said he, agonised: "look who's talkin' to Jum at the shup! It's the Reverend McNeil, our Parish Meenister."

Both Dougie and his Captain (with their wives) were members of the same congregation in Glasgow. The difference between their membership of it, however, was that though the Minister did not approve of the Captain's predilection for a dram, he was aware of it — and prepared to tolerate it. The Mate, on the other hand, had for many years now successfully pretended to both his wife and his Minister that he was of a Rechabitic and therefore strictly teetotal persuasion.

"He must have been wi' the excursion perty and recognised the vessel when they came ashore," Dougie continued. "I canna let him find me like this, he'll smell the drink on me and it's no chust that he'll put a bleck mark on me for it wi' the Kirk Session, he'll tell the mussis and my life wull not be worth living, I can assure you.

"I'm awa' to hide. Tell him I'm not on the shup this trup, tell him onything you like."

"Shame on you Dougie," said the Captain, "I thought you told us back there in the Inns that no Meenister would effer keep you from boarding *your* shup? You cannot surely have forgotten that aalready?"

"Forbye, he hass seen us!"

And with a cheery wave, he strolled down the quayside to shake the Minister by the hand.

FACTNOTE

In earlier generations superstition was rife in every fishing community from Cornwall to Shetland and took some quite bizarre forms. For some, it was unlucky to mention pigs (or pork, which must have somewhat restricted the choice of victuals on offer at mealtimes) and other animals which must never be talked of at sea included ferrets and rabbits.

Whistling on the quayside when the wind was from the east was another taboo in some ports, while refusal to sail on a Friday was more widespread. Sticking a knife into the mast (for wind) was a good-luck omen for some, a bad-luck certainty for others.

Almost universal were the superstitions associated with the clergy of all denominations. To meet a minister or priest on the road to the harbour was bad enough, to have one come aboard the boat for any reason was a portent of certain disaster.

'Sunday Boats' became a notorious feature on the Firth during the last decades of the 19th century. The Licensing Acts then in force forbade the sale of alcohol on the Sabbath save only to so-called 'Bona Fide Travellers' or to Hotel residents. But a number of enterprising (or to put it rather more accurately, avaricious) Glasgow publicans spotted that the restrictions of these Acts did not apply to ships: and realised that there were enough thirsty Glaswegians to make an investment in a battered old paddle-steamer a most rewarding speculation.

Their resulting Sunday fleets consisted of boats which had no pretensions to be family cruising vessels — or indeed cruising vessels in *any* sense. They were floating shebeens but (and here was the ace card) they were *legal* shebeens, and earned huge profits for their owners. Andrew McQueen summed up the whole sorry state-of-affairs very accurately in his *Clyde Steamers of the Last Fifty Years*, published in 1924:

'Travellers by these boats were almost entirely drouths out to secure the alcoholic refreshment denied to them ashore. The boats were simply floating pubs, and their routes and destinations were matters of little moment. It is probable that, when they arrived home, a large proportion of the passengers had no very definite idea as to where they had been.'

From the excesses of the 'Sunday Boats' (and the *Dunoon Castle* was the most ill-reputed of them all) came the development of the temperance steamers: and the amendments to the Licensing Acts in the late 1880s which banned sales of alcohol on Sundays aboard any vessel returning to her port of departure on the same day, and effectively closed down the Sabbath breakers.

12

That Sinking Feeling

Para Handy laid down the previous day's edition of the *Glasgow Evening News* (the most up-to-date account of the world and its ways presently available in the Harbour Inn at Ardrossan) with a snort of disdain.

"I chust cannot think what the Navy iss coming to, I said it to Dan a meenit ago" he confided to Dougie. Macphail was standing up at the bar talking to one of the engineers off the *Glen Sannox*, which had just completed her last run from Brodick. "What sort o' men are they employin' ass captains or helmsmen nooadays? Here iss another Naval shup agroond on the Lady Rock in the Firth of Lorne.

"Where the bleezes iss the Admirulity recruitin' these days? At the weans' boating pond at Kelvingrove? That makes three of His Majesty's Shups grounded on the Lady Rock skerry this year alone, and we're no' into October yet. It's not even ass if the rock wassna well enough lit, you ken that it is fine enough yourself, Dougie: you've seen it often: mony's the seck of winter coals we've humphed ashore there.

"At this rate poor King Edward'll be runnin' oot o' shups to send up there — or onywhere else."

"It's probably the same shup aal the time, Peter," observed the Mate. "or mebbe the same skipper. For there iss some shups, and some men, that chust seem to have a jinx on them.

"Did I neffer tell you aboot the mustress's Uncle Wulliam? He's retired noo, but he wass a deckhand, then a mate, and finally a skipper on wan or ither o' the Hays' boats aal his working life and given what befell him it's a miracle the owners kept him on for mair than a month. It wass wan disaster efter anither!

"At least when he didna have the command, he couldna really do aal that mich damage and it tended to be sma' beer.

"When he wass deckhand, mony times when he would be throwin' a line ashore for the longshoremen or the pier-hands to catch hold of, he'd throw it short and then discover it wassna even the right line: it would be chust a spare length of rope he'd flemished-doon *beside* the right line — for tidiness by his way of it — that wassna attached to onything on the shup, and they lost coont o' the fathoms and fathoms o' good rope he cost them, lyin' at the bottom of the river.

"More than wance, when he wass ashore himself to put a bight of a mooring-line over a bollard, he would pit it on wan that wass already cairrying the hawser of a steamer and you know yourself what the steamer crews can be like. They chust threw the top rope over the side of the pier, and Uncle Wulliam's vessel went driftin' off — if they were lucky.

"If they were *unlucky*, the bight of their line got aal fankled wi' the hawser of the steamer, so that wherever she went, they went too. The steamer crews never bothered to unfankle it, for them it wass chust a fine amusement, takin' poor Uncle Wullie's shup in tow ass if it they wass takin' a dug for a waalk on a leash. Wan time the *Inveraray Castle* towed them aal the way from Port Bannatyne to Colintraive before the Officers on the brudge of the paddle-steamer realised that they wassna alone in the Kyles!

"Ass Uncle Wulliam moved up the ladder o' command wi' Hays, and only the good Lord knows how he ever did, his capacity to make a mess of things increased dramatically. The mair he wass given to do, then the mair there wass that could go wrong, and maist usually it did."

"I canna understand how John Hay put up wi' it at all," put in the Engineer, who had rejoined his shipmates. "He wisna a man famous for his tolerance, wis he?"

"Right enough," said Dougie. "The faimily aalways used to say that Uncle Wulliam must have had some kind of a haud over John Hay, that he'd caught him wi' a drink in him on a Fast Day, or tellin' fibs to the Board o' Tred.

"But it wassna that at aal, of course: it wass chust that John Hay liked to have a man aboot the place that wass like a clown at a circus, good for a laugh so long as the herm he did wassna too serious, and it made John Hay feel important, like wan o' they auld medevial kings wi' his own Court Jester.

"But, ass I say, when Uncle Wulliam wass made Mate, there wass more scope for disaster.

"He showed that in fine style. His very first assignment ass a Mate went wrang — I canna chust mind the way of it — and for the next few years he wass shufted from wan shup o' the Hays' fleet to anither, none o' the skippers wanted him for long because something wass aye goin' to pieces when he wass aroond. Finally he was berthed on a puffer that was sent to the wee pier at Sannox, at the north end of Arran, for a cargo o' barytes ore from the mine up the glen.

"It iss a horrid cairgo to load and unload: mercifully we've neffer had a contract for't on the *Vital Spark*. What you may not know, then, iss that it iss a most terrible *heavy* cairgo. A bucketful o' barytes weighs an awful lot mair then a bucketful of onything else you care to name. So ony shup hass to be very careful how mich of it she takes on board, and her captain hass to work oot the load very carefully.

"Onyway, in came Uncle Wulliam's boat on the high tide, and they put her alangside the jetty and ass the tide went oot she beached herself, for there wassna mich watter at the inner end o' the pier.

"The boat wass chust a three-hander and wance she wass berthed, and still no sign of the quarry men comin' wi' the cairts of barytes, the skipper told Uncle Wulliam that he would leave him in cherge while he went to the Inn at Sannox vullage for a wee refreshment, and off he went and took the enchineer with him.

" 'If onybody frae the mine arrives,' said the skipper, 'tell him I'm at the Inns and whenever he wants to get the loading sterted, he can send for me, it's jist hauf-a-mile away. In the meantime, jist you keep an eye on the boat — and dinna you daur touch a thing,' he added emphatically, for Uncle Wulliam's reputation for makin' trouble had come before him.

"Chust ten minutes efter they'd left, the furst o' the Sannox Mine cairts appeared wi' two big Clydesdales in the shafts, and a squad o' men to help load the shup.

"There wass a kind of a chute wi' a funnel on tap of it fixed to a trolley on the quay, and the whole shebang could be swung roond and pointed doon into the hold of any vessel lying alangside. Then the ore wass chust shovelled from the cairts into the funnel and went whooshing doon the chute like snaw off a dyke and into the hold.

"Aal the crew of any shup had to do was point the mooth o' the chute in the right direction and get the trolley it wass moored to moved effery now and then so that the ore wass evenly spread in the hold.

"So when the first o' the cairts arrived, the foreman leaned over and shouted 'Puffer ahoy! Hoo mich o this dam' stuff can ye take?'

"Uncle Wulliam wass chust aboot to give the man the captain's message, when he thought to himself that it would be a grand surprise for his skipper to come back and find the chob aal done for him: mebbe it would be good for Uncle Wulliam's career too if he showed the unitiative.

"So, instead o' doin' what he wass told like a sensible chap would have done, he shouted back 'Chust you go ahead and fill her up wheneffer you're ready!'

" 'Fill her *up*?' said the foreman, quite flummoxed. 'Are ye sure ye ken whit ye're daeing?'

"Uncle Wulliam drew himself up to his full height and adjusted his peaked kep (he'd bought a white-topped wan ass soon ass the news of his promotion cam' through) and replied sherply: 'You concentrate on looking efter your horses, and allow me to know what iss best for the shup!'

"The foreman shrugged: it wassna his affair. For the next two hoors the Clyesdales and their cairts kept the barytes comin' doon to the shup, and by that time the hold wass full quite to the brim.

"The foreman got Uncle Wulliam to sign a sort of a paper givin' the tonnage she'd taken aboard, and off he and his men went.

"Chust as the loading sterted, the tide had turned and aal this time since then the flood had been coming in. The first inkling Uncle Wulliam had that something wassna right wass when he realised that the water wass creeping up the side o' the shup and the shup wassna moving at aal, she was stuck fast on the bottom as she had been at the foot o' the ebb. She wass that overweighted doon there wass no way at aal that she wass going to float!

"By the time the skipper and enchineer came back from the Inns the only parts of the shup that wass above watter was the mast, the wheelhoose, the ventilators and the funnel.

"It took them three days wi' buckets and shovels at low tide to empty enough barytes oot o' the hold for the shup to be able to refloat herself."

"And Hay's didna seck the man, not even efter that?" asked Para Handy in astonishment.

"Not them," said the Mate. "I can only think they believed that secking him would bring ill-luck on the firm — or that greater responsubility would mebbe improve the man, for it wassna aal that long efter the Sannox uncident that they gave him a shup of his ain.

"He wass to tak' her into Auchentarra on Loch Linnhe for a cairgo of granite from the wee quarry there.

"They cam' in at the peak o' high tide: the jetty was near awash wi' it and they had to lie off for an hour for the ebb to tak' some watter away and give them a chance to berth and make fast.

"Next morning they began to load up, but the quarry wass a good mile from the pier, and they had chust the wan cairt, wi' chust wan horse, and it took a couple of days to get the chob done.

"They took the granite doon to Oban, unloaded it at a private wharf at the sooth end of the bay, then back again for anither load from Auchentarra aboot three days efterwards.

"Wance the shup wass full to the line again, Uncle Wulliam made his farewells wi' the quarrymen, and cast off.

"This time they only got two hundred yerds oot towards the mooth of the bay when she grounded! What Uncle Wulliam had not realised wass that when they'd put in the previous week they'd come in on the spring tides, and the soundings he'd taken then on the way in, and back oot again, wassna the normal ones.

"There wass a sand-bar across the mooth of the bay which neffer had more than 10ft of soundings at normal high watter. But at the springs, there wass well over 16ft of watter on it at high tide.

"When Uncle Wulliam lifted his first cairgo, he'd come in and gone oot on the springs, drawing 11ft aft when she wass loaded, but wi' plenty mair than that under the keel he'd done so withoot any bother.

"This time, though, he wass well and truly stuck. It would be two weeks before the tides wass near enough the springs to give the shup enough watter to refloat herself. Meantime they had the choice of either throwing the cairgo overboard to free the shup, or sitting it oot.

"Uncle Wulliam telegraphed to the Hays' office in Kirkintilloch for instructions. Raither to his surprise, their reply was to tell him no' to dump the cairgo, chust to bide where he was and wait for the springs.

"He wass surprised: I neffer wass," the Mate concluded. "I think that Mr Hay realised it would be less dangerous for the company and its shups, no' to mention the world at large, chust to leave Uncle Wulliam stuck on a sandbar somewhere in Lorne for a fortnight, raither than have him goin' aboot loose."

"Well, Peter," observed the Engineer: "now ye'll mebbe stop fretting aboot the Admirulity. At least they havna got Dougie's Uncle Wulliam on their books. Jist as weel, or we'd be doon to wir last torpedo-boat-destroyer if his record in the merchant fleet wis onything to go by!

"Mebbe that wis why Hay never sacked him: perhaps the guvernment paid a subsidy to keep him oot of the Navy!"

FACTNOTE

There were three steamers named *Inveraray Castle* on the Clyde during the 19th century, and it is even thought that one of them was built as early as 1814, just two years after Bell's pioneering *Comet*.

The third ship of the name is the best-known. She was built in 1839 and was in service for almost 60 years, during which period she was twice taken into dry-dock and lengthened — a not unusual practice at that time.

She is believed to have spent her entire career on the Glasgow to Inveraray run — out one day and back the next — and provided the sort of passenger (and light cargo) service to the smaller piers and remoter communities which was beneath the dignity (or beyond the capabilities, due to their sheer size) of the giants of the steamer fleets.

Most of the Clyde puffer fleet belonged to John Hay and Company of Kirkintilloch. That business was in operation for almost 100 years and over that period the firm owned more than 90 of the little boats. They built most of what they owned, too, at their Kirkintilloch yard. Ross and Marshall of Greenock were another significant owner, starting as shipowners later than Hay but remaining in the business longer. They too nearly celebrated their centenary.

UNLUCKY FOR SOME — Here is Naval Patrol Boat 13 well and truly aground somewhere around Kintyre in the first decade of this century. Built in 1907, powered by Parson turbines, these little craft — 185ft in length but with a beam of only 18ft — were capable of 26 knots. Number 13's luck did not improve: she was lost in 1914 although not through enemy action, but collision with another naval vessel in the North Sea.

There was indeed a barytes mine in Glen Sannox and the ore was notoriously heavy for its bulk. Extraction of the mineral began in 1840 but at some point later in the Victorian era the whole operation was closed down by the then landowner (the Duke of Hamilton) on what seems to have been purely aesthetic or ecological grounds. A surprisingly late 20th century knee-jerk reaction to find a century earlier!

After the First War the mine was opened once again. It had its own private jetty just outside Sannox village and, by then, a light railway to haul the ponderous raw material down to the waiting puffers. The mine closed for good shortly before the outbreak of the Second War but it was during this period of its history that the ore really *did* 'sink' an unfortunate puffer and its unsuspecting or inexperienced skipper. Indeed, I am indebted to a reader of my first collection of Para Handy tales for relating to me his own recollections of just such an unexpected incident at the little Sannox pier!

Strangely, I cannot find the bay of Auchentarra, with its dangerous sandbar lurking to trap the unwary, in any maps that I have of the Loch Linnhe area.

13

A Boatman's Holiday

I was standing on the pier at Rothesay passing the time of day with Para Handy, whose beloved vessel lay in the outer harbour waiting the arrival of the local contractor's carts so that a cargo of road-chips could be unloaded.

It was early on a scorching August afternoon: the capital of Bute was already overwhelmed with visitors but their number was in process of being substantially augmented by the crowds who could be seen streaming ashore from the *Iona*, calling on her way to Tarbert and Ardrishaig, having left the Broomielaw at noon on the afternoon run which supplemented the *Columba*'s morning service on the route during the peak season.

"You would wonder where they are aal going to stay," remarked the Captain, watching as fathers struggled down the gangplank with the family's tin trunks and hat boxes while elsewhere on the pier anxious mothers desperately waved a rolled-up umbrella (only the very foolish ever came to Bute without one) to try to catch the attention of an unengaged shore porter with an empty handcart who could wheel the luggage along the esplanade to their chosen hotel.

"There iss times when I think that the island will chust up and sink under the sheer weight o' the numbers. If there iss ony hooseholds in the toon that iss not sleepin' in their beck yerds whiles the hoose is earning coin from towerists packed in hauf-a-dozen to the room, then they must be gey few and far between."

"What do you and Mrs Macfarlane do yourselves when it comes to holidays, Captain?" I enquired, curious: "presumably you have seen enough of the West Coast resorts all the other 50 weeks of the year, and choose something very different?"

"Mery and I very rarely go awa' at aal," Para Handy said. "I am no' mich of a traiveller, other than at my work. And if I can get the twa weeks o' the Fair off, then we ha'e Gleska almost to oorselves. Half the city hass gone doon the watter somewhere and the toon iss deserted.

"You have no idea how peaceful it iss in the Botanic Gairdens, or Gleska Green, or Kelvingrove, when there iss no crowds. And it iss the same wi' the shops, and the tea-rooms, and the picture palaces and aal the rest. There iss no crowds to fight your way through, and the shopkeepers and the rest is most obleeging, they're dam' gled to see ony customers at aal when the maist of their regular tred iss spending their money on sticks o' rock and Eyetalian ices somewhere aboot Innellan or Saltcoats.

"Certainly Gleska's no' a place you'd think to tak' your holidays in ony ither time o' the year but I assure you, in the second hauf of July, you could go a lot further and do a lot worse."

"An interesting concept, Captain," I said: "I confess I have never thought of it that way. In any case, I admit that I enjoy a change of scenery and surroundings, myself."

"Oh, we are not total stay-at-homes," said Para Handy. "We have been doon to England, we stayed at Bleckpool for a week wan year. It iss a strange toon, full o' the English, and the maist of their hooses is built oot o' brick wi' nae harling, it looks like a hauf-feenished building-site.

"We went doon by train frae Gleska, and when we got there we took a horse-cab to the hoose we wass booked into, for it wass a fair step oot of the toon centre.

"Aal the way through the toon Mery kept pointin' oot the number o' temperance hooses to be seen, they wass clustered at every street corner. I'd noticed it myself, and I wass getting a bit anxious aboot it, I can tell you.

"But Mery wass delighted, and she remarked to the cab-driver that Bleckpool must be wan o' the most abstentious holiday-resorts in the country, and the chentlemen that owned the temperance hotels deserved to be congratulated for their convictions.

" 'It's not chust exactly what you're thinking, Ma'am,' said the cabbie: 'though in one sense *convictions* is the right word to be using.

" 'You see, of aal the dry hooses you see, aboot hauf of

them *wants* a licence but cannae get it frae the magustrates because o' the reputation they have: and the other hauf *used* to have a licence — but lost it for the way they wass running the hooses, chust drinking shebeens they wass, wi' constant fighting and noise and broken glesses and the polis aye being called by the neighbours, and clamjamfreys and shenanigans every night.'

"That raither changed Mery's opeenion aboot Bleckpool and she wass gled to get oot of it efter the week — though I managed to find some cheery company roond aboot the pier. But wild horses woudna drag Mery beck!"

~

The Captain shrugged. "I must admut that I am not chust exectly comfortable staying in a hotel myself.

"Mony of the big wans are so highly-polished and stiff-necked that you are feart to sit on the chairs or waalk on the flairs in case there iss an extra cherge on the account, and the staff are aal so high-falutin' that you are feart to ask them for onything and, when you do, their accents is that posh you could cut them wi' a knife and you canna under-stand wan single word they are saying.

"And the smaal wans that I have been unlucky enough to stay in have usually been run by a man wi' a problem wi' drink and a wife that canna cook, so you get short-measure at the bar and short-shrift in the dining-room.

"The staff is either ower 80 and that wandered and trauch-led that the guests think *they* should be serving *them* raither than the ither way roond: or else they're laddies of aboot 12 years wi' weel-scrubbed faces and a habit o' picking their teeth wi' a matchstick when they think nobody's looking.

"I mind fine wan time a few years back, before the *Vital Spark* wass built, I wass working for a man that owned two or three boats that sailed oot o' Girvan. And did wan o' them no strand herself — or more accurately, did the man that wass supposed to be in cherge of her no' strand her, and him doon below in the fo'c'sle with aal the rest o' the shup's company and enchoying a refreshment when she ran agroond — on a sand bar in the Soond o' Raasay, on her way to Portree from Kyle.

"McTavish, him that owned the boat, secked the entire crew the meenit he got the report of it. I wass on my leave break at the time myself. This wass long afore I got married, of course, and I wass chust perambulating aboot Gleska and having a gless noo and then in wan o' the Hieland public hooses aboot the toon.

"McTavish caaled me back from my leave and sent me up wi' an engineer and a hand to bring the shup back doon to Girvan. I can tell you, I was not at aal happy aboot the chob. We had to get her refloated first, she wass still on the sand: and then we had to hope the propellor wassna damaged: and aal the time we would be aware of the owner waatching efferything that wass going on, through his agent in Portree.

"If things didna work oot then heaven help us, for he wass a short-fused man withoot an ounce of Chrustian charity in him, and he'd secked mair men for less reason than a Tarbert trawlerman's had sair heids on a Sabbath morning.

"We went up by train to Mallaig, and got there late afternoon. There wass only two boats a week to Portree, wan sailing the morn's morning — which iss why he'd sent us up that day — wi' the next no' due till fower days later.

"Lord help us if we missed that boat! And she sailed at half-past five in the morning! There wass a kind of a night-clerk in the Hotel, a man of 75 if he wass a day, very shaky on his feet and as deaf as a post.

"We made sure we wass early to bed, I can tell you. We had a room on the furst floor o' the Hotel wi' three beds in it, at the head of the stairs from the main haall.

"While the other two went up to make their ablutions, I went in search of this night-clerk.

"I found him cleaning the boots o' the commaircial chentlemen who wass the Hotel's only ither patrons, in a basement room wi' no light but wan solitary candle.

" 'We've to get the Skye steamer at half-past-five', I bellowed in his ear, 'and we daurna miss it! Ye'll need to mind to gi'e us a caall at half-past-four. Room three at the heid of the stair.'

" 'Aal right,' says he, 'that's no bother. Room three, heid of the stair, half-past-four for the half-past-five steamer — and ye dinna need to shout, I'm no deaf!'

"We found out later that, come the morning, he had forgotten which room wass to be knocked for the steamer, and he chust went to the tap o' the hoose — room 33 — and worked his way doon. You can imachine the abuse he got alang the way!

"But it took him a long time to work his way doon for the

ither chentlemen wass ill to rouse, them no' expecting the caall in the furst place, and verra displeased indeed when they were given it.

"When he finally knocked on the door of room three it wass too late.

"I woke up wi' this voice shouting through the keyhole: 'Are you the chentlemen that wants the caall for the early boat?'

" 'Yes,' I yelled back. 'Thanks! we'll be down for our breakfast in a jiffy.'

" 'Och, ye needna fash yersel's', he shouts: 'tak' your time, you've plenty of it. It's six o'clock and she's well on her way to Kyle by noo. She left hauf an hoor ago. There wass no need to waken you at aal, I chust did it because you asked me to.'

"So," concluded Para Handy, "that wass wan 'holiday' that cost me my chob, for MacTavish brought in a crew from Inverness and we were secked. I should chust have stayed in Gleska and taken my leave."

∿

With an imperious blast on her powerful steam whistle the *Iona* announced her intention of departing and the admiring flotilla of small yachts and rowing boats which had been gathered around her gleaming black hull like pilot fish round a whale scattered hastily as the steamer's bow and stern ropes were cast loose from the pier bollards and the paddle-blades began to turn.

At that moment came an anguished feminine cry of "Wait, wait for us, please: please wait!"

Turning, the Captain and I saw a strange little cavalcade come hurrying from the esplanade, along the connecting roadway to the pierhead.

In the van was a woman of perhaps 40 years, gesticulating quite frantically with an umbrella. Hers were the shouts.

Behind her, making the best speed he could, was one of the town's shore-porters with his barrow. On it lay the lady's luggage — and one other accoutrement: the lady's husband. Fast asleep and with a contented smile on his face, his rosy cheeks suggested how that contentment had been achieved, and why the couple were in grave danger of missing the steamer.

The *Iona's* Captain, on the wing of the bridge, took the

scene in at a glance — and gently nudged his vessel back towards the quay for the minute necessary for the lady and her luggage to be gallantly assisted aboard across the paddle-box by two of the ship's crew: and for the husband to be less ceremoniously taken in a fireman's lift and dropped onto a convenient bench.

Para Handy sighed.

"There is no justice, is there? We went sober to our beds and lost our chobs. That chentleman probably neffer went to his at aal last night and not only did he catch his ship, it wass his wife that he has to thank for that.

"If that had been Mery and me, I doot the mustress would have gone aboard and left me at Ro'say pier wi' a label roond my neck printed, 'Not wanted on Voyage'.

"And you know, she would have been quite right!"

FACTNOTE

Blackpool has been a favourite holiday destination for generations of lowland Scots and its 'Golden Mile' with its end-of-the-pier-shows, the tower, the ballroom, the funfair, have entertained millions and still attract the summer hordes at the end of this century. I wish the Clyde resorts had been as fortunate in fine-tuning and marketing their appeal for them we might still have had steamer fleets!

Of all the famous Clyde names, only that of the veteran *Iona* comes close to eclipsing the legendary *Columba*.

She was the third steamer of that name to be built for the Hutcheson fleet at the Govan yard of J & G Thomson in a space of just nine years!

The first *Iona*, launched in 1855, put in just seven seasons on the Clyde when her speed and manoeuvrability were noticed and she was bought by the American Confederate States for service as a blockade-runner in the Civil War. Ignominiously, however, she never got past the Tail o' the Bank, being run down by the steamship *Chanticleer* off Greenock when she was running without lights. As soon as she had been sold to the Americans a second *Iona* had been ordered from Thomsons yard, but this one never even entered service before she was snapped up by agents of the Confederacy. She got a little further on her voyage to America than her predecessor, though not much: she foundered off the island of Lundy in a Bristol Channel storm.

I suppose we only had a third *Iona* actually on the Clyde

because the American Civil War was coming to its end as she was being completed!

She was the largest vessel on the river at the time of her launch and for style and opulence she was not to be surpassed till 1878 when David MacBrayne, now controlling director of the Hutcheson fleet, ordered (again from Thomson's Govan yard) the incomparable *Columba*, a full one-fifth again bigger than *Iona* but very much based on her proven, successful design.

Columba had a long career as MacBrayne's adored flagship before going to the breakers in 1936 at the venerable age of 58, but here she had to give best to *Iona* which had seen an astonishing 72 years service when she, too, went for scrap that same year.

Who could have foreseen a hundred years ago that industrial, commercial Glasgow would indeed become a serious holiday destination — though Para Handy and his wife did not have the lure of such delights as the Burrell Collection or the restored Merchant City or the Mackintosh legend to tempt them!

THE ELEGANCE OF HORSEPOWER — *The suspicion is that this photograph was commissioned from the MacGrory brothers on the day that its Campbeltown owner-driver took delivery (probably by a steamer and possibly even by a puffer) of this handsome Hansom-cab, a fashionable conveyance designed in the mid-19th century by its eponymous inventor Joseph, but in fashion till well into the early years of the 20th century.*

14

Santa's Little Helpers

I encountered Para Handy and Hurricane Jack quite unexpectedly as they emerged from the Buchanan Street doorway of the Argyll Arcade late on Christmas Eve, the Captain's oldest friend clutching a large rectangular parcel wrapped in shiny brown paper printed overall with the name of the shop on which every schoolboy's hopes would that night be concentrated — the Clyde Model Dockyard.

"Last minute shopping indeed, Captain," I exclaimed : "and from the Clyde Model Dockyard itself! Who is the lucky lad?"

Para Handy, looking rather embarrassed, just mumbled something unintelligible and made to move off but Hurricane Jack, laying his burden carefully on the pavement, straightened up with a sigh and remarked pointedly, "It iss real thirsty work, this shopping business : and a rare expense ass weel : I'll tell you that for nothing."

Sensing a story, I persuaded the two mariners to join me for a seasonal dram in a convenient hostelry in neighbouring St Enoch's Square. But it took a second glass to start the flow of the narrative, and then a third before the whole sorry tale was unfolded for me.

It had all begun three days previously...

$\sim$

A freezing fog had enveloped the lochside village all day, and darkness was rapidly closing in on the short December afternoon when the indistinct silhouette of a steam-lighter loomed out of the gloaming and the fully-laden little vessel eased its way into the basin at the Ardrishaig end of the Crinan Canal.

In the wheelhouse of the *Vital Spark* Para Handy breathed a sigh of relief as he bent down to call into the engine-room at his feet. "Whenever you're ready, Dan," he said, and with a rattle and a clank the propeller-shaft stopped turning and the puffer drifted the last few feet onto the stone face of the quay.

"My Cot," said the skipper, as Sunny Jim leapt ashore with the bow mooring rope and slipped its bight over the nearest stone bollard, "I wass neffer so relieved to see the shup safe into port. Ever since we came round Ardlamont I have been frightened that every moment wud be our next."

Indeed it had been an uncomfortable passage up Loch Fyne, for it was there that the weather had closed in on the puffer and Para Handy had steered his course towards Ardrishaig more by instinct than anything else in fog which restricted visibility to less than fifty yards.

"It's chust ass well that Dougie iss not here," said Hurricane Jack, materialising out of the gloom on the cargo-hatch just forward of the wheelhouse. "A fine sailor when we are safe in port but tumid, tumid when we are at sea."

It was four days before Christmas and Dougie the family man had bargained with the bachelor Jack to stand in for him on this unexpected last-minute charter to Inveraray with a cargo of coals. Not that the Mate himself was particularly keen to spend the festive season cooped up with ten screaming children in a tenement flat in Plantation, but the Mate's wife was determined that he should do so, and she was certainly not a lady to be argued with lightly by anyone, and least of all by her husband.

Once the puffer was safely berthed, Para Handy went ashore and up to the Post Office to send a wire to McCallum, the Inveraray coal merchant, explaining why his cargo had been delayed.

McCallum's response, delivered to the *Vital Spark* half-an-hour later by a diminutive telegraph boy, proved that the spirit of the season of peace and good will to all men had not reached certain quarters of Upper Loch Fyne.

"You wud think that we was responsible for the fog," complained the Captain as the crew made their way up the quayside towards the Harbour Bar. "Well, all I can say iss that he will get his coals tomorrow if it lifts, but I am not prepared to risk the boat chust to keep Sandy McCallum's Campbell customers happy."

~

Next morning the fog had indeed dispersed and the puffer made an early start for Inveraray. Since one and all were anxious to get home in time for Christmas, the unloading of the coals was achieved in record time. As soon as the cargo was safely ashore in the early afternoon, and carted to McCallum's ree, the crew prepared to set sail at once without even a cursory visit to the bar of the George Hotel.

However, just as Sunny Jim was loosing the last mooring rope, the owner of the Hotel himself appeared on the quayside, quite out of breath, and carrying a large cardboard box.

"I heard you were at the harbour, Peter : I wonder if you would do me a kindness," he asked, "and deliver this for me? It's my nephew's Christmas present — my sister's laddie — and it should have gone up to Glasgow yesterday on the steamer, but with the fog the *Lord of the Isles* turned back at the Kyles and I've no way of getting it to town in time other than with yourself.

"My sister's house is just off Byres Road, and I'll give you the money for a cab..."

~

"Would you take a look at this!" cried Hurricane Jack fifteen minutes later, emerging from the fo'c'sle with the box — minus its lid — cradled in his arms, and an excited grin on his face.

Para Handy was about to protest at the cavalier way in which Jack had satisfied his curiosity, but when he saw the contents of the box for himself, he peremptorily summoned Sunny Jim to take the wheel and hurried for'ard to join his shipmate.

The box contained a magnificent train-set — a gleaming green and gold locomotive, three pullman coaches, and a bundle of silver and black rails.

"My chove," said the Captain enthusiastically. "Iss that not chust sublime, Jeck! There wass neffer toys like that when I wass a bairn and needin' them, or if there wass, then I neffer saw them.

"I'm sure it wouldna' do ony herm if we chust had a closer look at it aal..."

In no time at all, the rails — which formed a generous oval track — had been laid out on the mainhatch, the carriages set on one of the straight sections : the two mariners were peering curiously at the engine itself.

" 'Marklin, Made in Chermany'," said Para Handy, reading the trademark stamped on the underside of the chassis. "Clever duvvles, but I canna see the key and I canna imachine chust how on earth we're meant to wind the damn' thing up."

Hurricane Jack took the engine out of the skipper's hands and looked closely at it. "This isn't a clockwork injin at all, Peter," he said at length, reaching to the box and taking out of it a small tin which he opened to reveal a number of round white objects like miniature nightlights. "It's wan o' they real steam ones. You put some watter in the wee biler, and then you light wan o' these meths capsules in the firebox, and off she goes.

"I'm sure it wouldna' do ony herm if we chust tried her oot chust the wan wee time..."

However, despite their best efforts, neither Para Handy nor Jack had any success in getting the model engine fired up.

"Can I not have a shot at it please, Captain?" called Sunny Jim plaintively from the wheelhouse, whence his view of proceedings down on deck was frustratingly limited.

"Haud your wheesht and mind the wheel, Jum," replied Para Handy brusquely, "and leave this business to men who are old enough to ken what they're doin'. But you could maybe give Dan a call and ask him to come up here for a minute."

It was of course the puffer's engineer who finally cracked the problem of propulsion and in a few minutes the little train was chuffing importantly around and around the oval track, the three seamen on their hands and knees, spellbound, beside it.

Jim's repeated pleadings to be allowed to join in the fun were totally ignored.

"Is that aal there is to it?" Jack asked after a while. "I'm sure she wud run faster withoot all they carriages..." An experiment which was soon put to the test, and as soon shown to be true. Even that improvement, however, palled after a few minutes more.

"I'm sure and she wud be able to go faster if we took her aff the rails," suggested Para Handy : "and she'd certainly be able to go further..."

Moments later, with Para Handy on his knees at the after-end of the mainhatch and Jack at the fore-end, Macphail having retired to his lair with a snort of derision, the rails had been packed away and the little locomotive was racing to and fro the full length of the hatch, set on its way by one of the mariners, and then caught at the far end by the other, turned about, and sent on the return trip.

"Careful, Jeck," cried Para Handy : "dinna drop it, whatever you do!"

"Can I no' come doon and have a wee shot wi' it?" pleaded Sunny Jim again from the wheelhouse, and in that one fatal moment the damage was done.

Para Handy turned irritably to remonstrate with his persistent deckhand and as he did so the little engine, racing back from Hurricane Jack's end of the hatch, hurtled off it as it reached the momentarily unattended after-end, bounced once on the deck and, in a gleam of green and gold, soared over the low bulwarks of the puffer and sank, with one briefly echoing plop, into the salty depths of Loch Fyne.

"Jum!" yelled Para Handy accusingly. "Wull you chust look and see whit ye've been and gone and done noo..."

~

"An expensive high-jink, Captain" I said as we parted company on the corner of Argyll Street and Union Street. "But so long as you deliver the new set safely, and so long as neither giver nor receiver ever find out that you had to buy it, or why..."

"Chust so", said the Captain somewhat shame-facedly, and he and Hurricane Jack went off in search of a cab while I made my way back to the newspaper office.

~

It was several weeks before the *Vital Spark* was in Inveraray again but one February morning she lay at the outer end of the pier loading a cargo of pit-props.

Just after mid-day the owner of the George Hotel came down the quayside and called to Para Handy, who was supervising the work of the derrick from the deck. Dan Macphail was at the winch and Hurricane Jack and Sunny Jim were up on the pierhead roping bundles of the timber together.

"I just wanted to thank you for delivering that Christmas gift in Glasgow for me, Peter," the hotelier shouted. "Very much appreciated, and the laddie just loved his train.

"Funny thing, though : I must be losing my memory I think, for he wrote me such a nice letter about the train set and its fine *red* engine when I would have sworn blind that I had bought him a *green* one."

"Aye," Sunny Jim began : "But the toy shop wis sold richt oot o' the greeeeeaaaAAAAAH...!"

"Sorry, Jim" said Hurricane Jack loudly and pointedly, lifting the metal-shod heel of his heavy boot from where it had crashed down onto the toe and instep of the deckhand's left foot. "Ah didna see you there..."

FACTNOTE

The Clyde Model Dockyard in the Argyll Arcade, the L-shaped indoor shopping mall which links Buchanan Street and Argyll Street, was so much part of the myth and folklore of West of Scotland schoolboys of my own and previous generations that it almost comes as a surprise to find that it *doesn't* have an entry in the Collins Encyclopedia of Scotland.

Argyll Arcade today is inhabited by nothing but wall-to-wall jewellers, but go back a generation and it housed a wide range of shops of which the Model Dockyard was the undisputed mecca.

Its window displays were legendary, the stuff of magic, dreams of the unattainable. Before plastic came to destroy the quality and character of toys the magic names of Hornby, Meccano, Trix, Mammod, Dinky, Basset-Lowke, Marklin, Frog and other legends of railways, roadways, airways and seaways in miniature dominated that plate-glass paradise and its groaning shelves.

At Christmas, even in the decades of continuing shortages which stretched well into the fifties, the Dockyard somehow managed to acquire stock which eluded lesser contenders, and scrums of anxious youths fought for places at the windows to see what was available before rushing home to pen anxious lists for their own personal present providers — before the limited, but quite priceless, stocks ran out.

I was living many miles from Glasgow when the Dockyard finally closed: victim presumably of the mass-produced, mass-marketed toys which for all their greater availability in shopping malls everywhere — and their relatively greater affordability — seem inconsequential and insubstantial trivia in comparison to those earlier delights.

Those who remember the solid chunkiness of a post-war Dinky Toy taxi-cab (any colour you wanted so long as it was black and green or black and wine) with its uniformed driver seated in his cab, open to the elements: or the challenge of getting the best from Meccano sets with which everyone else seemed to be so much more adept than you were: struggling with balsa-wood ship or aeroplane kits: the acrid smell of modelling paint and varnish: the surprisingly versatile rubber Minibrix, precursor of Lego and a valuable adjunct to Hornby Gauge 0 train layouts.

Those who remember such delights will never forget them, and will only regret that the toys which thrill their own children seem at once made so slipshod and slapdash (though technically out-of-sight), and so ephemeral (though imperative possessions for their one brief hour of fashionable fame) by comparison.

15

The Black Sheep

T he disdain with which the Deck Officers of many of the crack paddle-steamers, and the officials at the more fashionable Clyde resorts, treat the puffers which cross their paths and frequent their harbours is as nothing compared with the calculated and insulting pretensions to superiority which are often directed at the little boats and those who work on them by the private yachts which they encounter — and the larger the yacht, then usually the larger the degree of derision with which they are treated.

Such opprobrium, however, comes not from the *owners* of the yachts but from their *crews*. This is particularly cruel, for as often as not these crewmen are of the same stock and background as the crews of the puffers, and the gabbarts and steam-lighters, which are the butt of their jibes and sneers.

I suppose it is merely symptomatic of the inadequacies of human nature that many who succeed in 'bettering' themselves, whether financially or socially, should then desire to kick away from beneath them the ladder by which they climbed to such new and giddy heights — and to pretend that they never had anything in common with those less fortunate occupants of the lower rungs of that same ladder (namely their former colleagues and equals) at the same time.

And no individual can be more cutting in these circumstances than one who only *pretends* that he has improved himself, but knows full well that, despite superficial outward appearances, he has in fact signally failed so to do.

Para Handy, fortunately, was a man of a kindly and

forgiving nature, and though he could be hurt by the unfeeling comments of former acquaintances who had moved on from the rigours and frustration of the coastal cargo trade, he was not prone to harbour grudges and was more likely to forgive and forget than to remember and plot revenge.

There are, however, exceptions to almost every rule and in this instance Para Handy's exception was Donald Anderson.

Anderson was a small, dark-haired and dark-featured individual with twitchy movements and a shifty look. He rarely if ever smiled and when he did (usually at the discomfiture or distress of another) it was, to trot out the old cliche, with his mouth only and not with his eyes.

Yet it had not always been so. Para Handy's very first posting afloat, as deckboy on a sailing gabbart trading out of Bowling, had been shared with Donald Anderson and the two lads, who were both of the same age, had struck up an immediate friendship.

In part they were drawn together by the unfamiliarity of their new surroundings, the uncertainty as to what the future held for them, and the sometimes unreasonable treatment meted out by the senior members of the gabbart's crew. In part, though, they had much in common despite the startling difference in their backgrounds — Para Handy brought up in a remote corner of Argyllshire, Anderson the unmistakable product of inner-city Glasgow. For the two years they spent on the gabbart, the two were inseparable.

Their paths diverged when they reached the age of 18.

Para Handy, determined to chart a career in the mercantile arm of shipping, signed on as deckhand on a larger gabbart carrying a wider range of cargos over longer distances.

Donald Anderson, when he learned of this, gave the very first indications of the sort of man he would one day become.

"Ye dinna catch me dirtyin' ma haun's ever again if I can help it," he said cuttingly. "Ah'm fairly dumbfoonered at ye, Peter Macfarlane. Ye can keep yer gabbarts frae noo on for me, for Ah've got took on by MacBrayne as a steward in the third-class saloon on the *Grenadier*, regular hoors, a fancy uniform jaicket and three meals a day, and that's only a start. So you can be thinkin' o' me, and the dufference between wis, each time you is shuvveling coals or roadstone or some other filthy cairgo in some god-forsaken Hielan' hell-hole on a cauld January day.

"Ah actually thocht ye'd some sense, but ye're naethin' but a Hielan' stot efter a', and that's whit ye'll stay."

"I dinna care much aboot clothes and ootward show, but you may as weel may get yoursel' into a uniform jecket if that is what you want, but it's for sure that you will neffer get your own command as a kutchen-porter if you live to be a centurion," was all that the young Para Handy replied, and Anderson gave him a foul look and they went their separate ways.

~

Over the years, Para Handy heard snippets of gossip about his former friend, and they occasionally encountered each other in some corner of the west.

Anderson did not keep his job with MacBrayne for long, for once into his steward's uniform his attitude to the patrons of the third-class accommodation to whose needs he was supposed to attend became quite insufferably patronising — only ministering to the whims of the gentry in the first class lounges and saloons could merit *his* attentions and match *his* pretensions — and after just three months he was looking for another post.

He then spent twenty years going foreign — on the Greenock to Nova Scotia service of the Allan Line as a senior steward, by his own account. The truth was more mundane. Once again found wanting in his care of the paying passengers, he was demoted to acting as mess 'boy' for the ship's engineers. He passed many fruitless and frustrated years trying to 'improve' his position by obtaining a cabin post with one of the other transatlantic shipping companies but his record, resentment and reputation always preceded him, however, and he stayed where he was.

"At least his uniform fits him, even if his estimation of his own importance doesna," remarked Para Handy to the Mate one day after they had encountered him in a dockside public house in Govan. "I am chust sorry for the Allan enchineers, it must be like bein' danced attendance on by a yahoo wi' a superiority complex. How they keep their hands off him I chust cannot think."

By the time Para Handy had his own command,

Anderson was back on the Clyde, having tried the patience of the Allan Line and its engineers just once too often. He drifted from one unhappy job to another — a washroom attendant at the St Enoch Hotel, a doorman at the Mitchell Library, a porter at Central Station, a boating-pond steward at Hogganfield Loch, a park-keeper at the Botanic Gardens. Anderson would take *anything* — as long as it gave him a clean-hands and non-labouring occupation, a uniform, and the opportunity to fawn ingratiatingly upon his superiors and treat contemptuously those he saw as his inferiors.

And through the passing years and the ups and downs he lost no opportunity, when their paths crossed, to sneer at the chosen career of the skipper of the *Vital Spark*, belittle his status, and contrast their circumstances to his own imagined advantage.

~

Late one Friday evening Para Handy guided his command gently through the narrow dock entrance at Rothesay and into the outer of the two harbours which lay sheltered by the great length of the town's main steamer pier.

Apart from a few small fishing smacks lying against its inner face for the weekend and a couple of skiffs bobbing to moorings in the centre of the basin, the only other occupant of the harbour was a handsome, yellow-funnelled steam yacht of similar length to the Vital Spark, but with a much narrower beam and a graceful look about her which the unfortunate puffer could never hope to emulate.

"Ready when you are, Dan," the Captain called down the speaking tube to the engine-room, and Macphail cut the power to the propellor and the *Vital Spark* drifted the last few feet onto the quay wall.

The accident was the merest trifle, the result perhaps of a sudden, slight flaw of wind catching the port quarter of the puffer — for she was in ballast, and riding high enough in the water to present a sail-like profile to a surface breeze: but whatever the reason, as the way came off her she gently — ever so gently — nudged her bows against the stern of the yacht and tipped that vessel just fractionally to starboard so that her fenders squeaked against the stone quay, and her main halyards slapped softly against her mast.

There were two immediate and contemporaneous results of this quiet coming-together.

From beneath the awning stretched across the fore-deck, where the owner and his party sat contemplating the peaceful charm of Rothesay over the rims of their cocktail-glasses, a tall figure rose to his feet and, glancing towards the wheelhouse of the *Vital Spark*, enquired in concerned tones: "Is everything all right with you Captain — no problems, I hope?"

At the same time a small, white-jacketed figure came hurtling out of the stern galley shaking his fist in the direction of the *Vital Spark* and mouthing a torrent of abuse. It was Donald Anderson.

Para Handy, ignoring him completely, doffed his cap with a nod of the head to the owner, and apologised for the mishap. "I am chust anxious aboot the yat," he concluded.

"Please don't concern yourself, Captain. The *Carola* is a sturdy little ship. I should know — I built her myself! And she has taken much more punishment many, many times when I've misjudged my approach to a jetty!"

And with a smile he turned away — and to Para Handy's relief and satisfaction sent Anderson (who had recognised the Captain and now stood glaring malevolently at him) back down below with a curt word and an angry gesture.

~

The following afternoon the *Vital Spark* came bucketing round the north end of Arran into Kilbrannan Sound in a strong south wind. The barley she had loaded at Rothesay was destined for one of the Campbeltown whisky distilleries.

Dougie caught Para Handy's arm and pointed towards the Kintyre coast. "Is that no' that yat we saw in Rothesay?" he suggested anxiously. "And does it no' look as if she's in trouble of some sort?"

Indeed the *Carola* it was, and — plainly drifting uncontrolled and without power — she was rolling alarmingly in the rising waves that came marching up from the stormy Mull to the south.

Fifteen minutes later the *Vital Spark* had passed a line to the yacht and begun to tow her back across the Sound to the shelter and safety of the bay at Lochranza.

~

At the yachtsman's insistence the crew of the *Vital Spark* (after a toilet supervised by her Captain, a toilet as thorough and as demanding as any they had ever inflicted upon themselves) dined on board the yacht that evening.

Para Handy had at first been most reluctant to accept the invitation and excused himself on the grounds that he and the steward of the *Carola* were acquaintances of long-standing but that they "didna get on".

"Don't concern yourself about that," said the yachtsman. "The man was only taken on temporarily for this one week, my regular steward being sick. And in any case, he's not on board any longer. I'd had more than enough of his insufferable behaviour before we reached Rothesay, and when I heard and saw how he treated you after that little incident last night, I sent him packing. I am used to having nothing but gentlemen on the *Carola* whether as guests or as crew, whatever their background may be. *Gentlemen!*" he repeated with emphasis.

"In fact," he observed at dinner, "I am absolutely certain that Anderson was responsible for the engine failure this afternoon and my engineer agrees. Somebody loosened one of the connecting rods so that after an hour or two it was bound to shear. It did not do that by itself."

"I think I might know where the polis could get a haud of him..." Para Handy began.

"No, not at all," said the yachtsman firmly. "There are some people not worth bothering about even to see them getting their due deserts. Some people are beneath contempt. And that man is one of them."

Para Handy could only nod in agreement.

FACTNOTE

The career of MacBrayne's *Grenadier* was a perfect illustration of just how far-ranging that company's operations were.

She spent several years on long-haul services out of Oban to the far North West Highlands, and latterly she was employed on the day-trip business of the bread-and-butter Oban money-maker, the excursion to Iona, for the Abbey and a touch of the mystery of the Celtic Church: and on to Staffa, for Fingal's Cave.

In winter she was often brought down to the Clyde to take over the daily Ardrishaig service from the *Columba* and she was the only MacBrayne paddle-steamer to be requisitioned for service in the First War. Returned to the Oban station in the 1920s she came to a tragic end, burned out at the South Pier in 1927.

Donald Anderson's grudging service at the Mitchell Library would probably have been deployed in the second building which that institution occupied, in Miller Street, from 1889 to 1911.

The Library moved in that year to the purpose-built premises which it has occupied ever since. The Mitchell was originally endowed by a Glasgow tobacco merchant and has become one of the largest Libraries in Britain — despite not having the right of the British Library or Trinity College Dublin to a free copy of every book published in the U.K. Its Glasgow Room is a goldmine of information, from the trivial to the earth-shattering, about the West of Scotland: and the staff the most knowledgeable and user-friendly in the business.

The steam-yacht *Carola* was built (possibly as an 'apprentice piece') in the yard of Scott of Bowling for the family of Scott of Bowling in 1898. 70ft long, and powered by a two-cylinder compound engine, she was used by the family for day excursions on the Clyde. Despite the fact that she had no cabin accommodation she was also used for longer excursions, sometimes as far as Oban by way of the Crinan Canal. She would undertake those journeys in a series of day-long stages, the family and their guests going ashore each night to sleep in a local hotel while the crew bunked down on board.

Derelict and abandoned in the River Leven, she was about to be broken up when she was rescued and taken down to Southampton to be restored by an English enthusiast.

Subsequently purchased by the Scottish Maritime Museum and brought back to the Clyde, she offers the opportunity for quiet contemplation of the river, in summer, from the decks of what is perhaps the oldest remaining sea-going steam yacht afloat.

16

On His Majesty's Service

It was a pleasantly sunny May morning, but Para Handy watched the Postman coming along the quayside at Bowling Harbour with some distaste, for he could see, clutched in that worthy's right hand, a buff-coloured envelope obviously intended for delivery to the *Vital Spark* and, in all probability, addressed to her Captain. Para Handy's experience with buff-coloured envelopes was that they were usually the harbingers not of good or welcome news but of unwanted ill-tidings, most usually of a monetary nature.

"What iss it this time," he demanded petulantly, "another bill from Campbell's Coal Ree? Ah've only jist paid for the last lot of assorted stanes he delivered in April."

The postman, handing over the envelope, shrugged apathetically and made off without a word.

Para Handy watched his wiry figure step briskly out along the quayside and back towards the village.

"You would think," he observed to the Mate, "that Lex Cameron would treat me wi' chust a little more respect, given what I know aboot him that his bosses at Post Office headquarters up in George Square dinna: and what they might want to do aboot it if they did!"

"What's that, Peter," queried Macphail, joining the other two on the main-hatch.

"Last Chrustmas Eve it wass," said the Captain, "right here in Bowling. You two — and Jum — had gone ashore for a refreshment while we wass waiting to go up the Canal to Port Dundas, but I had stayed on board in the fo'c'sle wi' a mutchkin of spirits to make up a hot toddy for myself, for you'll mind that I had a terrible dose of the flu at the time, and wass feeling pretty sorry for myself.

"Onyway, Lex Cameron came alongside up on the quay wi' the mail, and gave a bit of a whoop to see if there wass anyone on the shup, so I shouted on him and doon he came. Since it wass Chrustmas the least I could do wass to offer him a dram, ass any Chrustian chentleman would do, and he perched on the end of Dougie's bunk and drank it, and then made such a production oot of banging his empty gless doon on the table that I had to gi'e him anither.

"That wass when I realised that the man wass fairly in the horrors wi' the drink, and he had aboot ass much spurits aboard him aalready ass would have filled a bucket, but he didna have Hurricane Jeck's agility when it cam' to carryin' them.

" 'Are you aal right, Lex?' says I, 'I think maybe you should get yourself hame before you do yourself a mischief.'

" 'Ah canna dae that,' says he: 'the wife'd kill me if she saw me in this condeetion, Ah'll be a' right, jist help me up the ladder, Peter, and Ah'll get on wi' the roond. It's aye the same at Chrustmas, my regulars a' have drams waiting for me for the sake o' the season, and if Ah dinna drink them they would think Ah've taken offence at them.

" 'Jist see me ontae the quayside and point me at the vullage and Ah'll no' tak' anither drap o' spurits, Ah'll jist get the roond feenished and go and sleep it aff at ma brither's hoose.'

"I neffer saw Lex for a month or more after that," the Captain continued, "and when next I did I asked him how he'd got on that Chrustmas Eve, had he got the mails aal safely delivered and made peace with his mustress.

" 'Ah made peace wi' the mustress a' right, Peter,' says he: 'but there wis no way I could huv feenished the round, Ah wisna fit for't by then.'

" 'So what did you do,' I asked: 'did you get wan of your mates to feenish it for you?'

" 'Dod, no,' says Lex: 'Ah could hae got the sack straight off for bein' fu' and in cherge o' a load of mails. No, there wis only wan thing tae dae, and Ah done it. Ye ken there's a mail box at the harbour entrance up yonder? Weel, I jist emptied my bag of a' the letters and packets in it, and posted the whole lot back again, and went hame.'

"And that's the man who canna be bothered to give me the time of day," concluded Para Handy with disgust, and he examined the small brown envelope suspiciously. "Whit does *OHMS* mean?" he enquired, studying the imprint on its top left corner.

"*On His Majesty's Service* of course," said the Engineer.

"And for why would King Edward be writing to me," asked Para Handy incredulously, "for I'm sure I'm no' in his obleegement in any way."

"Dinna be so daft," said Macphail. "It's no a letter frae the King, that jist means it's an offeecial letter o' some sort. It wull be frae the Tax Office, or the Customs and Excise men, or something like that."

Para Handy shivered apprehensively. "I am sure I am beholden to nobody for nothing," and he ripped the envelope open and pulled out the flimsy sheet which it contained.

It was merely notification of a minor amendment, with regard to the lighting of Pilot Vessels, to the Merchant Shipping Acts of 1892, 1897 and 1904.

"Well, that iss a great relief," said the Captain. "I neffer see these brown unvelopes but my hert sinks. I mind the trouble my mither's cousin Cherlie got into wance wi' the Tax people when he had that big ferm at Dunure, it wass the ruination of the man, and him the only member o' the femily that wass effer likely to mak' serious money.

"The trouble wass he hadna paid a penny piece of Income Tax for years, but eventually they caught up wi' him and he got a whole series of abusive letters demandin' to know whit way he hadna been keeping in touch and letting them know how he wass getting on, and threatening the poor soul wi' aal sorts of hellfire and brumstone if he didna pay up fast.

"I wull say this for Cherlie, he could aalways tell when he wass in real trouble, and he recognised that this wass the time for drastic action, so he pulled his tin trunk oot from under the bed, counted oot two hundred pounds, put them into a paper poke, and took the train from Ayr up to Gleska an went to the Tax Office.

" 'Cherlie Mackinnon from Dunure Ferm,' says he to the man at the desk by way of introduction, 'and I've been getting a wheen o' letters from ye, so I thocht I'd best come and see you to straighten it aal oot.' And he tipped the money oot o' the poke onto the desk counter.

" 'Two hundred pound,' he says: 'and I think that should see us straight. So, if you're happy wi' that, I'll be on my way back to the ferm': and he headed for the street door.

"The clerk wass aal taken aback but he recovered himself enough to shout to Cherlie, 'Wait a meenit Mr Mackinnon, I'll have to give you a receipt for this money.'

"Cherlie wass almost in the street by this time but he

stuck his head back round the door and said, 'No, no, my mannie. You mustn't do that! That's *cash* — for peety's sake, you're neffer goin' to pit that through the *books*, are ye?'

Para Handy shook his head sadly. "Poor Cherlie, the Income Tax people went into his affairs wi' a most duvvelish ill-wull till he wass left with nothin' but the breeks he stood up in, they took the ferm off him to pay what they said he owed, and that wass the end of the only chance of a puckle money that either the Mackinnons or the Macfarlanes effer had aboot them!

"It iss chust a pity that Cherlie didna have the natural sagiocity and deviousness of Hurricane Jeck, for likely he would have had the ferm yet!

"While Jeck had the happy knack of spendin' money as if it grew on trees and aal he effer had to do wass chust wander oot and pick some more, he wass also pretty skilfull at keeping it oot of the hands of the Revenue and the Excise Officers.

"Wan time, when he wass wi' the Allan Line, he had bought himself a smaall barrel of white spurit from a private enterprise still run by an acquaintance o' his in Plantation, and installed it in the fore-cabin of the vessel he wass on. He wass a popular man wi' his shupmates that trup, and his price for the gill wass very fair.

"When they put in at Halifax in Nova Scotia Jeck still had a mair than half-full barrel o' illicit spurits in the fo'c'sle, and no intention at aal of surrendering it to the Canadian Excisemen, though he knew that they would be coming on board to search the shup. What he did wass, he got an empty whusky bottle from the Officer's Mess and filled it wi' watter that he coloured wi' a wheen o' burnt sugar so it looked like the real stuff.

"When the Excisemen came aboard and doon to the fo'c'sle — with the barrel of spurits lying on a trestle in the corner, quite openly, and wi' a spigot at the fore-end of her — Jeck admutted straight away that he had some undeclared whisky that wass due for a surcharge.

" 'But chust the wan bottle, chentlemen,' he said, producing the bottle o' coloured watter from his locker, 'and I wull gi'e ye a wee taste so ye can assess it yourselves for strength and cheneral cheerfulness, but ye'd better watter it doon a bit for it iss strong stuff!' And did he no' get two glesses, and pour a gill or thereby of the coloured watter into them, and then chust as cool ass you like wander over to the barrel o' white spurits and fill the glesses up from the spigot! And the two Excisemen smacked their lips and said that yes, it wass a fine bottle of spurits, but there would be two dollars duty to pay, and when Jeck paid it they went off quite jocco, neffer for wan moment jalousing that there had been a barrel in the corner of the fore-cabin wi' aboot 12 *gallons* of whusky in it!

"The only time that I effer heard of Jeck getting the worst of an encounter wi' the Customs or the Excisemen wass when he came back to Liverpool on that same trup.

"The barrel of spurits wass near enough finished but Jeck wass dem'd if he was going to leave ony of it behind. So the morning they docked he got ootside as much of it as he possibly could."

"And knowing Jack," interposed the Mate, "I would imagine that was a pretty impressive intake."

"Chust so," agreed the Captain: "in fact that wass his undoing. When he'd taken what he could carry internally, ass you might say, there wass still about two bottles-worth of spurits left in the barrel so he got two empty bottles, filled them, wrapped them in two dirty shirts, rammed them into the legs of his rubber boots, and stuffed the boots into the very bottom of his dunnage-bag under a pile of jerseys and oilskins and the like.

"Then he hoisted the bag onto his shouthers, and off like a full-rigged ship to the Customs Shed. By the time he got there, what wi' the fresh air and the amount of good spurits he had on board, for the first time in his life Jeck didna really know whether it was the Old New Year or a wet Thursday in Crarae.

" 'Have you onything to declare?' asked the Customs man, poking the dunnage-bag Jeck had laid on the coonter.

"Jeck beamed on him with immense kindliness. 'Have I onything to declare?' says he, glowing with the greatest of good-wull to aal men, 'yes indeed I have, but I am a sporting chentlemen and I will give you a chance to make some money on it.

" 'I'll bet you a pound you canna find it!'

"Poor Jeck spent the rest o' the day in some sort of a cells in the Customs-shed sobering up while they decided what to do with him, and he missed his train to Gleska.

" 'I tell you, Peter,' he said to me later: 'if the Government go on at the rate they're goin' now they wull run oot of things to tax! A chentleman iss not a free man in this country any more, he iss hounded for his money from wan day to the next.

" 'Where will it aal end? Aboot the only things they havna taxed yet are horses or bicycles to pay for the roads, or pianos or harmoniums in the hoose to pay for their enter-tainment value, or the watter in the teps. That would be the final insult — it's bad enough paying tax on whusky, chust imagine if you had to pay tax on the watter to pit in it!' "

Para Handy got to his feet and stretched. "Anyway, the owner wull be taxing us for idling awa' the day if we don't make a start. And I dinna want to stert gettin' broon unvelopes from him, apart from the wans wi' the pey in them!"

FACTNOTE

The original idea for this story came not just from the firm conviction (held, I am sure, by many) that with only a very few exceptions buff-coloured envelopes are not worth the bother of opening them, but also from the very vivid memory of a postman who served an office in which I once worked — but wild horses will not make me reveal which town that was in!

He did indeed arrive with our mail one Christmas Eve, rather the worse for wear, and he did indeed partake of a dram or two at the party which was in full swing that day in what was otherwise a rather conformist place of work, and after leaving the office, he did indeed post the contents of his satchel in a handily-placed letter-box — and go home: via the pub.

The first Allan Line ship to cross the Atlantic from Greenock sailed from that port in 1819. She was a small brig, the *Jean*, but she was forerunner of the huge fleets of vessels which flew the Allan Line flag independently across the Atlantic for almost 100 years. Though Glasgow remained their head-office Allan Line ships also provided services across to North America from Liverpool and Le Havre. The business was bought over and amalgamated with Canadian Pacific in 1915.

Typical of the larger Allan ships to be seen on the Clyde in the first decade of this century was the *Grampian*, a 10,000 ton liner built by Stephens of Linthouse for the Canadian service. While undergoing a postwar refit at Antwerp she was virtually gutted by fire, handed over to the insurers, and finally broken up four years later in 1925.

I don't know what it is about Customs at airports or seaports but it seems that even the most innocent person will suffer a harrowing guilt on the way through the Green Channel.

I always imagine that there is a large hand suspended in space above my head pointing unmistakeably in my direction, and I shiver yet at the recollection of coming through the Green Gate at Glasgow Airport when our family were kids, and the two of them looked up at me and shouted in piercing voices that seemed to echo round the hall for an eternity 'Is this where they're going to stop you and search you, Daddy?'

Para Handy would find it hard to believe that almost everything in sight is indeed taxed nowadays. They maybe haven't taxed horses for using the roads — but they've hammered cars. And though pianos are, I think, still exempt, TVs have taken a bit of a beating.

God forbid that they should ever tax books!

A COMPANY AT CARRADALE — Just disembarked from the Kinloch *are Campbeltown's Boy's Brigade unit, en route to their summer camp. Not 'On His Majesty's Service' but seeing themselves as very much a serving and serviceable organisation, the movement was near its peak at this period and was a valued asset in the local community and a formative influence on youngsters from country and city alike.*

17

All the Fun of the Fair

Tarbert Fair was in full swing and a great press of people was constantly moving hither and thither: along the shore road from the steamer pier to the inner harbour, where excitement at the finishing line of a rowing race was reaching fever pitch: from the inner harbour back to the steamer pier, to meet arrivals off the incoming *Lord of the Isles*: and from every direction to the centre of the town and out along the West Loch Tarbert road towards the showground and amusement park.

Finely turned-out open carriages accoutred in highly-polished brass and gleaming leather, their immaculate horses driven by a smartly-dressed coachman and occupied by young ladies in their brightest finery and twirling parasols, contrasted strongly (and strangely) with the carts in from the country — crammed with four generations of the same family, work-begrimed, drawn by a single patient Clydesdale. Poles apart in every regard but sharing the same excitement and sense of occasion on Tarbert's annual big day.

Aboard the steam-lighter tucked into the innermost recess of the coal harbour, ablutions were in progress as her crew made ready to join in the excitement. She had berthed just an hour earlier, after a helter-skelter dash (or the nearest thing to a helter-skelter dash of which she was capable) from Carradale, where she had been discharging cement.

Macphail, still querulous and ill-tempered after the exertions he had been called upon to make in piling on the coal in a vain pursuit of the extra knots demanded by the Captain, was in the *Vital Spark*'s bows with a blunt safety razor and the ship's mirror, scraping at his face with an expression of considerable concentration and periodic protests as he nicked his skin.

Captain and Mate shared the puffer's ablutions bucket at the fore-end of the main hatch. Dougie, despite Para Handy's caustic comments as to the superfluity of the gesture (given the almost total absence of hair upon his head) was shampooing vigorously, while his commander was using copious applications of soft-soap to rid his hands of a layer of caked-on cement.

Sunny Jim alone was ready for the fray. His melodeon lay at his feet as he stood on the after-end of the same hatch and amused himself (and several passers-by on the quayside) with a brisk display of step-dancing for which his whistling provided the only music.

"Will you lot get a move on," he cried in exasperation a few minutes later, when he stopped to draw breath. "It's a fair that's on for wan day, no' a fortnight, and besides for all the good you three auld fogeys are likely to get oot of it, ye're a' jist wastin' yer time."

Para Handy was on the point of retaliating caustically to these unkind remarks when there came the tuneless toot of a rather feeble ship's whistle and another puffer appeared round the head of the jetty and drifted down towards the *Vital Spark*.

"Oh no," said the Captain, swivelling round to inspect the new arrival, "oh no, for peety's sake. It's the *Cherokee*! I had raither hoped they had emigrated wi' the Klondike men, but then I should have kent better. We'll neffer be rid o' Rab Gunn, the man's like the proverbial bad penny."

Gunn's *Cherokee* was one of the few skipper-owned puffers to be encountered on the river, though in fact she spent most of her time on the Forth and Clyde and Monklands Canals, ferrying coals from the mines to the furnaces of the Lanarkshire steel mills, and finished iron and steel from there to the shipyards on the upper Clyde. That meant that, thankfully, her path only rarely crossed that of the *Vital Spark*.

The origins of the strained relations between the two skippers were lost in history, though Para Handy's constant references to Gunn as a 'lowland loon' and that worthy's dismissal of his rival as a 'Hielan' haddie' did little to smooth the way to peace and harmony.

This antipathy extended to the two crews as well. Gunn's Mate, Big Fergie, was an ox of a man with an arm like a side of beef and a temper on a short fuse, of whom gentle Dougie kept well clear. Morrison, the Engineer, was a mean-spirited man with a weakness for gambling and a reputation for cheating at cards while the Deckhand, known simply as Towser, was a swarthy young man with gold ear-rings and long, straggly hair.

"Ah'm amazed yon rust-bucket o' yours is still afloat," roared Gunn from his wheelhouse as the *Cherokee* eased her way into the berth immediately astern of the *Vital Spark*. "Ah heard she'd been hit and sunk by an oaring-boat aff Skelmorlie!"

"Iss that so," said Para Handy huffily, hastily completing the last of his own toilet and hurrying to join his crew, who now stood waiting him on the quayside: "well, that chust shows you that you shouldna believe a word you hear in those disgraceful low-country shebeens you spend your days in!

"I am more than a little surprised to see you in Loch Fyne at aal, there's no caall for coal-gabbarts up here. And besides wi' your navigation abulities I didna think they let you loose outside the Canals for even you canna get lost in there, aal you have to do is follow your nose. It's different oot here on the real river. Are you sure you havna taken the wrong turn at the Garrioch Heid, are you no' meant to be in Ayr right noo for a load of nutty slack from the mines aboot Cumnock?"

"Very cluvver," riposted Gunn. "You are much too smart for your ain good, Macfarlane. I wuddna normally gi'e you the time o' day aboot it, but jist to pit you in your place Ah'll tell ye for nothin' that the *Cherokee* is on her way tae Inveraray for a cairgo o' baled wool frae the Argyll estates. Ah'm sure an' you wush you could get a classy job like that but you've nae chance wi' yon tarry old hooker o' yours."

Para Handy drew himself up with dignity. "Classy chob? You mean you caall shuftin' a few bales of greasy wool a *classy* chob? We are off later tonight to the heid of the Loch to load a *real* classy cargo furst thing tomorrow at Cairndow! The cases and baggage of the biggest shooting perty of English chentlemen effer seen in Upper Loch Fyne. Tarry old hooker, indeed!"

And, turning away, he picked his way across the quayside — an operation which had to be undertaken with some care, as it was in the course of being resurfaced in places

119

and stacks of cobblestones and low pyramids of roadstone had been deposited where repairs were being carried out.

~

The crew returned to the puffer at dusk, foot-weary but more than content with life after a splendid day at the Fair.

The Engineer's years of shovelling coal had stood him in good stead at the Test-Your-Strength Stall and his mighty hammer blow had sent the wooden shuttle flying up the vertical post to ring the bell at the top with a reverberating, satisfying clang: and won him a bottle of whisky which, in the euphoria of his success, he had generously agreed would be shared with his colleagues.

Sunny Jim, relying on his nimble-footedness to see him through, had put himself forward at the Boxing Booth (to the horror of the pacifist Mate) and successfully survived three rounds against the promoter's protégé, largely by virtue of running rapidly backwards round the ring, but had nonetheless qualified to win the half-crown on offer for the achievement, and used it to treat his shipmates at the Harbour Inn on their way back to the boat.

Even the lugubrious Dougie, cautiously investing his six-pence to enter the incense-filled tent of The Mystic Maharajah of Mysore, had emerged happily when that necromancer (actually an out-of-work riveter from Yorkhill) prognosticated nothing for him but future success and early promotion. For the next month or so he was on the look-out, whenever the *Vital Spark* was in port, for the arrival of the telegraph boy bringing news of his posting to his own command — till he gradually forgot the whole affair.

Para Handy had enjoyed a particularly satisfactory day, for he had early on made the happy discovery that two of his cousins were on the Fair 'Committee' and had spent a pleasant hour or so in that crowded and convivial tent enjoying the hospitality of the Fair's organisers.

That happy atmosphere of universal goodwill was destroyed in an instant when the crew reached the edge of the quayside where the puffer had been moored.

There was no sign of her.

Para Handy blanched: "My Cot," he said, 'Issn't this the bonnie calamity! The shup's been stole on us! Whateffer wull the owner say!"

Sunny Jim caught hold of the Captain's sleeve and tugged

at it, pointing towards the stern of the *Cherokee*, where Rab Gunn sat on a coil of rope puffing contentedly at his pipe and looking on innocently.

"If ye're looking for that rust-bucket of yours," he said, "Ah think ye'll find her over at the steamer pier. We jist left her there wance we'd finished wi' her.

"You see, my boys decided to earn a penny or two from the towerists and we wisnae going to use wir ain boat, and spoil wir ain reputation. Wance the last steamer had left we set your tarry old hooker up as a sort of a floating funfair and gave them free trups roond the bay. But we made a fortune aff the entertainment! Big Fergie carried on a Boxing Prize Match doon in the hold and though wan fella caught him wi' a lucky poke in the eye for the rest o' the time he jist plain murdered them, it wis like takin' toffee aff af a bairn. Morrison ran a school o' Find-the-Lady on the foredeck and Towser wrapped himself in a couple o' blankets and did the genuine Gypsy Rose Lee in the fo'c'sle. We took in near on four pund, and the lads are aff to spend their share.

"Ah'm just staying on board to keep an eye on the shup, for Ah ken whit you Hielan' stots can be like when your temper's up!"

And with a sarcastic, satisfied laugh he stood up, stretched luxuriously, and made his way along the deck and down the hatch of the fo'c'sle.

Para Handy, dejected and at a loss for words, shook his head sadly and, motioning the crew to follow him, set off on the half-mile walk round to the steamer pier.

Once again, Sunny Jim caught him by the sleeve and pointed, but this time towards the assorted building materials which had been left on the quayside overnight by the construction gang.

"Captain," he whispered urgently, "is that no' a tar-biler over there? And iss that no a length of hose connected tae it, wi' a handpump on the side of the biler?"

"Aye," said the Captain, "what of it?"

"Well," said Jim "D'ye no' think, if someone were to tiptoe aboard the *Cherokee* wi' the end of yon hose while Gunn's asleep and before his crew get back from the Inns, and slide aside jist wan plank on the hatch, that we'd have a fine chance to get back at them...?"

~

Sharing the contents of Macphail's bottle of spirits in their thick tea-mugs was a welcome bonus, but the crew were in high spirits (for very different reasons) as the *Vital Spark* chugged out into Loch Fyne half-an-hour later and set her course for a moonlight run north to Cairndow.

"I chust wush," said the Captain, "that I could be in Inveraray tomorrow morning to see Gunn's face when they open the hatches to take that cargo of wool on board.

"Some chance! Not with three inches or more of liquid tar lying on the floor of the hold. That was a sublime notion of yours, Jum, chust sublime. There iss no getting away from it. I could wish though that there had been more tar in the biler than that but at least it will give them something to think aboot.

"There's no doot at aal now as to which shup is the tarry old hooker now, eh, boys? Gunn'll no' shout that at the *Vital Spark* again in a hurry!"

FACTNOTE

The second *Lord of the Isles* featured in my first collection of Para Handy stories. Launched from D & W Henderson's Meadowside Yard in 1891, she was an acclaimed and handsome ship which in no way could eclipse the Columbia, but which ran her close in terms of public loyalty and affection, and could almost — but not quite — match her for speed.

The Captain's reference to the Klondike has, of course, nothing to do with the operations and practices of the rusting and battered fish-processing factory ships which have followed the herring fleets round Scotland in recent decades, but everything to do with the great Canadian Gold Rush of 1897.

Only the Californian bonanza of the late 1840s exceeded the Klondike for madness and mayhem, but of course that was located in a (slightly) more accessible and (certainly) more amenable environment. And lasted just a little longer: the Klondike was over and done with in less than four years.

The Klondike River in the Arctic North-West of Canada, on that country's border with Alaska, came to public notice when gold was discovered in its creeks and those of its tributaries. Both the climate and the terrain were implacably hostile. Wintertime temperatures fell to 50 degrees below centigrade and the area of the strike could only be reached with the very greatest of difficulty, either up the Yukon river or by way of treacherous mountain passes from Alaska.

Yet despite those almost insurmountable hazards nearly 30,000 prospectors and camp-followers streamed into the area. Shanty towns sprang up overnight. In all probability the owners of the saloons and brothels did rather better out of the 'strike' than did any of the miners. Dawson City, the self-created 'capital' of the gold fever country, reached a peak population of about 20,000. Only about 300 households remain there today.

The country fairs which criss-crossed Scotland on their travels were the eagerly awaited event of the year in many of the most isolated communities and their 'attractions' did indeed include the notorious boxing-booths to which any local aspirants of the 'noble art' were lured (to provide entertainment for a paying audience) by the promise of a shilling or two if they could last a round — or three rounds, depending on the generosity of the proprietor — against the veteran thugs who were the stock-in-trade of the whole enterprise.

Cairndow Church, at the northern arm of Loch Fyne, has a unique octagonal parish kirk, built in 1820, which attracts visitors year round. The loch itself at this point is now heavy with the cages of salmon-farms.

ROLL UP, ROLL UP! — The annual Fair or Show was the highlight of the summer for many isolated Argyllshire towns and villages, and here the McGrory brothers have captured some of the atmosphere of those occasions. To the left, the tall post of the 'Ring-the-Bell' test of strength towers above the twin booths of conjurers, and to their right, catching the attention of the passers-by, is a boxing booth, the gloves for unwary challengers hanging from poles across its frontage.

18

Cafe Society

Mrs Macfarlane looked appraisingly at her husband over the rim of her breakfast tea-cup and came to a decision about something which she had been mulling over in her mind for some days.

"Peter," she said firmly, "I think it is high time that I invited Mrs Macphail and Mrs Campbell to tea. You spend most of your life with their husbands yet I've only met them once, very briefly, at our wedding. And," she added with a smile, "since I had a lot of more important things on my mind that day, I don't think I gave them the attention they deserved. It would be nice to get to know them a little better."

Para Handy grimaced.

"I am not sure that that iss such a good idea, Mery," he said hesitantly, picking his words as carefully as he could. "Effer since we got married I have made a point of keeping my home life quite separate from the shup. Besides, the three of you mightna get on, and that could strain relations between the menfolk, and it's herd enough ass it is bein' cuvil to Dan when the moods iss on him, or copin' wi' wan of Dougie's tirravees if he's had a bad weekend at hame."

Mrs Macfarlane bridled.

"Are you suggesting that I am difficult to get on with?"

"Not at aal, Mery," he said hastily. "You are sublime, chust sublime, and the wumman that couldna get on with you would be a sorry case indeed."

And so the necessary arrangements were made and, the following Thursday, when their men were buffeting through a March gale in the Sound of Mull, the three ladies took a lavish tea together at Mrs Macfarlane's neat flat on the second floor of a trim red sandstone tenement, just off

Byres Road, which boasted a quite astonishing wally close showing an unmistakable influence of the Orient in its design and colours.

The Captain's menage was accounted by the two visitors to be a most desirable and beautifully furbished apartment and was much admired, although in the course of conversation Mrs Campbell remarked that she understood, from what she had read in the papers, that electric lighting was about to be made generally available in that part of the city: and perhaps Mrs Macfarlane could persuade the Captain to make the necessary investment to add its advantages to the many the house already possessed. And Mrs Macfarlane agreed that this would indeed be a subject worth broaching with her husband.

The three ladies got on famously, and their cosy tete-a-tete in the Macfarlane menage was soon followed by a return invitation to Annie Macphail's Plantation home, where over an even more lavish tea a quite exhaustive discussion took place on the merits or otherwise of being domiciled so close to the river with its riveters and hooters and fog: above all, fog: with the balance of opinion finally coming to the conclusion that King's Park and its environs (to take just one example) was, really, quite close enough: and that Mrs Macphail would have to have a word with Dan on that very subject at some suitable occasion in the near future.

The ladies met two weeks later at Lisa Campbell's many-bedded pied-a-terre in Ibrox. The day was carefully planned by their hostess who succeeded in emptying the house of its 12 noisy siblings for the two hours duration of the tea-party by giving them each a jelly-piece and a penny for their fares and sending them on the long, slow tram-trip from Paisley Road West out to Airdrie, and back.

It was a ruse that had saved her sanity before this, and it did not let her down that afternoon. Nor did her catering, for she served a tea even more sumptuous than those proferred at Byres Road and Plantation, conscious that she was entertaining the widow of a baker who would have high standards in that department.

Once more the conversation ranged widely. Mrs Macphail, who was herself one of a large family of five brothers and four sisters and came originally from Bowling, stressed the great value of a house (be it ever so humble a house) somewhere in the country and with a garden of its own, when it came to allowing parents the luxury of a little peace and privacy from the noisy demands of their numerous offspring. Impressed, Mrs Campbell concurred with the Captain's wife's proposal that she really should speak to Dougie about the problem and canvass *his* opinion as to the feasibility of a move when he returned that night from Bowling.

So pleasant had these meetings been for the ladies that nobody thought to call a halt now that the wheel had come full circle, as it were. Indeed Mrs Macfarlane, who was now planning to be hostess a second time, hit upon a novel and really quite exciting idea in relation to their next get-together, and began to make preparations for it.

~

The Captain was home for the whole of the following weekend and there was a subject which he must — reluctantly — broach with his wife.

Reluctantly because he genuinely hated to do or say anything to upset her in any way at all: but reluctantly also because for all her aura of gentle kindness and unstinting affection, Mrs Macfarlane could, when roused, be found to have considerable backbone when it came to defending her position and her rights as a woman.

"Mery," he said, tentatively, when the dishes had been cleared away from the tea-table and the two sat quietly at their ease on either side of the parlour fire, "are you planning to have ony more o' these tea-pairties wi' Dan's and Dougie's wives?"

"Why, certainly," his wife replied, brightly: "such charming ladies, and we do seem to have so much in common — apart from our husbands being shipmates. We really look forward to meeting and I am planning something rather special for next time."

Para Handy scuffled his slippers on the rug. "Weel, Mery, it iss like this. The laads are upset aboot some o' the things you have aal been talking aboot, and the way they are now being nagged at aboot it aal."

Mrs Macfarlane bridled. "I am sure I do not know what you mean, Peter."

"It iss this business of hooses, the three of you agreein' that I should be puttin' in the electric for a stert: I am not made of money, you know that fine.

126

"And that Dan should mak' a move to get awa' from the ruver chust because it's foggier there than up at Hyndland or Gilmorehill. I neffer heard such umpident nonsense. Dan *likes* the ruver, he wis born and brought up on the ruver and he's no more intention of leavin' it than of emigrating to Canada. If Dougie wass here he would tell you himself. Forbye, Annie Macphail was perfectly content wi' their wee hoose there till you and Lisa Campbell got sterted on her.

"And then you are tryin' to get poor Dougie to move awa' frae Ibrox! Dougie canna *staun'* the country! The laad was brought up in Cowal, for peety's sake, and he saw mair rain in the first ten years of his life than maist men see in their three-score and ten. As he says, at least in the city there's aye somewhere fine and handy to tak' shelter if the heavens open, and usually somewhere that you can find some company to pass the day wi' and get a gless in your haund at the same time."

Mrs Macfarlane gave her husband a steely look.

"If we wasn't meant to try and better ourselves," she said with conviction, "the good Lord would not have given us ambition! If you had not had any ambition you would still have been a deckie on a gabbart."

"That iss not the same at aal," countered her husband. "It iss in the nature of a man to mak' the best he can of his *career* for the sake of his faimily but it iss neffer the place of the faimily to try to change his *character*, and that iss what the three of you are daein'. Dan would be lost away from the ruver and Dougie would be right oot of place oot o' the toon and if the three of you cairry on like this there wull be no *Vital Spark* and no crew for we'll be at opposite ends o' the country. Forbye, you wouldna like to be put to live somewhere you wassna comfortable wi' yourself, Mery. You wouldna want change chust for the sake of it."

"Nonsense," said Mrs Macfarlane sharply, "for a start I moved here from Campbeltown without making a fuss about it when we got married. It is a matter of adjusting and making the best of the circumstances wherever you find yourself, not complaining when there is nothing to complain about. Annie and Lisa have my full support."

And she retired, frostily, to iron the Captain's shirts in the kitchen ready for his departure the following morning.

∾

When Para Handy returned from an eight day trip to Islay and Jura, he found his wife in subdued mood.

"What ails you, Mery?" he asked anxiously as she greeted him at the door absent-mindedly, and turned away without proferring her cheek for a kiss.

She shook her head.

"Now, now," said the Captain. "Something's wrong. What have I done — or not done?"

"Oh, it's not you, Peter," she said at length, sitting on the arm of her chair in the parlour, "it's me. You were right about our tea-parties. We went about them all wrong, trying to outdo each other with the baking and the accessories and then trying to improve the poor woman's house that we were in. Well, we have all learned our lessons.

"This week was my turn to have Lisa and Annie round, but I had the notion to take them up town for a fancy afternoon spree and we went to Miss Cranston's Room de Luxe in Sauchiehall Street."

She shuddered at the memory.

"I have never been so embarrassed in my life! I knew I had made a mistake from the moment we went through the door!

"The place was full of nothing but society ladies from places like Bearsden or Whitecraigs or Eastwood or Milngavie. There were more fur-coats hanging on the racks at the door than you would find running about in a zoo, and as for the hats!" — she shook her head in disbelief — "the hats! Lisa and Annie and I felt quite out of place among all that finery, for all that we were dressed in what we thought was our *own*."

Para Handy nodded sympathetically. "It iss chust what I have been trying to tell you, Mery: let us be happy with what we have and with where we were meant to be."

"But it got worse," said his wife, "the waitress that came to serve at our table was a Campbeltown woman I had been at school with and she recognised me, I could see that: but she pretended she did not, and ignored us as much as she could, and spilled the tea on the tablecloth when she put the pot down, and never brought us fresh hot water, or offered us extra cakes, the way she did at all the other tables.

"And when the bill came, I did not have enough money to pay it it was so huge, and had to ask Lisa and Annie to help out.

"I have never been so ashamed and angry all at the same time."

"And I am sure you neffer looked bonnier either," said Para Handy with some fervour, and comforted her, "for when the colour comes to your cheeks when you are upset or cross, there is not a prettier gyurl in aal Scotland. And besides, you were never out of place in there, you are a finer lady than aal the toffs o' Gleska pit together, and I am proud to be your man."

At which Mrs Macfarlane blushed most becomingly, and clapped her husband gently on the shoulder.

"Keep your teas wi' the other wives by aal means, Mery, for it iss good that you are all frien's. But neffer try to change the way the world is, and certainly leave well alane wi' the way we are, and Dougie iss, and Dan.

"We're aal Jock Tamson's bairns on the shup, and on shore, and that's the way we want it to be — and nobody is goin' to alter that — not even our wives!"

FACTNOTE

Of the ladies of the three senior members of the crew only Para Handy's wife Mary makes more than a fleeting appearance. There is just one brief veiled reference to Dan Macphail's domestic circumstances, though Dougie's wife makes her mark (in *The Mate's Wife*, one of the earliest of the original stories) when she turns up at Innellan pier on pay-day to collect the Mate's wages, 'with her door-key in her hand, the same ass if it wass a pistol to put at his heid'.

Para Handy tells us that she is down on the first steamer from Glasgow any Saturday that the puffer is inside Ardlamont (the outer margin of the Kyles of Bute) so she is not a lady to be taken lightly and certainly not one to whom one would willingly take home an opened pay-packet.

To introduce the three ladies to each other was a temptation impossible to resist.

Glasgow had certain catering institutions, including among their number the venue chosen by Mrs Macfarlane for the ladies' afternoon tea, which were unique to the city, or so at least it seemed, and which though they had their origins at the turn of the century, lived on into the second half.

For serious eating, whether of lunches or high teas, a Scottish speciality rarely encountered nowadays, there were the three restaurant businesses founded and operated by three redoubtable ladies, whose names were almost always given in full when their establishments were being referred to. These were the respected restaurants run by Miss Cranston, Miss Buick and Miss Rombach and though targeted at the middle to upper class family market they were also very popular lunchtime venues for Glaswegian businessmen.

A second, distinctive, Glasgow institution was the base-ment coffee-house, very much the preserve of the male, and the haunt of the lawyers, accountants and merchants who made up so much of the middle-class commercial backbone of the city centre. The chain of tobacco-shops owned by Mr George Murray Frame had in their depths a dark, wood-panelled, dimly-lit subterranean room redolent of coffee and tobacco smoke and crammed full in mid-morning (and most other times of the day) of men in dark suits, whose dark topcoats and bowler hats festooned the wooden hallstands at the foot of the stairs which led down from the shop above.

The formidable Miss Cranston was one of the early patrons of Charles Rennie Mackintosh and her (and his) Willow Tea Room, in which every detail of interior design bears his stamp and seal, is a major attraction still in Sauchiehall Street.

For Richer, for Poorer — No two photographs from the MacGrory Archive better illustrate the yawning gap between Edwardian rich and Edwardian poor than these dramatically contrasting depictions of the crofter or smallholder in his donkey-cart and landowner with shiny top-hat in his pony and trap. The Trabant and Ferrari of 90 years ago!

19

The Sound of Silence

P ara Handy studied the telegram which had just
arrived from the owner of the *Vital Spark* with
details of her next assignment. "Lighthooses!" he
exclaimed petulantly. "More of him and his dam'
lighthooses: I dinna care if I never see wan again ass long
ass I live."

The puffer was lying at Rothesay where I was changing
steamers for a long-promised visit to old friends in Lamlash,
and the Captain had seen me on the quayside when I disembarked from the *Lord of the Isles* and invited me on
board for a mug of tea. Our exchange of the gossip of the
river as we sat side-by-side in friendly and relaxed familiarity on the vessel's main-hatch had been passing the time
very pleasantly until we were interrupted by the arrival of
a Telegraph Boy complete with scarlet bicycle and low,
black, chin-strapped pillbox hat.

"So what's the call of duty this time, Captain?" I
enquired, as that mariner angrily tore the flimsy telegram
into shreds and consigned the fragments to the winds.

"Well," he said: "at least it's no' coals this time, for that
is the worst cairgo of them aal, ass I have told you before
now. But this wull run it close for we're to tak' in the oil in
barrels for the generators at the lights on the Ailsa Craig
and roond the Mull o' Kintyre, and I sometimes think, from
the way the crew behave and the sheer tumidity of them
aal, that we iss an explosion waiting for somewhere convenient to happen when that is oor cairgo.

"We daurna smoke on deck by Dan's way of it — and him
wi' a fire going in the stokehold that wouldna have disgraced Emperor Nero: and Dougie iss that nervous that he

132

iss not at aal happy if Jum hass the galley stove goin' in the
fo'c'sle to boil a kettle for oor teas or potatos for oor denner
so we feenish up livin' on mulk and rabbit-food.

"I neffer, effer eat ass much in the way o' lettuces and
raw carrots and that sort of rubbish in a whole twelve-
month ass I do on a single week's fuellin' run to the
lighthooses — and aal chust because my crew are feart o'
havin' an open flame on the shup. They are chust feart for
their lifes! If Dougie wass here he would tell you himself.

"I aalways tell them that a load of whusky, though it
might be a much more welcome cairgo for aal sorts of reasons, iss chust ass likely to blow them to Kingdom Come ass
a load of kerosene or paraffin — but wull they lusten? Wull
they bleezes. You are talking to a brick wall wi' them."

~

It was therefore with some anxiety that I first came
across the accounts, a week later, of an accident which had
befallen a steam-lighter in the course of her duties in servicing the lighthouse which guides mariners safely past
Davaar Island at the mouth of Campbeltown Loch and into
the welcoming shelter of that capacious harbour.

It appeared that the vessel involved — un-named in
those first reports of the mishap carried in the earliest editions of the *Glasgow Herald* — was carrying kerosene to
the light-station. She was struck by an errant starting-flare
fired from the trim motor-launch acting as floating club-
house and starter's office for the Campbeltown Yacht Club's
annual regatta, which was in process of setting the yawl
class off on a triangular course from the island to Peninver
on the Kintyre peninsula, across to Blackwaterfoot on
Arran, and back to the finishing-line at Davaar.

The rocket had landed on, and set fire to, a small heap of
waste rags on the puffer's foredeck. Onlookers reported that
within seconds a middle-aged man, thought to be the Mate
of the vessel concerned, had dived overboard followed
immediately by a young deck-hand and, just a fraction
later, by an older man who had been seen scrambling out of
the engine-room hatchway at the stern of the boat.

This left on board just one man, presumed to be the skipper of the vessel, who had been alone in the wheelhouse
when the flare struck.

By the time this man — described by at least one paper

as the 'hero of the day' had run to the foredeck to extinguish the flames with a bucket of water hauled from the sea, dashed below to the engine-room to set the machinery to the off position, and returned on deck and made for the wheel-house, it was too late. The puffer ran firmly aground on the sandy tidal-flats below the lighthouse, and stayed there till the next high-tide floated her off that same evening.

"I wass bleck burning ashamed for them aal," said Para Handy bitterly the next time I met him, and questioned him about the incident — for of course, as later editions of the paper had confirmed, the steam-lighter involved in the incident was indeed, as I had suspected from the first, the unfortunate *Vital Spark*.

"Not wan scrap of courage or initiative between the three of them," he continued, "but they did weel enough for themselves right enough! Aal three of them was picked up by the Yat Club's safety-launch and taken into Campbeltoon and treated like royalty, ass if they had been real shupwrecked sailors and no' chust three faint-hearts that had shamelessly neglected their duties to save their necks! And there wass I marooned on the shup, nothing could get alongside her till the tide turned, and there wass-na so mich as a drop of wholesome Brutish spirits aboard, nor the makin's of a hot meal neither.

"Meanwhile that crew of mine wass safe ashore bein' wrapped up in warm blankets at the Mussion to Seaman's Hostel, and coaxed to tak' chust the wan more wee hot whusky drink, and spoon-fed wi' soup and chicken, and generally made heroes of."

I agreed with the Captain that it must really have been an infuriating experience.

"Aye, and outfuriating ass weel," he protested, "for when they wass interviewed by the chentlemen of the press when we got back to Gleska two days later (and no disrespect intended to yourself, Mr Munro, you'll understand) here and did the reporters no' sort of agree wi' them that the only reason I had stayed on board wass that I couldna sweem and that the three o' them had had to dive off to get a boat to rescue me, because our own skiff had a hole in her from where *I* had hit her onto a rock skerry aff the mooth of the Sliddery Water when *I* wass oot poaching in Arran the previous night.

"Dam' leears — we wass *aal* oot poaching in Arran the previous night!

"Onyway, I have made it clear to the owner: I am not cairrying kerosene effer again wi' that lot and I am gled to say that in aal the circumstances, he has agreed to that."

"Well, that should reduce the visits you have to make to the lighthouses, Captain," I said: "and given that you don't like them, that should suit you fine."

"Aye," said Para Handy, scratching his ear. "They chust do not agree wi' the Macfarlanes and I am not surprised. Look at my brither Keep Dark, noo — he wass six months in wan o' they rock lights aff the Pacific coast of America. Keep Dark went foreign for mony years, and wan time in the nineties he hit rock-bottom in San Francisco, poor duvvle, he wass ashore from wan o' they nitrate cluppers, they wass on passage from Valparaiso wi' a load of guano. That iss the most desperate cairgo you could effer imagine! Loadin' it iss unspeakable and the smell of it is in effery cranny o' the shup, you cannot escape it at aal.

"And that very first night Keep Dark got kind of separated from his shupmates and found himself alone and up a back-alley in the derk which is no' the kind of thing you'd wush on your worst enemy in San Francisco. He got shanghaied poor duvvle, by a gang that wass crewin' up wan o' the Yankee Cape Horners — naebody would shup on wan o' them of his own free wull — and though he managed to sneak ashore three nights later afore she wass ready to put to sea, by that time his own shup had sailed without him and he wass stuck in America with only the clothes he stood up in.

"His luck changed, he met up wi' a man that wass in cherge of the lighthooses on the coast roond aboot, and him orichinally a Macfarlane from some wee vullage sooth of Oban. He offered Keep Dark a posting to wan o' the rock lights, ten dollars a month aal found, and of course my brither chumped at it.

"The lighthoose wass on tap of a rock chust off a long kind of a headland, and man but it wass a desolate place. There wassna a hoose within miles, and the landing on the rock in a wee bit skiff from the lighthooses relief shup wass a nightmare.

"The worst of it though wass the fog. Keep Dark said it wass fog even on from wan day to the next, it chust neffer lifted at aal week in and week oot, and effery 45 seconds your ears was split wi' the blatter o' the huge foghorn on the cliff edge not 20 feet from the keepers' living room at the foot o' the tower.

"There wass only two of them on the rock and they worked six hours on, six hours off round the clock: it wass a funny kind of a shuft, said Keep Derk, but you got used to it. You even got used to climbing up to the tap o' the tower wance effery half hour to trum the light, and mak' sure aal was hunkey-dorey up there — no' that it would really have mattered whether the light wass on or off, because wi' the constant fog the light wass aboot as much use as a teeto-taller at a Tiree funeral.

"What you chust *couldna* get used to, though, said Keep Dark, wass the foghorn. It near deeved him to utter distrac-tion, five seconds of sheer hell every 45 seconds night and day. It wass bad enough when you wass on waatch, but it wass when you wass trying to get some sleep that you felt like goin' up to the tap of the tower and throwin' yourself aff it.

"The other keeper wass an American caalled Purdie, a smert enough man, and he'd been on the station for years. 'Ye'll soon get used tae the foghorn,' he says to Keep Dark wheneffer he'd be complainin' aboot the din, 'and then you'll be like me — I neffer, effer hear it nooadays. It chust forms a pert o' the naitural background ass far ass I am con-cerned and I am totally unaware of it goin' aff at aal. Wait you and you wull see.'

"Keep Dark didna believe him, he wass at his wut's end wi' the din and he wass even thinkin' aboot tamperin' wi' the foghorn's automatic mechanism to shut the dam' thing up, even if it wass only for a half-an-hour.

"In the end, he didna need to. It did it for him! Wan night he wass on duty and Purdie, who slept like a log from the moment his heid touched the pillow, despite the fact that that dam' foghorn wass shakin' the very foondations o' the tower wi' the racket it wass making, wass snoring chently in his bunk ass peaceful ass if he wass in a boat drufting on some silent and deserted loch.

"Keep Dark wass sitting at the table reading an old news-paper and trying to pretend he couldna hear a thing when — withoot him knowing onything aboot it at first — there must have been some kind of a mechanical failure on the clockwork motor that ran the foghorn and set it aff auto-matically (it wass aal worked wi' some kind of a fantoosh self-winding hydraulic enchine) and it broke doon.

"So there wass Keep Dark, coonting in his head till the time the next blast was due — you got that you did that withoot even noticin' it, he said, it wass some kind of a defence system the body put up — and when he got to '41,42,43,44,45' and braced himsel' for the roar o' the horn, nothin' happened.

"Total, blissful silence for the furst time in the three weeks he'd been on the tower.

"What *did* happen, though, wass that Purdie wakened in a flash and leaped oot o' his bunk in a panic shouting '*Whit in the name of Cot wass* **that**?'

"Lighthooses!" said Para Handy firmly. "Dinna talk to me aboot lighthooses. They are nothin' but a trial and tribulation. If Keep Dark wass here, he would tell you himself."

FACTNOTE

Para Handy's family are only hinted at in Neil Munro's original stories, but at least we know that he was one of ten sons, 'all men except one, and he was a valet'. We are told the by-name of four of the others. They were (and it would be a fascinating if unproductive exercise to speculate how they got such unlikely nicknames) the Beekan, Kail, the Nipper — and Keep Dark.

Did Keep Dark get his sobriquet by virtue of the fact that he had worked on a lighthouse? Probably not, but that is my excuse for featuring him in this tale!

Davaar Island lies like a cork in the neck of a bottle at the entrance to Campbeltown Loch, its cliffs pierced with caves in one of which a local artist, Alexander Mackinnon, secretly painted — in 1887 — a representation of the Crucifixion which still forms a place of pilgrimage today. A shingle spit almost one mile in length connects Davaar to the mainland and although it appears to offer a safe and dry crossing, many walkers have been caught out by the flooding tides and it needs to be approached with caution.

The island gave its name to the Campbeltown Shipping Company's eponymous screw-steamer, launched in 1885. She was a beautiful little ship with a clipper bow, figurehead — and twin funnels set close together aft of the bridge. In 1903 she underwent a series of alterations which included replacing the twin funnels with a single smokestack. She gave four decades more of service before going to the breakers in 1943.

The first British maritime incursions to the Pacific were the 18th century naval or privateering expeditions in search of the fabled treasure galleons of the Spanish colonies in Peru and the Philippines.

Over the next century the clipper trade to and from the Pacific coast of South America was founded on three cargos — copper ore from the mines of Central Peru, nitrates from the arid deserts of Chile, and guano from the bird-islands offshore. Poor Keep Dark was sailing before-the-mast at the peak of these detested contracts.

All were loathed by the crews as foul cargos to be avoided when possible — nitrate was particularly susceptible to fire, for example — but the guano cargos were unquestionably the worst.

Guano was formed, quite simply, by the droppings of a thousand generations of seabirds as it accumulated on their isolated, uninhabited and uninhabitable breeding rocks and islands lying offshore. On some islets the guano deposits of millenia were more than 200ft deep.

LEAD KINDLY LIGHT — This is Davaar Lighthouse, on the eastern tip of Davaar Island at the entrance to Campbeltown Loch, and plainly there is some sort of regatta in progress. The two-funnelled steamer heading towards Campbeltown is the Davaar *of 1885 and we can date the photograph as prior to 1903 for in that year she was reboiled and as a consequence of that alteration, her twin funnels were replaced by a single, broader smokestack. Her passenger lounges were enlarged and extended at the same time.*

20

Twixt Heaven and Hell

The *Vital Spark* came lolloping into Loch Broom, and Dougie heaved a sigh of relief as they were drawn into its sheltering arms and the white-capped waves of the open sea dwindled into the distance astern. In ballast (she had come to the northerly port of Ullapool to load a consignment of cured herring in barrels for Glasgow) the puffer had been accorded a lively reception by the notorious waters of the Minch from the moment she had passed out of the protection of the Sound of Sleat.

"Man, but your tumid, Dougie, tumid!" said Para Handy from the wheel, "neffer happier than when you're safe inside the Garroch Heid. But the shup wass built to tak' this and more."

"Maybe the shup wass," replied the Mate, "but I am sure and I wass not. It iss at times like this that I think it would be no bad idea to look for a shore chob. At least the grund stays in the wan place and you are not aalways lookin' for something to hold on to, to stop you bein' thrown across the room!"

"Ah'm no' so sure aboot that," said Macphail, poking his head from the engine-room hatch. "Depends whaur ye are. Take Sooth America for unstance, when Ah wis there wance wi' the Donaldson Line there wis that many earth-quakes goin' on, the streets wis heavin' like wan o' the penny-rides at Henglers's, and if ye went ashore for a refreshment, ye daurna pit yer gless on the table for fear it wis cowped."

Para Handy snorted. He had a very low threshold of disbe-lief in the matter of the Engineer's tales of his world travels and on more than one occasion had poured total scorn not just on the particular experience being recounted, but on the whole notion of Macphail having ever been further from the tenements of his native Plantation than the Irish Sea.

"Well, there's nothin' earth-shattering aboot Ullapool," said the Captain. "For they are aal aawful Hielan' up here, the only excitement o' the day iss when the mail comes in from Inverness and it iss usually a week late even so. If it wassna for the herring-boats in season to help keep the place cheery, it might ass weel close doon for aal that ever happens."

Indeed the town itself, a couple of streets of neatly presented white buildings on a promontory which terminated in the harbour itself, seemed asleep. The few remaining East Coast boats which came to the port for the brief herring season were at sea, and the only signs of commercial activity were the darkly-smoking chimneys of the two curing stations, all that were left of the once huge numbers of processing factories which had crowded Ullapool before the virtual collapse of the fishings thirty years previously.

"My brither Alec, the wan that wass in service and we didna talk aboot, Napkin Heid we cried him, he wass a year butling at wan o' the big Estates a few miles north o' the toon," Para Handy continued. "He didna have a high opeenion o' the place at aal, and the man he wass working for wass the worst of it. The Laird had a quite dreadful reputation: he wass a most terrible man for the drink: he wass a gambler at the cairds and a maist unsuccessful wan at that: and the parlour-maids — not chust in his ain hoose but in aal of the big hooses, and even the Manse too — learned soon enough to run for their lives if the Laird wass aboot and wi' a dram on board.

"He wass the despair o' his poor wife. She was more than twenty years younger than him, a kindly soul Alec said, but no match for the Laird, and efter Alec had been in the man's service for six months or thereby, the poor wumman chust upped and left him and went hame to her own people in Dingwall and took the weans wi' her.

"That wass when things started to go really doon hill at the Big Hoose, Alec said. There wass nobody to even try to keep the man in check, the drinking perties went on aal night, and the cairds wass played seven days a week, for there wull always be disreputable cronies to gather roond a man like the Laird ass long ass he has his money.

"Within a couple of weeks of the wife leaving, Alec wass the only servant left at the hoose, aal the wummen had fled, and Alec himsel' had had mair than enough of it and was lookin' oot for anither place.

"The Meenister took to comin' oot to see the Laird, he thought it his Chrustian duty to save sich a dreadful back-slider, and tried to persuade him to get back on the straight and narrow.

" 'To bleezes wi' your straight and narrow,' said the Laird. 'Is it no' enough that I come to the Kirk releegiously every Lord's Day?'

" 'You may come to the Kirk,' said the Minister, 'but you always sleep through the service, and the congregation iss beginning to complain aboot it.'

" 'Nae doot,' replied the Laird, 'but that'll only be because of my snoring keeping *them* awake. What else can you expect when you preach nothing but hellfire and brum-stone? Lustenin' to wan o' your sermons would turn milk sour.'

"From that you can imagine that relationships between the Laird and the Manse wass very strained."

The *Vital Spark* was now less than a hundred yards from the harbour and Para Handy, calling down for the engines to be stopped, let her drift slowly towards the stone quay. Sunny Jim moved forward and made ready to leap ashore with the bow rope.

The reception committee waiting on the quayside to wel-come them to Ullapool consisted in its entirety of two very small, dirty and ragged urchins of about eight years of age, one engaged in throwing stones at the wheeling seagulls, and the other picking his nose.

"What wass also clear to Alec by now," the Captain con-tinued once the mooring process was complete and the crew retired to the fo'c'sle to brew up a pot of tea, "wass that the Laird wass chust destroyin' himself wi' drink.

"But it wass a fever that took him before the drink had had the chance to feenish the chob. For three days he lay at death's door, but if you thought that would have concentrat-ed his mind on higher things, you can think again. He kept a bottle hidden under the bed and made sure Alec had it topped up: he wass aalways tryin' to grab hold of the nurse that the local doctor sent in to look efter him: and whenever the Meenister, good Chrustian soul that he wass, came to see him, he cursed him and his whole Kirk Session to bleezes.

"Then came the morning when Alec answered a knock on the door to find the Minister on the step.

" 'A fine day, Alec,' said he as my brither took his coat. 'And how is the Laird this morning? I do hope his temperature is no higher than it was last night?'

" 'I wass speculating aboot that very thing myself, Meenister, and hoping chust the same ass you: though I wouldna be counting on it,' said Alec. 'for I think it could well be a great deal higher by now. You see, the Laird passed awa' at three o'clock this morning.'

"So there wass Alec withoot a billet, though a relieved man to have got oot of his last one. But the Meenister put in a word for him wi' the owner o' the Bay Hotel, here in the toon, and he took Alec on as Head Porter. The Hotel's still here, but it iss changed oot of aal recognition for it has a drinks licence noo but when Alec worked there it wass a Temperance Hoose.

"Alec could tak' that or leave it, he wassna *for* drink the way Hurricane Jeck iss, for instance: and in spite of aal the months of misery wi' the Laird, he wassna *against* it neither.

"What he *wass* against, though, wass the miserable kind of a clientele the Hotel attracted for the maist o' them wass the sort of folk that looked ass if they'd neffer had so mich ass wan single day's enchoyment out of life. Good Templar families on holiday: or commercial travellers of the Rechabite persuasion (and little enough business they could expect to do in Ullapool, what with the shopkeepers no' wantin' to offend the sensubilities of the fushermen that made up the maist of their regular custom by havin' ony truck wi' teetotallers): or Meenisters — Meenisters maist of aal.

" 'It wass that miserable in that Hotel, Peter' he said to me after he'd got oot of it, 'that in comparison wi' it, a day in an undertaker's office would have been mair like a night at the Music Halls for cheneral hilarity and entertainment.'

"Mercifully he didna have to thole it for long, for he got the seck wan November morning chust a couple of months after he'd started.

"There was some kind of a Presbytery Convention in the toon and Ullapool wass chust hotching wi' gentlemen of the cloth, there wass dog-collars on effery street corner and needless to say the Bay Hotel was chammed to the rafters wi' them. If it had been a gloomy place afore, it wass like a wet day in Rothesay noo, prayer-meetings in effery room and faces efferywhere ass lang ass the Parliamentary Road.

"That morning was the third day of the Convention and Alec wass at his wut's end, but he wass up at the crack o' dawn ass usual and laid a fine log fire in the big open fire-place in the main lounge, then took up his post at the Porter's Desk in the front hall.

"Pretty soon the Meenisters began to come doon stairs in ones and twos and foregaither, ass they did the first thing effery morning, for a wheen o' prayers and a lugubrious unaccompanied psalm or two in the lounge. That wass usually feenished by quarter to eight or thereby, and at eight o'clock it wass Alec's duty to go through the various public rooms wi' a gong, to summon the residents to their breakfasts in the dining-room.

"When he went into the lounge to do chust that, there wass mair than a dozen Meenisters in their bleck frock-coats and white collars clustered aboot the fire, some o' them toasting their backs at it, others warmin' their hands, for it wass a frosty cauld morning outside and the Hotel wass far from warm.

" 'Yes,' one of the older Meenisters wass saying ass Alec came into the room, 'I enchoyed a positively apocalyptic dream last night — I dreamed that I wass in Heaven!'

" 'And what wass Heaven like,' asked one of the younger ones.

" 'It wass very much like our Convention,' replied the older man solemnly, 'a meeting-place and a gathering-place for the faithful and the penitent.'

"Alec told me later that he chust could not have resisted the temptation that now overwhelmed him. He coughed, and the group round the fire turned towards him.

" 'That is aal most interesting, chentlemen,' said he, 'for I too had a most prophetic dream last night. But where you, Sir, dreamed of Heaven I dreamed that I was in Hell.'

"There was a pause till one of the chentleman asked: 'And what was *that* like?'

" 'It wass chust exactly like the fire in this hotel lounge,' said Alec brightly, 'you could hardly see the flames for Meenisters!'

"He wass oot on the street wi' his tin trunk within 20 minutes but it was the very best thing that effer happened to him. Not only did he get oot of the Bay Hotel and oot of Ullapool, but he took a tumble to himself and gave up working in service and got a proper chob.

"He's a potman at the Horseshoe Inn in Gleska now, happy ass larry, and quite reconciled wi' the rest o' the faimily, for the maist o' my cheneration o' the Macfarlanes wouldna talk to him whiles he wass in service.

" 'It iss like a new lease of life, Peter,' he told me the last time I saw him, and the latest word iss that he iss getting married next month to wan o' the barmaids."

"Well, there you are Peter," said the Engineer, laughing: "you were wrong in what you said a while back — it seems they do get earth-shattering events happening in Ullapool! Jist ask your brother — Ah'm sure he'd agree!"

FACTNOTE

Para Handy's (unnamed) brother is referred to (working as a valet and disowned by the his nine siblings) on the very first page of the first of Neil Munro's original tales — *Para Handy, Master Mariner*. I felt that following the tale of Keep Dark in the previous chapter such an unlikely relative had to be worth investigating!

Ullapool was founded on fishing, has had two hundred years of feast and famine as the herring shoals have come and gone and come back again, but now earns its keep almost entirely from tourism. Though Loch Broom in recent years has been crammed with catchers and mother-ships from almost every country of Northern Europe and some from even further afield, only a tiny handful of small wooden vessels are locally owned and crewed (almost exclusively for shellfish) and no shore-based curing stations remain. The processing of the catch is now carried out on the fleet of klondykers anchored out in the Loch.

Just as Neil Munro's home town of Inveraray was designed and built from scratch as a planned entity by the Duke of Argyll in the 1740s when his new Castle was also constructed and the old Castle and Village demolished, so Ullapool too is an artificial creation.

Here, though, the builder was not a local landowner and the motive was not for the sake of elegance and prestige. Ullapool was identified as the perfect location for a fully integrated fishing town ideally placed to exploit the huge herring shoals of the Minches.

Thus the town came into being in 1788, the brain-child of the British Fisheries Society, with the necessary constituent parts for catching the fish, processing the fish, and servicing the fleet. Thus there were, in addition to the curing stations, a variety of other shore-based operations including boat-yards and ship-chandlers, cooperages and net-works. In season not just the boats but the majority of the shore-workers moved into Ullapool in those days when an army of workers spent each year following the herring shoals on their mysterious migrations around the coasts.

In 1974 Ullapool replaced Mallaig and Kyle of Lochalsh as the terminus for the direct sea-crossing to Stornoway. One perhaps unforeseen side-effect of that decision was that it placed the Inverness to Kyle Railway Line, world-famous for the stunning beauty of its meanderings across some of the most evocative and remote landscapes in the United Kingdom, but economically very fragile, under almost constant threat of closure. So far the conservationists have managed to fend off the pragmatists but its long-term future is still far from assured.

21

A Matter of Men and Machinery

Dougie, who was seated atop the wheelhouse with paint-pot and brush, touching up the black boot-topping on the puffer's funnel, pointed over the puffer's bows and observed: "This must be him comin' noo."

Para Handy turned round from the sternpost, where he had been making some minor adjustments to the rope fenders, and peered along the empty cobbled vista of Yorkhill quayside towards the distant dock gates.

A small figure, hunching forward slightly as he walked and clutching a shabby canvas holdall, was rapidly drawing near the *Vital Spark* with quick, purposeful paces.

"He looks hermless enough," observed the Captain, "and there iss not much of him, to be sure!"

The Mate slid down from the wheelhouse roof and joined him against the rail on the puffer's port quarter. The approaching figure took the last few paces which brought him abreast of the two shipmates and leaned down towards the vessel, whose deck was a few feet below the level of the quay.

"I am sure I must have mistaken my instructions," he observed to the pair quietly in a soft voice with the clipped tones of the east coast discernible in it. "and taken a wrong turning somewhere in the docks. You are not by any chance Captain Peter Macfarlane? I think, surely, that you can't possibly be."

"Oh but I am," said Para Handy cheerfully. "And you'll be Angus Napier? The Docks Office told me to expect you some time this afternoon. Welcome to the smartest boat in the tred. This iss Dougie Campbell, my Mate. Throw us your portmanteau and come aboard. I can assure you we are mair than pleased that you are here, for we have been marooned in this wulderness for the last two days."

With a strangely twisted expression on his face Napier complied with these instructions slowly and uncertainly, and clambered down the iron ladder set into the face of the quay and onto the deck.

He looked about him almost apprehensively.

"And this is really the *Vital Spark*?" he enquired in a doubtful voice, "and you're expecting an engineer...?"

~

Forty-eight hours previously misfortune had struck the puffer or, more accurately, her engineer when Dan Macphail, at home in Plantation for the weekend, had been suddenly taken ill with severe stomach pains which were quickly diagnosed by the doctor summoned by his anxious wife as appendicitis.

Now Dan languished in the Western Infirmary awaiting a decision about an operation and the owner of the *Vital Spark* had been forced to look for a relief engineer. The ship, meanwhile, lay idle at Yorkhill fully-laden with the annual cargo of winter coals ordered by their Laird for the islanders of Canna, unable to fulfill her obligations under that contract till a temporary replacement for Macphail could be found.

"Could you and your Mate not manage the conning and the running of the vessel?" had been the owner's first question when Para Handy reported the situation at his office on Monday morning. "I am sure that between the pair of you you're as familiar with the engines as Macphail himself, and there is little enough to do except keep the furnace fired."

"Not I!" exclaimed Para Handy in some horror. "I leave aal that side of the business to Macphail. My place iss on the brudge o' the shup, no deevin' aboot amang aal the coals and grease and bilers like wan o' the bleck geng on the *Lusitania*. It iss the naavigation and cheneral management of the vessel that iss my responsibility, and a heavy one it iss.

"Besides, you wouldna want the *Vital Spark* to end up the same way as Wullie Jardine's *Saxon* did a year or two back?"

"What happened to her?" enquired the owner, curious.

"She was dam' lucky no' to be sunk." said Para Handy. "Wullie had a furious argument wi' his engineer, old Erchie Begg, one November night when they wass berthed in Dunoon and had gone ashore for a smaal refreshment, and they fell oot aboot their relative importance to the shup.

" 'Caal yourself an enchineer do you,' howled Wullie when Erchie suchested that because of his qualifications he was the key man on board. 'Ah've seen better-qualified men than you drivin' a dustcairt for the Gleska Corporation. *You* run a shup indeed! My Lordie, you couldna even run a tap!'

" 'Iss that so,' retorted Erchie, 'well then I would like to see you tryin' your hand at the controls o' the engine-room. Ony fool can *steer* a boat, Lord knows, Ah did it in my bath when I was a bairn, but it tak's brains to *drive* wan, and you couldna drive a nail intae a plank.'

"There wass more, much more, in the same comradely vein for the two wass in their best insultin' trum what wi' the refreshments they had taken and the upshot of it aal wass that they agreed that, next mornin', the Engineer would tak' the wheel ass they left the Coal Pier at Dunoon, whiles Wullie would be doon below makin' sure the engines didna break.

"What had seemed a good idea at midnight wass very much less attractive at seven o'clock on a dark winter mornin' but the two o' them wass that thrawn neither would admit it, and Wullie went doon to the engine-room while Erchie sauntered into the deckhoose and grabbed the wheel and pretended to himself he'd been doin' it aal his naitural.

"The Mate, who'd been told to keep well clear and leave the two eejits to their ain devices, cast off the bow and stern ropes and she began to druft off the pier-head. Erchie rang doon for full-speed ahead and Wullie tried to mak' some sense of aal the levers and gauges in front of him.

"For a few minutes there wass no sound apart from a series of muffled curses from doon below, then there wass a grindin' and a crunchin' and the propellor began to turn. For a while both men thought efferything wass hunky-dory, till there wass a loud screech on the whustle to the engine-room and Erchie roared doon the voice-pipe 'You auld goat! You've got her goin' astern instead of aheid!'

"Next thing came the crunchin' and the grindin' sounds aal over again, followed by silence and then mair cursin', lots mair cursin', wi' chust occasional bursts of the shaft turnin' for a meenit and then stoppin', and then turnin' again, till finally in a last flurry of un-Chrustian language Wullie admitted defeat and yelled up the voice-pipe for Erchie to get back doon below and sort things oot for he chust wassna able to cope wi' it at aal.

"There was a short silence, then Erchie called quietly doon the pipe 'Weel, Ah dinna think there's mich point in me comin' back doon right noo, Wullie, for Ah'm pretty sure Ah've chust run her onto the Gantocks onyway.'

"And indeed he had, right at the top of the tide, and it wass a full twelve hoors before they wass able to float her off again!

"Naw," concluded Para Handy firmly. "We're no sturrin' till we get an engineer." And, in view of the evidence which he had just had put so graphically before him, the owner agreed with some alacrity that Para Handy should register the temporary vacancy with the employment exchange at the Clyde Docks Office as a matter of urgency.

∼

The bemused Napier set foot on the puffer's deck with an air of reluctance and stared about him in disbelief, pulling off his jauntily-tilted blue peaked cap to scratch at his head with all the signs of an inner turmoil.

Para Handy led him to Macphail's dark subterranean domain. The East Coast man looked even more distraught as he cast his eyes over the cramped engine-room with its single bunker, its single furnace, single boiler, single-pistoned power unit and single propellor shaft: its ramshackle tangle of dank pipes stained here and there with rust and marked by dark streaks of oil: its basic controls and almost total absence of instrumentation of any description.

"There she is, then," said Para Handy with some pride. "Iss she not the beauty?"

There was an awkward silence.

"Is this *it*, then?" Napier asked finally. "I mean, where's the rest of your crew for a start..."

"Oh," said the Captain, "Jum wull be back at any meenit, he has chust gone ashore for some provisions ass I was determined to mak' a start ass soon ass you got here. We have lost two days already and our customer is becoming impatient at the delay, he has been sending telegraphs to the owner's office to say so."

Napier looked no more at his ease. "So — er — this 'Jum': is he my stoker, or my greaser, or my machine-man? And whichever he is, where are the other two? And how the blazes does your regular man find enough space for them all to carry out their duties in a cupboard like this?"

Para Handy stared at the relief engineer uncomprehendingly.

"Jum iss our deckhand and cook," he said: "and a good cook he has become over the years, you will be well fed aboard the shup I can assure you! But Jum has no business effer to be in the enchine-room at aal: it iss your own responsibulity entirely and neither Jum nor nobody else wull interfere with that, I can promise you ."

Napier gaped on the Captain. "D'you mean to tell me you are sailing with jist one man in the engine-room? What happens when he's asleep in his bunk?"

"What do you mean 'what happens'?" retorted the Captain. "What do you think happens? Nothing happens! When he's off-watch then efferybody's off-watch."

Napier blanched. "When I saw the vessel, I had to admire your courage in undertaking the voyage and I was prepared at least to consider sailing with you for I've never been known to shrink from my duty. But with no proper crew — man, you're all mad! You will never, never make it to Canada in this tub!"

"*Canada*," exclaimed Para Handy. "For peety's sake, who the duvvle said onythin' aboot Canada? What do you think this is — the Allan line? We're chust takin' some coals in to *Canna*. Does Dougie look the sort of a man who would risk the North Atlantic in anything smaaller than the *Olympic*? As for me, a Macfarlane neffer shurked, but there are lumits!"

The other looked mightily relieved. "Well," he said, "I have been sent here under false pretences, for I'm a deep-sea man myself, waiting to take up the Chief's post on the new Ben Line ship that's fitting out at Fairfields right now, and when I asked at the Docks Office yesterday about the chance of a berth to fill in the time, they told me that you were looking for an engineer for a round-trip — to Canada!

"That clerk must have cloth ears! And I must say you gave me the devil of a fright! What's more, I take my hat off to your own engineer: I'm too spoiled by having a huge squad at my beck and call. I could no more run this engine-room on my own than I could navigate to

Australia — your man's worth his weight in gold and I hope you realise it."

～

Para Handy and Dougie were delighted, on their return to the boat thirty minutes later after they had treated Napier to a dram to compensate for the waste of his time, to discover that not only was Sunny Jim back — as expected — and frying sausages in the fo'c'sle, but Macphail himself was esconced among his engines and examining them anxiously to see if they had come to any harm during his absence.

"Dan!" cried the Captain, beaming with enthusiasm, "we are fair delighted to see you back! What happened to the appendix?"

"Appendix my eye," replied the Engineer. "It wis naethin' but a bad spell o' indigestion and the Hospital wisnae weel pleased wi' ma ain Doctor for gettin' it wrang.

"Huv I missed much?"

"Nothing at aal, Dan," said Para Handy. "Nothing at aal. There wass some talk of takin' her to Canada" — the Engineer paled — "but, och, it came to nothing, it wass chust a baur. Let us chust get some steam up, and we will tell you aal aboot it some other time."

FACTNOTE

The Gantock Rocks lie about half-a-mile south-east of Dunoon Pier and must have claimed many maritime victims large and small over the centuries, particularly in poor visibility and rough seas. Although they are now well-lit, and in spite of all the modern aids to navigation, they still do — as was demonstrated by our last and much-loved paddler *Waverley*, which was stranded on the reef but fortunately with no casualties and no serious damage to her hull.

The largest ship ever to have been sunk by the Gantocks was the Swedish ore carrier *Akka* which went down in April 1956. Six of her crew were lost in the tragedy, which was apparently caused by steering-failure when she slowed down in order to pick up the river-pilot for her voyage upstream to Glasgow. The 5,500 ton ship, with an overall length of 440ft, struck the reef on her port side, ripping a huge hole in the hull, and remained afloat for only a matter of a few minutes.

The White Star liner *Olympic* was built in the Belfast yard of Harland and Wolff and handed over to her owners on May 31st 1911, the same day on which her sister *Titanic* was launched. An overall length of nearly 900ft ensured that these new ships far exceeded their German and Cunard rivals in size as well as in the opulence of their accommodations. They were designed to deliver profits as well as prestige, though, being powered by newly-developed engine systems which combined efficiency with economy, and capable of carrying 2,500 fare-paying passengers in three classes.

Hidden from these passengers were the echoing caverns of the engine room and, worst horror of all, the stokehold where (till the use of oil-fuel rendered their thankless, repetitive tasks redundant) armies of men laboured on the back-breaking work of coaling the furnaces for the 29 boilers which powered the ship.

Known in the shipboard slang of the period as the 'Black Gang', most of the stokers employed on the British Transatlantic fleet were Liverpool Irish. Harsh conditions bred harsh men and stories of quarrels and sometimes lethal fights — usually among themselves, though occasionally with other members of the crew and even more rarely with particularly brutal Officers — are a part of the legend and lore of the age. However they invariably maintained good relations with the galley, which they provided with fuel and whose fires they helped maintain. In return, the cooks passed to the stokehold men what became known as the 'Black Pan' — uneaten food left over from the sumptuous menus provided to First Class Passengers.

The 'Black Pan' was at its bounteous best during spells of bad weather — the more prolonged, the better!

22

May the Best Man Win

Para Handy and Dougie were seated in Castle Gardens in Dunoon watching the world go by on the esplanade below them. It was the middle of July, the weather was set fine, and the town was packed with holidaymakers and day visitors. A quarter of a mile away at the Coal Pier a thin drizzle of smoke rose skywards from the black-topped red funnel of the *Vital Spark*, awaiting a consignment of logs to be carted down from Glen Masson.

There was a sudden buzz of interest on the thronged pavement and a scatter of applause, and a wedding-party came into sight and headed for the Argyll Hotel. Bride and groom occupied the first carriage-and-pair and in a second one, following closely behind, were bridesmaids, the best man, and the ushers.

"A wedding," sighed Para Handy sentimentally. "I can neffer see wan but I think aboot my own."

"And I neffer see wan but I try to forget aboot my own," said the Mate gloomily.

"Neffer!" said Para Handy, "Lisa iss a fine, managing wumman if a bit headstrong chust now and then, and you have a family to be proud of. Brutain's hardy sons!"

"Aye," replied the Mate, yet more gloomily still. "All twelve of them."

Para Handy felt it was time to focus his companion's attention elsewhere.

"Hurricane Jeck wass best man at a weddin' in Oban a few years back," he observed. "Man, they still taalk aboot it in the toon to this day!

"I wass ashore myself on leave at the time, and met Jeck hurryin' up Buchanan Street towards the railway station.

" 'The very man,' says Jeck. 'I have time for chust the wan wee gless before my train leaves, and I need your advice, Peter.'

"Jeck had been asked earlier in the week by an old frien' of his from Barra if he wud be his best man, he wass being merrit next day in Oban on a Kilmore gyurl, and this wass Jeck heading for the train for the two of them wass to meet up in Oban that night, and stay over at the Crown Hotel before the wedding the following morning.

" 'What it is, Peter,' says Jeck, quite flustered, 'iss that I havna a notion whit's expected of me. You know me, Peter, I've made dam' sure never to be tied doon, and the result iss that I have neffer effer been at *any* wedding in my naitural, neffer mind my own!

" 'So tell me, what's a best man, and what's he to do?'

"Weel, I gave Jeck a quick run through on the duties and the responsubilities o' best men: he didna like the bit aboot answering the toast to the bridesmaids, said he wassna much for public speaking, but I told him not to worry, by that time in the proceedings efferybody would have had a gless or two and the place would be fine and cheery.

" 'The most important thing you have to do, Jeck, is to get the bridegroom to the kirk on time, smertly turned oot, and above aal else — sober. Every bride's mither aye thinks that nobody is good enough for her lass, and if the gyurl's intended turns up late, and looking ass if he had been dragged through a hedge backwards, and reekin' o' spurits, then I promise you that that merriage iss off to the worst of aal possible sterts.'

" 'Thanks Peter,' says Jeck, looking at the clock in the public hoose we wass in, 'I wull remember. On time, smert, sober. You can rely on me!'

"And with a quick shake o' the haund, he was off like a whippet to catch his train.

"It wass some months before I heard what way things had gone for Jeck and his frien' in Oban. The news wassna good and the cheneral feeling wass that neither was the prognostications for the merriage.

"The groom wass a MacNeil from Castlebay, a fine, cheery chap wi' shouthers on him like an ox, by name o' Wullie. He wass in the Navy at the time, and he'd met the bride the previous summer when the fleet wass in Oban, and she wass workin' ass a waitress at a wee temperance hotel at the back o' the toon. The two of them met at the

Argyllshire Gaithering in August and by the time Wullie's ship sailed at the end of September, he wass an engaged man. The gyurl — Constance, her name wass, but she answered to Connie — wass a MacRobb from Kilmore.

"Her faimily didna take too kindly to the news that she wass engaged to a sailor — though they'd neffer met him and didna really know mich aboot him — but Connie assured them he wass a true and considerate chentleman, and then she spent the winter saving money and gaithering together aal the bits and pieces for her bottom drawer.

"Wullie couldna get ony leave till the wedding itself, so aal the arrangements had to be left to the MacRobb faimily. They booked the kirk — St Andrews, on the esplanade: and promised a fine reception efter, wi' places for 40 o' Wullie's faimily and frien's from Castlebay.

"On the evening Jeck arrived in Oban Wullie wass all on his own for the Barra fowk wass comin' to Oban overnight on the steamer and wudna get there till the morning. So they had agreed that efferybody would mak' their ain way to the Kirk, and chust meet up there for the service at eleven o'clock.

"Jeck met Wullie at the Crown Hotel, ass arranged, and the two of them exchanged news, aal very quiet and restrained, and had a fish tea in the hotel dining-room.

" 'I am seeing you're early to your bed tonight, Wullie," said Jeck firmly, 'for it iss my responsubility to deliver you to the Kirk on time and in appropriate trum for the occasion.'

"And the two of them agreed they would have chust a ten minute stroll on the esplanade, and then go to their rooms.

"This wass the point at which things sterted to go seriously wrong for, while they wass at their teas, they hadna noticed that a naval cruiser had come into Oban Bay and when they got to the esplanade, the toon wass chust hotching wi' seamen, and worst of aal, it wass the shup Wullie had been on till chust three months earlier, so aalmost efferyone o' the navy that the two of them encountered on the pavements wass a friend of the groom's — and when they heard that he wass getting married the next day, they chust wouldna tak' no for an answer in relation to the matter of a gless of somethin' to celebrate.

"I would like to think that Jeck did his best to protect Wullie from himself, but I am chust not sure. It would have been hard enough to protect Wullie from *Jeck* in normal circumstances. And I do not know exactly what happened, for the two main players in the game have no recollection of it, for reasons that wull become obvious, and I canna very well ask the Navy to hold an unquisition into it aal.

"The pair foond themselves press-ganged by aal Wullie's former shupmates, and soon they wass in among a lerge perty of sailors visiting aal the public hooses of Oban wan by wan, and bringing an unfectious air of goodwull and happiness wi' them whereffer they went.

"The following ten hours or so iss a mystery and Jeck's next connection wi' reality cam' at aboot nine o'clock the followin' morning when he woke up, fully clothed, underneath wan o' the airches o' McCaig's Folly above the toon. Efter less than a meenit — he wass aalways very quick makin' a recovery from this sort of situation, he'd had lots o' practice — Jeck remembered where he wass, and why. And realised that there wass no sign of Wullie!

"But chust then, he heard somebody snoring, very loud, and a wee investigation resulted in the discovery of Wullie asleep under the next airchway, and in a terrible state! Jeck realised that *he* probably looked jist as bad, but he hadna a mirror aboot his person. Wullie's clothes was aal damp and stained green wi' the gress he'd slept on, he'd lost his collar and tie, his hair wass a mess and he wass in sair need of a shave. Possibly worst of aal wass that for some reason that Jeck could not fathom or remember, Wullie had a whupper o' a bleck eye.

"Jeck woke him urchently and reminded him whit day it wass.

" 'My Cot,' says Wullie, 'we must get back to the Hotel and get bathed and shaved and changed. It's less than two hours to the wedding!'

"If Jeck had thought things couldna get ony worse, he wass very wrang. When they got to the Hotel, the proprietor wouldna let them in. Apparently they'd rolled up to the hotel aboot two in the mornin', wi' a whole perty o' sailors, demanded drinks aal roond, and threatened his person when he refused. They had only left when the owner sent for the polis.

" 'Well at least let us get oor clothes,' Jeck pleaded. 'The man iss getting married at eleven o'clock.'

"'Heaven help the bride,' said the hotelier, 'but I'll gi'e ye back yer stuff — wance ye settle the bill.' Jeck and Wullie went through their pockets — but they didna have a penny piece between them.

" 'In that case,' said the hotelier, 'I'm holding onto your luggage till ye pay what's owin'. That's the law, that's what I'm entitled to do, and that's what I'm doing.'

"Jeck pleaded and better pleaded, but the man wouldna budge an inch. The two of them made the best attempt to tidy up they could in the waash-room at the station, then hurried out along the esplanade to the Kirk.

"I dinna ken what the Meenister thought, but he said nothing though he had bad news for Wullie. 'I didna realise you wass coming over in advance' (Wullie hadna a clue what he meant by that) 'but the rest of your folk are coming on the overnight boat, aren't they?' he asked and Wullie nodded. 'Weel, I'm afraid to tell you she had a biler failure and she'll no' be in Oban till two this efternoon. I presume you wull want to put the weddin' off till then?' And when Wullie said no, just to go ahead, the Minister looked puzzled, and said he would have to send word to the bride and her party, but they could be there in under half-an-hour. Wullie didna understand that, neither.

"So it wass twenty minutes past eleven when Wullie and Jeck took their places at the fore-end of the altar, wi' naebody in their side of the Kirk at aal, and naethin' but strangers — the bride's pairty — on the ither.

"The organ struck up *Here comes the Bride* and Jeck and Wullie wass aware of the gyurl and her attendants comin' up the aisle and when they reached alangside and Wullie turned to smile at her he foond himsel' lookin' at a total stranger. 'Who on earth are *you*?' screamed the bride, and Wullie said he could ask her the same thing. The Meenister near threw a fit and said angrily to Wullie, 'What sort o' shame are you bringin' to St Antonys wi' a stupid prank like that!' 'St Antonys' yelped Jeck, 'I thought this wass St Andrews?'

" 'Naw, said the Meenister, furious, 'St Andrews is a hunner yerds further along the front. *Our* groom is a fine young man from Colonsay and his faimily, but the boat has broke doon, which iss why I couldna think how *this* groom got here at aal.'

"So Jeck and Wullie were an hour late for the real weddin', and by that time the bride wass chust gettin' ready to go hame for she thought she'd been left at the altar. She wass ready enough to tear Wullie to bits, whateffer his condition or excuses, but when she saw the state of him and the best man, and gaithered what had been going on, she near enough *did* go hame.

"Eventually the wedding went ahead. Things didna get ony better efterwards, neither, though by noo Jeck wass past caring and in any case the trouble wass being caused by Wullie's faimily.

"What neither Wullie nor Jeck, nor the faimily, had known wass that the MacRobbs and their kin wass strict teetotallers, very staunch Rechabites to a man, and the reception wass in the Oban Temperance Halls without a refreshment in sight.

"The MacNeils spent their time ignoring the bride's pairty and complaining loudly about the lack of Highland hospitality and how they'd been brought aal the way from Barra under false pretences and I am ashamed to say that some of them went out to the toon for a gless, and brought several bottles back wi' them for the rest o' the company.

"By the time it cam' time for Jeck's speech there wasna mich point makin' it for the maist of the MacRobbs had gone hame and the few that hadna — the younger, bigger men — wass having a donnybrook wi' the MacNeils: and the bride was in hysterics in the ladies' cloakroom.

"So if you effer get depressed thinking aboot your ain wedding, Dougie, then think aboot *that* one. That'll cheer you up!"

FACTNOTE

Castle Gardens remains a very pleasant spot from which to watch the passing show, though sadly there are few movements of shipping on the river and Dunoon Pier, onto which the Gardens look directly down, once a crossroads of steamer services both complementary and competing, now offers no spectacle other than that of the arrival and departure of the regular Cal-Mac boat from Gourock.

The Glasgow to Oban Railway, in the days when Hurricane Jack made the journey, would have taken him to the west coast port by way of Stirling, Callander and Killin Junction on one of the most scenic railway journeys in Europe.

By 1965, despite some half-hearted attempts by BR to attract additional patronage by putting observation cars — some with a conductor/guide — on the peak summer services, it was obvious that the Beeching Axe would include

THE WEDDING PARTY — In my factual companion to Para Handy's world In the Wake of the Vital Spark *I used as one of the illustrations a photograph of a different Campbeltown wedding and was thrilled and quite fascinated to receive a letter from a lady who could identify most of the 'sitters' as her own forebears. Can anyone help out in the same way with this splendid period piece?*

this beautiful but tortuous route. The Dunblane to Crianlarich section was closed, the track uprooted, and trains for Oban henceforth left from Glasgow Queen Street and travelled up Loch Long and Loch Lomond on the much shorter former LNER line to Crianlarich and on to Oban.

McCaig's Tower, to give it its proper name, is an incongruous but very distinctive feature of the town's sky-line overlooking the bay and the Sound of Mull, and offering from its elevated position fine views of what are perhaps the most dramatic sunsets in the West.

A replica, albeit on a reduced scale, of the Colosseum in Rome, work started on it in 1897, and the stated intention of the excercise was that of providing work for the unemployed labourers of the district. This was the first but it certainly has not been the last of purported 'job creation schemes' which have been a feature of the Highland economy on many occasions since.

The big difference here, however, was that the funds for this project came, not from the public purse, but from a retired Oban businessman, one John McCaig, who was himself a shareholder in the Oban and Callander Railway Company — and the owner of the town's North Pier. The project was never carried through, work ceasing in 1898, and since rumour has it that had it been finished it was intended as some sort of monument and mausoleum for the McCaig family, it is probably just as well.

The Argyllshire Gathering, held every August, hosts some of the top Solo Piping competitions and is very much a key date in the social calendar for the great and good of that part of Argyll, whose Duke is its hereditary Chieftain.

23

The Appliance of Science

With almost every year bringing some further, dramatic advance in the range of navigational and mechanical instrumentation and infrastructure (and domestic comfort) available to mariners the world over I have always been forcefully struck by the apparent failure of even the most basic improvements to the sailors' lot to come (or be brought) to the attention of Captain and crew of the *Vital Spark*.

Year on year that most kenspeckle component of the entire Clyde puffer fleet remains firmly anchored to the anachronistic maritime technology of the year in which she was launched, even in terms of her domestic arrangements.

Thus (to take just a few examples) the revolution of wireless communication has passed her by, as has the more widespread installation of the repeating engine-room telegraph: the now normal provision in the wheelhouse of a handsome, brass-cased instrument combining compass, chronometer and barometer: the switch to electrical incandescent lighting: the provision of running water from a central tank: and the use of bottled gas for the purpose of cooking.

Aboard the *Vital Spark*, therefore, Para Handy still puts in to the nearest village blessed with a Post Office to communicate by telegram with his Head Office, and gives his instructions to the engine-room either verbally, or with a tap of the boot on Macphail's flat cap. A small pocket compass of very dubious accuracy is the sole aid to navigation, and the battered tin alarm-clock hanging by a string from a nail in the fo'c'sle the only rough guide to the real time.

Weather prediction is always accomplished first thing each morning by sending Sunny Jim up on deck to see if it is raining or not. Dougie still trims and curses dimly-flickering, temperamental oil-lamps for the ship's navigation and safety after dark. On deck, Sunny Jim rinses out dirty pots and dishes in a bucket of sea-water, and down below in the fo'c'sle he cooks on a smoking coal stove.

Thus the facilities enjoyed aboard the speeding *Columba* are as far removed from those deployed on the wretched puffer which she regularly leaves in her wake, as the accoutrements to hand in the douce terrace houses of Kelvinside are an advance upon the amenities of a Hottentot hut.

Given Para Handy's blind devotion to his command this was not an easy topic to broach, but encountering the mariner on Dunoon pier recently I took the opportunity to draw to his attention the favourable reception accorded to the recently-electrified tram service on Bute, and asked whether he foresaw, in the near future, any likely major improvements to the maritime services on the Firth — and particularly to the lot of the puffer-men who provided so many of them.

"None that I can really think of," he replied, catching hold of my elbow as he did so and steering me gently, unobtrusively and almost absent-mindedly (though with unerring accuracy) in the very precise direction of the Licensed Refreshment Room located at the eastern end of the pier.

~

"But surely there are many things which would help make life easier for you," I continued a minute or so later as the barman wiped our corner table with a damp cloth before setting our glasses on it. "What about weather prediction, for instance. A barometer would allow you to make some sensible judgement about likely conditions over the next twenty-four hours…"

"Barometer!" exclaimed the Captain, almost choking on his drink. "Don't talk to me aboot barometers. They are nothin' but a snare and a delusion, as it says in the Scruptures.

"The owner sent one doon to the vessel a year or two back wi' a wee note ass to how to work it, and said it would help us plan our week better if we had some idea of the likely condeeshuns when we wass at sea. I am not a thrawn man, so though I didna like it I hung the dam' thing up in the fo'c'sle and effery mornin' and effery evening I would be lookin' at it to see what it said.

"It aalways pointed to the same thing. *Set Fair*. It didna matter if we wass marooned in Tobermory wi' a howlin' gale, or stranded in the fog in Ardrossan Harbour, or gettin' snowed on like we wass in the Arctic, but us chust in Colintraive. *Set Fair*. That was the message even on, month efter month.

"I stuck it oot, for it wassna my property and anyway I had learnt chust to ignore it, but we had Jeck wi' us for a couple of trups and I tell you he took ass ill to that dam' barometer ass if it had been a temperance campaigner in the Yoker Vaults at the Gleska Fair Weekend.

"He finally snapped one mornin' when we wass comin' doon from Arrochar. It had been rainin' on like a second Flood for three solid days and we wass aal on a short fuse ass a result. Mebbe I should have seen the warnin' signs the previous night, for Jeck had spent maist o' the evenin' swearin' at the barometer ass if it wass personally responsible for the doonpour.

"Chust before mid-day I wass in the wheelhouse, wi' Jeck and Dougie off watch in the fo'c'sle, when suddenly the fore-hatch crashed open and Jeck came clatterin' on deck wi' the barometer clutched in baith hands.

"He jumped onto the main hatch and held the barometer high over his head wi' its face to the sky, and the rain wass harder than ever and the clouds wass that low you could have touched them wi' an oar.

" '*Set Fair!*' bellowed Jeck. ' *Set Fair*, is it, ye eejit! Weel maybe ye'll believe the evidence o' yer ain eyes noo, ye leein' blackguard!' — and he fair shook the implement in his hands and thrust it up and into the worst o' the rain — 'Tak' a good look at that. *Set Fair* my auntie!'

"And wi' a final roond o' curses I wouldna give myself a red face by repeating, he swung the barometer round above his head several times for luck and sent it hurtling up and oot and over and into the loch and oot of oor lives forever.

"Naw, I am not a great man for any o' these new-fangled gadgets at aal, for you almost neffer find them to be aal they is cracked up to be. I am chust perfectly content so long as I am provided wi' the staples that have made us Brutain's hardy sons," the Captain concluded, mournfully staring into his now empty glass with a pointed purposefulness to which I felt it best to respond.

~

Para Handy's frustrations with the recalcitrant barometer, however, were as nothing compared with the encounter with the new technologies which he experienced a couple of weeks after our conversation in Dunoon.

The incident is best related as it was reported in the columns of the Greenock Telegraph in the following terms, which I here reproduce by kind permission of the Editor of that respected journal:

A NEAR MISS AT ARDNADAM
(National Press please copy)

After exhaustive enquiries by the piermaster concerned, the steam gabbart *Vital Spark* has been held solely responsible for the regrettable incident at Ardnadam Pier at 10 p.m. last Saturday night which resulted in minor damage to the structure of the pier and to the upperworks of the paddle-steamer *Dandie Dinmont*, which was berthing at the time. Of more immediate concern was the mental and physical distress occasioned to a large number of excursionists, of both sexes and all ages, who were waiting on the pierhead to board the steamer for their scheduled 'moonlight-cruise' return journey to Craigendorran.

It transpired that, as part of a planned refurbishment of the puffer, her owner had contracted with the Ardnadam Foundry for the supply of a new remote-control signalling apparatus between wheelhouse and engine-room: and a steam-whistle of improved design and performance.

These had been fitted under the supervision of the Captain and Engineer of the steam lighter, though we understand from the foreman of the Foundry that there had been constant bickering and altercation between the two as to the most effective way of achieving satisfactory installation of the new equipment.

With benefit of hindsight it is now apparent that certain grave errors and miscalculations occurred and that neither piece of equipment was correctly instated.

The results were unfortunate to say the least.

As the *Dandie Dinmont* approached, the Captain of the steam lighter, which had been tied up alongside the head of the pier, loosed his moorings and signalled for dead slow astern in order to move slightly inshore to leave a clear berth for the steamer. Unhappily it is now apparent that the signalling device had been installed back-to-front and the instructions which were displayed in the engine-room in fact called for emergency full-speed ahead.

The puffer collided bow-first with the paddle-box of the approaching steamer but, mercifully, the damage was slight as even at maximum revolutions the acceleration of this type of vessel is notoriously ponderous.

On realising what had happened (though not, unfortunately, why it had happened) the engineer of the puffer engaged full speed astern, at which the vessel proceeded to bear down on the pierhead, now crowded with the steamer's intending passengers.

In the wheelhouse the vessel's Captain, powerless — in the time available — to prevent the imminent collision with the pier, pulled sharply on the lanyard of the new steam-whistle to sound a warning.

Unfortunately the valve-pipe from the boiler which was intended to power the whistle had been erroneously connected not to the tubing at the base of the whistle shaft, but to an old, narrow and disused ventilation pipe which led directly into the base of the vessel's smoke-stack.

As a result, instead of producing the intended warning whistle, deployment of the lever which should have controlled that instrument sent a great blast of scalding steam straight up the shaft of the funnel and resulted in the immediate and widespread emission of an enormous cloud of smoke and soot of quite volcanic proportions which, in the prevailing wind, was deposited thickly onto the pier and onto the persons and clothing of all those standing upon it.

It is understood that several parties are consulting their lawyers as a result of this contre-temps, and that when last seen the Captain and Engineer of the steam-lighter were on the point of exchanging blows on the mainhatch as the vessel, still under power but not apparently under control, drifted out from the pier and vanished into the darkness.

~

I was glad that some weeks passed before I again encountered the Captain.

In the meantime, although I cut out the newspaper's report and pasted it carefully into my commonplace book, I have made a mental note never again to broach with Para Handy the subject of the new technologies.

I would hate to see him blow his top again.

FACTNOTE

Till the very end of their era, the puffers were the most basic of vessels, embellished with few refinements and even less evidence of modern technology.

They relied on the seamanship, experience and total familiarity with the waters they sailed which were the hall-mark of their skippers and their crews. Indeed as more one than former puffer man has told me, that instinct was often more to be relied on than the best efforts of modern science. Those most gifted were able to 'feel' a storm coming in from the west, or 'sense' the imminence of fog before it closed in — and take the appropriate avoiding action in good time.

Ardnadam Pier, some 70 yards from shoreline to pier-head, was the longest of the Clyde piers. Indeed it still *is* because it has survived as a result of having been the pier which served the US Navy throughout their 30 year lease of the anchorage of Holy Loch as the North Atlantic base for their quite unholy nuclear submarines. Improved and refurbished, scrupulously maintained as a result of its total-ly unforeseen strategic importance, the venerable pier is today in immaculate condition, set fair to celebrate its 150th anniversary in 2008.

The communities centred around Holy Loch and its immediate environs, were — at the zenith of communica-tion by water on the Clyde — the very heart of commuter-land both in terms of travel to work (in Glasgow), and travel to shop (either in Greenock or closer at hand in Dunoon.) As a result, within a space of just a few miles on the Cowal shore of the Firth, there were steamer piers at Blairmore, Strone, Kilmun, Ardnadam, Hunter's Quay and Kirn. All had regular communications with the principal Cowal pier at Dunoon, and with the railheads of Gourock, Greenock and Craigendorran, as well as the Broomielaw or Bridge Wharf in the heart of Glasgow itself.

The *Dandie Dinmont*, launched from the Partick yard of Messrs A and J Inglis of Pointhouse in 1895, was the regular Holy Loch steamer for most of her working life. Named, like all steamers in the North British Company's fleet, after a character from one of Sir Walter Scott's novels, she was 195' overall with handsome saloons fore and aft. Her contemporaries in the North British fleet included the remarkable *Lucy Ashton*, a product of the *real* 'Upper Clyde', built by Seath's of Rutherglen in 1888. Only MacBrayne's *Iona* — broken up in 1936 after no less than 72 years in service — could be regarded as a more potent link to the Victorian era. 'Lucy' survived two World Wars and was only withdrawn from service in 1949, still within the living memory and, above all, the practical experience of countless Clyde enthusiasts.

24

The Gunpowder Plot

Many residents of the West Highlands are angry at the way in which successive governments have used the area as a convenient dumping ground for industrial activity of a risky nature — such as the manufacture of explosives: or for testing the efficiency and effectiveness of a wide variety of experimental maritime or martial hardware — from submarines to land mines.

Many *more* residents would be equally angry if they were aware of such activity in the first instance, but it is in the nature of government to admit little and divulge less, and as a result obfuscation of the truth is nowadays an art form in political and military circles.

Thus one of the better-kept secrets of the Ardlamont peninsula is the presence, in the tiny clachan of Millhouse on the narrow winding road from Tighnabruaich to the Otter Ferry, of a not insubstantial manufactory of black gunpowder — established two generations ago in 1839. It is indeed from this very enterprise that the little village derives its name, though the majority of visitors passing through it (and there are, sadly, very few of these despite the general growth of tourism on the fringes of the Firth of Clyde) are unaware of its presence. They assume that the group of buildings enclosed within a high dry-stone wall and just visible from the road, through a barred iron gate bearing a nameboard reading simply 'Mill', are intended for the more acceptable and less controversial activity of grinding corn or barley.

Even Para Handy himself, regular habitue of the Kyleside piers though he is, never ventured inland of Kames and thus remained in total ignorance of the existence of that

Gunpowder Mill until the bizarre chain of events, which are here related for the first time, were set in motion by a peremptory summons to the offices of the owner of the *Vital Spark*.

The Captain made his way along the Broomielaw in the direction of those rarely-visited premises with considerable trepidation, mentally reviewing the events of recent weeks with the aim of identifying in advance the (hopefully minor) peccadillo for which he was about to be called to book.

He need not have worried. The owner himself greeted him in the lobby and, throwing a comradely arm over Para Handy's shoulder, ushered him into his inner sanctum, sat him down, and offered a cigar from the humidor atop his leather-inlaid desk.

"We have been commissioned to undertake a rather unusual and challenging contract, Peter," said the owner: "and it was at once clear to me that only the *Vital Spark* could be trusted to fulfil it satisfactorily."

Para Handy positively glowed with pride.

"There is a vessel wrecked on the Burnt Islands to the west of Colintraive," the owner continued. "Just a small schooner, but her cargo must be recovered urgently. The salvage team have reported to her owners that the only type of ship able to come near her is a puffer, which can get alongside and then ground on the shoals when the tide goes out."

He spread out a sea-chart — one of the very few that Para Handy had ever seen — on the desk between them.

"A larger steamship would have far too much draft to come into this channel even at high tide, and of course no sailing vessel with any sort of keel would be able to ground on the ebb tides without heeling over to such a degree that she wouldn't be able to work her derrick.

"It's either a steam-lighter, or nothing."

"Well you need have no fear at aal on that score," said Para Handy confidently, "for the *Vital Spark* iss more than capable of doing the chob."

"Good!" The owner smiled expansively. "I was sure that would be your reaction, Peter: and I am sure too that there could well be a modest bonus for her Captain once the job is complete."

There was a pause as the implications of that last, and unrehearsed, statement sank in to both parties.

"So what iss her cairgo, then?" asked Para Handy — more out of a desire to fill that embarrassing silence than from any real concern about the matter.

"Butter," said the owner after a moment. "Salted butter: from Islay, in barrels for export."

At which juncture the owner shuffled his feet noisily under the polished mahogany desk, and twisted uncomfortably in his swivel chair before ringing the bell at his right hand and, when his clerk put his head round the frosted-glass door from the outer room with an enquiring glance, instructing that worthy to fetch the bottle of whisky from the safe and pour two generous drams.

~

"Are we no' puttin' in to Colintraive for the night?" queried Dougie with some surprise as the smartest boat in the coasting trade hiccuped past that attractive settlement at eight o'clock the following evening.

It was a pleasantly mild late September gloaming and the lights of the little Kyleside village twinkled invitingly in the gathering dusk, those of the Inns on the low ridge above the pier particularly conspicuous and especially promising of a warm welcome and good company.

"Owner's orders," said Para Handy. "He iss frightened that there could be something stole from the wreck — from her accoutrements or her cairgo. Remember what Hurricane Jeck got up to in the Kyles wi' yon steam yat the *Eagle* that her owner abandoned at Tighnabruaich! He strupped her of efferything that wassna nailed doon — and maist o' the things that wass as weel! So the owner wants us to moor chust off of Burnt Island ass a deterchent to ony o' the light-fingered chentry, and then to go alongside her and ground on the ebb at furst light tomorrow to transfer the cairgo."

Once they had dropped anchor 50 yards from the sorry-looking remains of the two-masted schooner *Caroline Anne*, her foremast broken off at deck level and lying athwartships with rigging and sails trailing overboard in a tangle of sodden rope and canvas, Para Handy — to the crew's disgust — produced a piece of paper from his trousers pocket and recited a watch roster for the hours of darkness.

~

Sunny Jim, on the dawn shift, was astonished to see — as

the light grew brighter — that there were crowds assembled on the water's edge to either hand. Those on the Bute shore had had an arduous walk over rough country to reach their viewpoint, for this northern tip of the island was barren and normally without any human presence. Today however a goodly number of men, women and children were to be seen on the rocky beach, many of them (just like their counterparts on the opposite shore) studying the *Vital Spark* closely through binoculars or telescopes.

When the puffer was successfully beached alongside the stranded schooner the unloading process began, as a cargo consisting of small wooden barrels was transferred from the hold of one ship to the hold of the other in netting slings. From the shore came great whooping cries of "Oooooh!" each time the laden sling was swung between the vessels, and a hearty cheer once its load had been safely lowered into the main-hatch of the *Vital Spark*.

"Ah cannae think whit's so interestin' aboot a cairgo o' butter firkins," protested Macphail for the umpteenth time, as another whoop marked the progression of a fully-laden net from schooner to puffer: "and it's no' as if they havnae seen plenty o' shups stranded on the Burnt Islands afore noo. There must be precious little doin' in Rothesay or along the Kyles if this is seen as entertainment for a family day oot!"

"They iss a funny kind o' firkin, forbye," said Dougie, "for I have neffer before seen Islay butter packed in barrels wi' a bleck Jolly Roger flag pentit' on the lids — usually it iss the picture of a coo."

"Naw," said Macphail with a snort, "that disnae surprise me at all, that's their trade-mark. Maist o' the fairmers in Islay are naethin' but a crew o' pirates: they'd rook ye blind sooner than look ye in the e'e. If ye'd mind whit we wis payin' for tatties in Port Askaig last month then ye'd hiv tae wonder that they dinna mak' ony visitin' seaman walk the plank aff the toon pier-heid as a deevershun for the lieges on a Setturday nicht.

"Onyway, if it's flags ye're on aboot, did you ever see wan as trauchled as thon auld rag hingin' on the *Caroline Ann*?"

And he pointed aloft to the schooner's mast-head, where a plain red burgee, tattered at the edges and stained by a continuing exposure to the weather of many years, flapped idly in a light southerly breeze.

At which moment, the last load having been swung

aboard the *Vital Spark*, Sunny Jim (acting on instructions given earlier by his Captain) launched the puffer's punt and rowed off towards Colintraive and its well-stocked Inn with a pocketful of change and two large tin canisters.

At the same time Para Handy himself, overhearing his Engineer's caustic remark about the schooner's burgee, glanced up at it in curiosity — and saw something which made him draw his breath in sharply, and scurry off into the wheelhouse.

~

"No, no, put your money away, there is no charge at all," said the Landlord of the Colintraive Inn as he filled the second of the *Vital Spark*'s canisters and Sunny Jim, who had been rummaging clumsily in his pocket for the money, looked up in astonishment.

"Just tell Para Handy that he has given us more entertainment this morning than we've had for many a month," continued the Landlord: "and besides, I had a wee bet that you *would* unload the cargo safely — so I have won a few shullings for myself, as the maist o' the folk thought that Peter would blow the shup to smithereens."

Jim croaked wordlessly as the landlord concluded:

"Aye, it takes a strong hand and a sherp eye to trans-ship near on fufty tons o' gunpooder just as calmly as if it had been barrels of herring — or butter, come to that."

~

On board the puffer Para Handy, ashen-faced, appeared at the door of the wheelhouse with a copy of Brown's Manual of Signals in his hand.

"Dougie, pit oot thon pipe this meenit. Dan, away you and dowse the fire in the enchine-room and the stove in the fo'c'sle and if either of you have matches aboot your persons then throw them over the side o' the shup.

"We are standing on a floating bomb! A red burgee flies ower a ship that's cairryin' explosives. Butter firkins my eye — we've chust loaded up wi' kegs o' gunpooder. We canna unload them again and I wull not abandon shup: neffer let it be said that a Macfarlane flunched at the hoor o' danger. But there iss only wan way this shup iss going up-river — and that iss under wind-power. Break oot the mainsail for there will be no fires aboard the vessel from noo on. I do not care how long it takes."

~

It took three days — for puffers, while notoriously slow under power, are positively plodding under sail.

The passage of the *Vital Spark* up river started out in convoy fashion as Sunny Jim, refusing point-blank to set foot aboard the vessel till her lethal cargo was safely unloaded, followed her in the punt, maintaining station a hundred yards astern. He finally bargained with his ship-mates for a tow-line in exchange for the two canisters of Colintraive ale, and slept through most of the subsequent voyage upstream.

News of the puffer's condition and cargo spread like wild-fire before her and, sporting her red burgee (a warning as potent as the hand-bell of a medieval leper) she was given a wide berth by all the traffic on the river. But she was cheered to the echo by the curious crowds on the bank — crowds which became denser as she neared the centre of the city, lured to this most unusual spectacle of a floating bomb by the reports carried in the *Glasgow Evening News*.

Her owner, uncertain whether to be outraged or flattered by the attention focussed on his wayward craft, met Para Handy on his eventual arrival at Finnieston with cautious cheerfulness.

This was only slighty diminished when it was made clear to him that the promised bonus, now that the entire crew of the puffer were privy to his deceptions should — far from being split four ways — now be multiplied four times. He cheered himself up with the thought that the original Gunpowder plotters had paid a far higher price for *their* deception.

FACTNOTE

The Cowal peninsula and the shores of Upper Loch Fyne seem to have been singled out as highly convenient dump-ing grounds for undesirable military activity for more than a century.

The US Navy has only recently withdrawn its Polaris Submarine Base from the Holy Loch just a couple of miles from Dunoon — a presence which made not just the adjacent, innocent villages of Kilmun or Sandbank but the entire Central Belt of Scotland one of the most obvious potential targets for a primary pre-emptive strike by the former Soviet Union throughout the uneasy decades of the Cold War.

Our immediate forebears maybe did not have the misfortune to live with that particular threat hanging over their heads, but they were certainly no strangers to an unwanted military or armament facility deployed into their midst without so much as a 'by your leave'.

Thus at otherwise idyllic locations such as Furnace on Loch Fyne, Clachaig in Glen Lean west of Dunoon, and Millhouse, just inland from Kames on the Kyles, gunpowder and other explosives were manufactured over a period of close on a hundred years.

Operations at Furnace (where the established presence of a huge granite quarry had produced generations of locals inured to the thump and the threat of daily detonations) closed in the 1880s after a horrendous explosion left more than 20 dead.

The black powder manufactory at Clachaig lasted a decade or two longer and some of the original worker's cottages, renovated and restored, are happy homes today.

The Millhouse works were shut down only in the 1920s, despite a series of catastrophic accidents over the previous century which resulted in heavy loss of life and (if the contemporary newspaper reports are to be believed) were sometimes to be heard — and even felt — as far away as Rothesay and Inveraray.

The finished products from Millhouse ware indeed shipped out on schooners from a private jetty at Kames, to which the kegs were transported on horse-drawn carts — their wheel rims at first cushioned by leather and, later, by rubber.

Anyone who has seen that classic edge-of-the-seat 1950s French film *Les Salaires de Peur* (The Wages of Fear) about truckers offered premium payment to drive potentially lethal loads of nitro-glycerine several hundred miles across unsurfaced roads in mountainous terrain will have some idea of how the drivers of those carts may have felt as they went about their duties!

25

Nor any Drop to Drink

In the balmy, early evening of midsummer's day, the *Vital Spark* lay against the inner face of Inveraray pier. In the afternoon the thermometer had touched 80 degrees fahrenheit, without so much as a whisper of wind, and even now, at six o'clock, there was not the slightest promise of any freshness in the air and the heat remained overwhelming.

The puffer's crew were spreadeagled on the main-hatch: Para Handy, vainly seeking some shade in the wheelhouse, leaned his elbows on the sill of its opened fore-window and surveyed the crowds thronging the pier and its approaches with a somewhat jaundiced eye.

Preparing to board the steamer *Ivanhoe* were the several hundred members of a special charter party. Special in more ways than one, for this was a strangely silent crowd. Though it included scores of children of an age-group which would normally be expected to be of a boisterous and undisciplined disposition, these particular youngsters were marshalled into subdued groups under the watchful eye of straight-backed ladies of an angular build, a frosty mien and a certain age — and all apparently sharing a taste for unseasonably drab and voluminous garments.

The balance of the company was comprised of perhaps one hundred couples, presumably the parents and grandparents of the silent children, conversing in small groups in a whisper, their heads down: occasionally, just occasionally, a few of the men-folk glanced wistfully towards the frontage of the town, dominated by the prominent white facade of the Argyll Arms Hotel. The last components of the party were about one hundred younger men and women who were also gathered in supervised clusters, all men in this one or that, all girls in these others.

Gliding through the crowd with beady eyes which seemed to peer everywhere and take in everything were a dozen or more stiffly erect figures in black frock coats, high-buttoned waistcoats, and tall, shiny-black stovepipe hats, and carrying tight-rolled umbrellas, the glint of white dog-collars (largely hidden behind full sets of Dundreary whiskers) the only departure from unrelieved black in their whole attire.

"A Good Templar's summer ooting," said Para Handy with a degree of acerbity, to nobody in particular: and he shivered in spite of the heat. "Now there iss a sight to mak' the blood run cold! There is chust aboot as much spurit of happiness, good-wull and harmony in that gaitherin' ass would fill an empty vestas box!

"They'll have been at the Cherry Park for a tent-meeting and a picnic, and then a march back doon the toon to the pier. Cheery days! Look you at aal they bible-thumpers wi' the chuldren, and aal they spunster wummen chaperonin' the lasses, crampin' their style and makin' sure they keep them awa' from the lads and dinna let ony couples go wanderin' off into the woods or up wan o' the closes. Then there's a wheen o' bleck-coated meenisters to stop the menfolk from sluppin' off to the bar of the Argyll Arms or the George Hotel for chust the wan wee Chrustian dram and a necessary refreshment on a thirsty day like this!

"I am thinking they would be better to hire in a whole pack of collie dugs and drive the puir duvvles through the town ass if they wass a flock of sheeps, for if you ask me that iss what they aal are, and that iss surely how they are treated by their weemen and their meenisters: if Dougie wass here he would tell you that himself."

Indeed the thronged pier dispersed an aura of gloom totally at odds with the brightness of the day, and in dismal contrast to the cheery joie-de-vivre and bonhommie which were dispensed in large measure to all and sundry by the typical excursion party.

Certainly the crew of the *Vital Spark*, and perhaps the whole of Inveraray as well, breathed a sigh of quiet relief when, at half past six and with the boarding process completed, there was a toot (even *that* a subdued one) on the *Ivanhoe's* whistle and the paddler moved out into open water and headed off back towards Ardrossan.

"In a sense," observed Para Handy half-an-hour later, as the crew settled onto a bench in front of the Argyll Arms Hotel and contemplated the play of light on the trees of Duniquaich over the top of a pint pot, "in a sense they only have themselves to blame, puir craiturs, but at the same time there iss many of the menfolk chust bludgeoned into the Templars, or maybe the Rechabites forbye, by their wummenfolk, wi' no chance at aal to mak' an escape. I mean, would *you* want to argue the rights and wrongs wi' maist o' the wummen we saw on that pier today? They certainly pit the fear o' the Lord in me. I am thinkin' that maist men would simply do what they wass told ass long ass the wummen wass around, and do what they wanted to do themselves ass soon ass they were on their own.

"And when you get them on their own, the maist o' the Templars men are chust ordinary mortals like the rest o' us."

"I'm sure an they didna bring mich business to the Inveraray Inns today, though," observed Macphail. "The Licensees' herts must sink to their boots when they see the *Ivanhoe* offshore. If she had been the *Lord of the Isles* wi' a works' ootin' frae Fairfield's yerd that wud hae been different, Ah'm thinkin'."

"You would be surprised, Dan," said Para Handy, "at chust how profitable a temperance excursion can be for the licensed trade if aal the arrangements are in the right hands."

Sunny Jim sensed a story.

"Go on, Captain," he prompted. "What d'ye mean?"

"It wass many years back," said Para Handy. "Hurricane Jeck and me wass crewin' a sailin' gabbart that turned a penny for a man in Saltcoats.

"We were to load a cargo o' bales o' wool from Lochranza, and we arrived there late one Friday evenin' and went ashore for a gless of something at Peter Murdo Cameron's Inn, chust along the road from the head of the pier.

"Cameron was in a bleck mood, that wass plain to see, and Jeck asked him what wass the matter.

" 'Chust my luck,' says Cameron, 'you can imachine how very few excursion perties we get comin' to Lochranza, the maist o' the steamer passengers we see iss those aboard the *Kintyre* goin' to or from Campbeltown. Precious few effer comes ashore *here* for a dram. If it wassna for the likes of you, Jeck, and the herring boats in season, and the workers on the big estate, there would be little point openin' a bar in Lochranza and little chance o' makin' a livin' from it.

" 'So when we heard yestreen that there wass an excursion comin' to Lochranza tomorrow — aal adults, too — on a special charter on the *Glen Sannox*, you can imachine that I got quite excited and ordered in extra supplies from the distillery up the road, and brought in more beer on the dray from Brodick this mornin'. It wass going to be like Chrustmas and Hogmanay rolled into one, I told myself. Then this afternoon we foond out what this excursion perty consists of. Chust Rechabites from Fairlie. *Rechabites!* And me with effery penny I could raise invested in drink for them. It'll be months before I clear the stock I've bought in, and the most of the beer will have turned sour, wait you and you will see.

" '*Rechabites*! They'll be the ruin o' me.'

" 'Tush, Peter Murdo,' says Jeck reproachfully — and he wass quite jocco — 'for a Lochranza man you are givin' up aawful easily. The average chentleman of the Rechabite persuasion has exactly the same proportions of a thirst as you or me, it is chust that he hass rather less of an opportunity to indulge it, especially when his wummenfolk are aboot him. Tomorrow you will have to see to it that the men get a run at the refreshments and you will do very well.'

" 'But that's just it,' cried Cameron. 'The wummenfolk wull be aal aboot them aal the time, and forbye Lochranza iss chust a wee place. They canna lose each other ass if this wass a lerge metropiliss like Campbeltown. They daurna come in to an Inns.'

" 'Well then,' says Jeck, 'you will chust have to cater for the wummen at the same time, and whiles they are busy at their teas and scones who iss to know what their menfolk might be up to? Get yourself up early the morn's morn, wi' a wheen o' your frien's (and wan or two wives ass well) and I will show you.' "

Para Handy paused to drain his glass, and look pointedly at the Engineer as he set it on the table in front of him. Macphail took the hint and signalled to a passing barman.

"I must admut," the Captain continued, "that I thought Jeck had taken leave of his senses. But I had reckoned without the man's cheneral agility. He wass sublime, chust sublime!

"On Saturday morning we were up to the Inns at first light. You will mind, Dougie, that there iss a big white board along the front o' the hoose with PETER M CAMERON'S spelt oot on it in big bleck-painted wudden letters, and then inside there iss a corridor, and off it, two big rooms — the bar to the right, and a room on the left wi' tables and chairs where ye can take your refreshments in peace and ring a wee bell when you are wantin' anither gless.

"What Jeck did wass to tak' aal the letters off the board along the front o' the hoose, mak' another 'O' oot o' the lid of a herring firkin, and hammer the letters back up on the board but this time so that they spelt oot TEMPERANCE ROOMS.

"Then he sent for a can o' white paint and a wee brush, and on the door in the corridor that led into the bar he wrote 'Coffee Room and Smoking Parlour — Gentlemen Only': and on the door to the sitting room he wrote 'Tea Room — Ladies Only'.

"And he got Cameron's wife, and three of her friends, to go and bake up a stock o' buns and scones and fancies that wouldna have disgraced a Baker's shop, and to fetch over aal their cups and saucers and plates and teapots and the like.

"He had Cameron put on his best Fast Day suit, and his wife a bleck dress and white peenie, and the two o' them wi' silver trays under their airms, and had them meet the excursionists at the heid o' the pier as they came off the shup at wan o'clock.

"Jeck himself stood at the Inns door and greeted the ladies wi' a most gracious bow that it wass a preevilege to behold, and ushered them aal into the big Tea Room.

"The chentlemen were asked to wait in the roadway till aal the ladies wass seated, and then Jeck invited them to come into the hoose.

"It chust needed the wan quick question at the entrance to find oot exactly what sort of refreshment the chentlemen were most anxious for, and ony that wass true teetotal-isators (and there wassna but a handful o' them) wass qui-etly taken into the hoose next door where Jeck had arranged wi' Cameron's neebour that she would provide teas for any o' the chentlemen that wass soft enough in the heid to want chust that and nothin' else.

"It wass a roarin' success! Cameron took more money in that day than he had effer seen before in a week, and his wife and her friends did such a great tred wi' the ladies in the Tea Room that she wass able to pit new curtains right through the hoose wi' the profits on it. A total waste o' money, Cameron thought that, but he couldna complain.

"Jeck had thought of efferything. When it wass time for the steamer to sail, and the chentlemen wass leaving the Inns by the back door, Jeck even had a boy there passin' oot pan drops and soor plooms to the chentlemen so their wives wouldna jalouse chust what kind o' coffee and tea *they* had been drinking!

"Cameron had even struck a bargain wi' the Lodge Secretary that they would come back again the next month. 'The best ooting we have ever had,' said that worthy, 'for you have opened up a new world to us, Mr Cameron'. And Cameron had the grace to admit that if it hadna been for Jeck there wouldna have been any sort of new world for the Rechabites to open up at aal.

"Jeck got a half-a-case of whusky for his troubles, and Cameron gave me a crate of Bass beer, and that evening we loaded the wool and set off for Gleska.

"Next time we called at Lochranza we found that the planned return trup had been caaled off. There wass some things that even Jeck chust couldna legislate for.

"The chentlemen had aal gone back on board smelling as sweet as a nut, thenks to the lozengers and the boilings that Jeck had dispensed. What he could neffer have foreseen or prevented wass that some of them wass that cheery they began to sing on the trup home — loudly. And it wassna Moodey and Sankey neither. When the wummenfolk heard a roaring chorus of *The Foggy Foggy Dew* come echoing throughout the shup from the fore-saloon where the chentlemen had gathered, they realised something wass going on and a few enquiries wass put urchently in hand wi' some bemused and befuddled husbands, and the game wass up.

"But it was a rare high-jink while it lasted!"

FACTNOTE

Victorian and Edwardian society had an ambivalent attitude to drink and its problems and an ambivalent way of coping with the situation as well.

These were the generations which saw the peak of the Temperance Movements (although they were in serious decline by the end of the 19th century) but at the same time they were also the years of almost unlimited and

THE SUMMER 'TRIP' — Not, on this occasion, anything as depressing as a Templar's Outing but, probably, either a School or most likely a Sunday School *picnic. These were common enough in the west of Scotland until well into the 1950s but are nowadays, I'm sure, a thing of the past. Higher standards of living and above all the wider availability of the ubiquitous motorcar mean that there is no novelty or excitement in an annual day-out by coach or steamer.*

unchecked consumption of alcohol.

Temperance movements were usually led by the 'middle' classes, the objects of whose campaigning were — inevitably, but all too frequently unjustifiably — the 'working' classes.

Drink was perceived as a social problem with well-defined class boundaries and the heavy consumption of those more fortunate in their circumstances was accepted with good-natured tolerance while over-indulgence by the 'lower orders' was railed against and vilified.

The two most influential Movements were the splendid-ly-titled Independent Order of Rechabites (British in origin and dating from the 1830s) and the Good Templars, import-ed from America in the 1870s. It is a fact that in both cases women were often leading protagonists. Where else, in the stifling chauvinistic atmosphere of the mid-Victorian era, could a woman hope to make her mark in the world? It was true also that there were as many backsliders and time-servers as there were genuine converts and followers among the male membership. Neil Munro makes several references to the standing of the Temperance Movements in the Para Handy, Erchie and Jimmy Swan stories. The Movements were accepted by then as legitimate targets for gentle humour — not cruel mockery: for mild parody — not merciless pillory.

There was even a brief nod in the direction of the teetotal lobby from the shipping companies. The *Ivanhoe* was a brave experiment, an alcohol-free vessel commissioned for and managed by a group of Clyde owners and operators — not for the benefit of the Temperance Movements, but for the sake of families whose enjoyment of the amenity of the Clyde was on occasion not just threatened but destroyed by the excesses of a raucous minority.

By the 1890s the problem of drink on the ships (which in any case history has probably, in retrospect, exaggerated) was more or less under control. The worst excesses had been snuffed out as operators improved supervision and control, and common sense and acceptable behaviour prevailed. The *Ivanhoe* reverted to the role of a typical Clyde steamer of her day.

Tea was no longer compulsory aboard her: but neither was strong drink.

26

Para Handy's Ark

Sunny Jim sighed hopefully. "Ah sometimes wush we could have some sort of an animal on the shup," he said. "A dug, for instance. It's aye cheerier when there's a dug aboot the place. I think it's thon constant tail-wagging: it's infectious."

"The only things infectious aboot dugs is fleas," said Para Handy sharply, "And we are not having a dug on the vessel, so you needna even think aboot it. I have not forgotten the sorry business wi' yon Pomeranian that you borrowed a few years back, Jum, and I have no intention of repeating the experiment."

"Aye," put in the Engineer innocently, "you're kind of unlucky wi' animals when I come to think o' it. There wis the dug: and of course there wis yon cockatoo…"

"I wull not be reminded of that incident!" said the Captain indignantly. "Mony's the sleepless night it cost me."

"…and there wis that coo at Lochgoilhead," continued the Engineer remorselessly: "and your so-called singin' canary, and the tortoise, and of course Jeck's Fenian goat, and…"

Para Handy, who had been perched on the edge of the main-hatch smoking a peaceful pipe while Dougie took a trick at the wheel, leaped to his feet with an angry snort and marched off towards the bows, where he made a great show of studying the pier at Carradale — their destination with a cargo of slates, and which was now in plain sight — with such concentration and interest as to suggest that he had never seen a similar construction in his life before.

"Aye," said Macphail to Sunny Jim, "he disnae like any

183

reminder aboot those episodes at all. The man's no' canny when it comes to animals. He's no' very canny when it comes to human beings either, come to that.

"But Ah doot he means it, Jum: aboot the only animal you'd be allowed to put on board this vessel wud be a goldfish in a bowl and even then he'd find some way of stoppin' you. Para Handy and animals jist disnae mix."

~

Late the following afternoon, with the Carradale slates safely ashore, the Captain received a telegram from the owner advising that their next cargo was a farm-flitting from Millport on the island of Cumbrae — its ultimate destination unstated.

The news did not greatly please the Captain, for farm-flittings were not his favourite consignment.

They required that the hold had to be carefully packed with any number of teachests crammed with clothes and linen and crockery and saucepans and all the minutiae of life, followed by the flotsam and jetsam of the farmhouse furniture, then — almost always — an awkward deck-cargo of a plough and a harrow and the carts which had brought most of the plenishings to the pierhead in the first place, and finally (just to top off the whole improbable mixture) the farmer and his family.

Para Handy therefore supervised the berthing of the puffer at Millport Old Pier the next day with ill-disguised displeasure, and looked around him for his cargo. There was no sign of it.

"That chust aboot puts the lid on it," he complained to nobody in particular. "Not content wi' contracting a vessel as smert ass the *Vital Spark* to luft a mixter-maxter cairgo mair suited to a common coal-gabbart, they cannot even arrange for the goods to be here ready for us when we arrive.

"How much longer are we going to be kept hangin' aboot Millport chust like we wass on holiday?"

The rhetorical question was soon answered.

A stockily-built, red-faced man in a suit of good tweeds walked onto the pier and up to where the puffer lay.

"Captain Macfarlane?" he enquired.

"Chust so," said Para Handy: "and you wull be Muster MacMillan. But where is oor cairgo?"

"Here they come now," said MacMillan, pointing to the pier gate and (before the startled Captain could respond by asking what on earth the man meant by referring to his cargo as 'they') a strange procession came into view, coaxed along by six or seven farmhands with sticks.

Para Handy stared in total disbelief.

There were half-a-dozen cows, at least 20 blackface sheep, a sturdy Clydesdale, a couple of sows (one with a litter of tiny piglets) and a surly-looking boar, a few geese, rather more hens and ducks, and a couple of border collies.

"There must be some mustake," the Captain spluttered, "we wass contracted for a ferm-flitting."

"And what do you think this is, Captain?" MacMillan asked. "It is certainly not a menagerie."

"But a ferm-flitting iss the furniture and the chattels," Para Handy protested. "Naebody flits the *animals*. They stays on the ferm."

"Not in this case, Captain," replied MacMillan. "I am moving my livestock to a new farm. It is perfectly straightforward."

"Not from where I am standing," Para Handy countered. "Forbye we havna the facilities on board the shup for lookin' efter live animals, even if we had the knowledge for it."

"But Captain," said MacMillan, "they will only be on board for half-an-hour. Our destination is Fairlie, that is all, and my own men will be travelling with the beasts. All of the loading and unloading will be their responsibility. You are being asked simply to steer the ship two miles across the bay to Fairlie Pier and you are being paid handsomely for it."

"The owner iss mebbe being paid handsomely" was Para Handy's somewhat caustic response. "There iss nothing in this for the poor crew. But, if it iss only for a couple of miles, and if your men wull handle the beasts, then I suppose we must chust grin and bear it.

"But I don't suppose your men are going to be responsible for cleaning up the mess on the decks of the smertest vessel in the coasting trade, though — eh?"

MacMillan ignored the suggestion, and at his signal the loading began.

An hour later Para Handy stared in pained disbelief from the wheelhouse window at the state of his beloved ship. The cattle were in the hold, lowered there by slings, and the

Clydesdale stood patiently beside the mast. The pigs had been confined to the bows with a hastily-improvised pen knocked together by the farmer's men from a few wicket gates, but the sheep roamed everywhere and the poultry disputed with them for the limited deck space available.

"This iss chust a nightmare," the Captain imparted to Dougie almost tearfully, "and I only wush that I could wake up and find oot that it wass!"

At that juncture MacMillan came along the quayside and Para Handy stepped out on deck to speak with him. "I am most grateful, Captain," the farmer said. "There will be two cattle-trucks waiting at Fairlie and my men will have the animals ashore in no time. There is just one small thing, though: please don't say that the cargo is from Millport. I — er — don't want some of my rivals over in Ayrshire to know that I am moving my stock out of the island.

"Nobody will be interested, but — just in case they do ask — I would take it as a personal kindness if you would simply say that the beasts are from Arran." And leaning forward, as if to shake the Captain by the hand, he pressed a piece of folded paper into his fingers — a piece of folded paper which, when Para Handy examined it in the wheelhouse a moment later, proved to be a five-pound-note.

"There iss something chust not right aboot aal this Dougie, and I am sure and I do not know what to make of it at aal. And what on earth am I going to say in Fairlie if they ask me where we are from? A Macfarlane doesna tell a lie for any man!"

"Well," said the Mate, pragmatically, "let's chust hope that nobody asks."

∽

Nobody did — because nobody needed to.

The *Vital Spark* was met, as she approached Fairlie, by a figure in dark blue uniform wielding a large magaphone and with a small crowd at his back.

"Puffer ahoy!" shouted the policeman. "Stand clear! You are not allowed to land those animals here, nor to tie up alongside. No other pier on the river will take you, either."

Para Handy paled, and turned to the farmer's foreman, who was crouched down, hiding, at the starboard side of the wheelhouse.

"What in bleezes iss goin' on here," he demanded. "Iss

this stolen property we are carrying?"

"Naw, it's worse than that," said the foreman wretchedly. "Wan o' the small ferms on the west side of Cumbrae has a suspected ootbreak o' foot-and-mouth disease, MacMillan foond oot aboot it yesterday, but since he'd already booked your boat to move his stock to a ferm he's bought at Hunterston, he wis jist hoping that he could get the beasts safely awa' and landed at Fairlie afore the news got oot. It seems he wis too late."

Para Handy's reappearance at Millport was met with an even angrier rebuff than he had received at Fairlie.

"The only reason that the polis iss no here to greet you in person, Peter Macfarlane," howled the irate pier-master, "iss that he has that scoundrel MacMillan under arrest for trying to move cattle oot of a controlled zone, and he is undergoing some prutty severe questioning doon at the polis office right now.

"If I wass you, I would chust get oot of here fast afore you're booked yoursel' ass an accessible after the fact, or whateffer the expression iss."

~

The next three days — the worst three days of his life, Para Handy maintains, and he will expound upon them at great length to anybody prepared to listen — have passed into the legend and lore of longshore gossip on the Clyde.

No port or harbour on the river would allow the puffer to enter or moor, far less unload a cargo which was becoming more and more restive and (it has to be said) foetid as well. Para Handy even made a bold effort to attract the attention of the press and through them, perhaps, the sympathy of the public by trying to take his floating zoo right up-river to the Broomielaw, but he was frustrated by two of the Clyde Port Authority's launches which forced him to turn back at Renfrew Ferry.

The one concession that was made by Authority was made not to the crew of the *Vital Spark* or the farmer's men but to her live cargo: feedstuff and water for the animals was delivered daily by another puffer especially chartered for the occasion by one of the animal charities. The human beings on board were reduced to a diet of salt herring and potatos.

Relief came on the fourth day when the results of all the

tests undertaken at the suspect farm on Cumbrae were completed — with negative results. A collective sigh of relief went up along the river and not just from the Clyde coast's farmers: there were some mightily relieved sailors as well, when the good news was finally communicated to the *Vital Spark* by one of the Greenock Pilot Cutters.

"You are more than welcome to land your cargo anywhere you like now, Captain," said her skipper: "and I would imagine that somewhere with a public house close at hand would be your first choice, after all that's happened?" And with a laugh he turned back to his own bridge and gave the order which sent the cutter swiftly on her way, throwing up an impressive foaming wake as she did so.

It was with great deliberation, but great satisfaction as well, that Para Handy, ignoring the protests of MacMillan's men and insisting on his right as master of the vessel to make all the decisions appertaining to her safety and convenience, reached that decision — and landed the animals back at Millport.

"Well, now MacMillan can stert aal over again," he observed to Dougie, "if onybody'll deal wi' him. Which I doot. He's pit *his* foot in his mooth chust the wan time too many, I'm thinking."

FACTNOTE

Dan Macphail's unkind references to his Captain's earlier misfortunes need no explanation for those who are familiar with Neil Munro's original tales. The watery fate of the unfortunate cockatoo is a classic.

The two Cumbraes lie just off the Ayrshire coast between Largs and Hunterston. Little Cumbrae has been uninhabited in historic times except by the keepers of its lighthouse, but Great Cumbrae was a popular holiday destination for many years and still attracts a loyal following. Millport, the capital, was served by two steamer piers but this did not save the resort from the so-called 'Siege of Millport' in July 1906 when the steamer companies refused to pay increased pier dues to the Town Council and withdrew all services.

Everything from puffers and motor launches to rowing boats and yachts was dragooned into service to convey holidaymakers (and business travellers) in and out of the island, for the effects of a protracted shut-out would be an economic disaster for the island. In July the resident population was swelled five-fold with the arrival of the Trades Fair visitors.

After some behind-the-scenes wheeling and dealing a compromise was reached and normal service resumed within the week. One has the feeling that the shipping companies themselves could not have afforded a protracted strike since not only would their steamers be losing revenue, thanks to the loss of all passenger traffic, so also would the railways which owned the steamers and which themselves normally carried the crowds from Glasgow down to the Ayrshire piers — at a considerable profit.

In the years before the Erskine Bridge and the Clyde Tunnel and the Motorway across the Clyde there were many ferry services for vehicles and passengers from the upper reaches of the river down as far as Erskine. Here and at Renfrew there were two chain-ferries, which pulled themselves undramatically but quite efficiently to and fro across the river by steam-powered pawls clanking their way along a fixed chain.

Both these vessels came in on concrete slips at either bank so the state of the tide was of no concern to them. Further up the river, where ferries operated to stone quays, significant tidal implications stimulated the development of the ingenious 'elevating ferries' of Finnieston, Whiteinch and Govan. Their carrying-decks were not attached to the hull which provided the flotation — they were in fact platforms suspended from three perpendicular girders to each side, port and starboard, raised or lowered by steam-winches according to the state of the tide, and so could always be docked at the same level as the quays.

27

Follow My Leader

The *Vital Spark* had just threaded her way through the narrows of the Kyles, en route to Tarbert with a load of salt for the curing stations, when the staccato beat of paddle-wheels echoed across the water astern of the puffer. Para Handy, at the wheel, turned to identify the approaching vessel.

A few minutes later, as the Captain feigned indifference under the pretence of studying the shoreline of the island of Bute to port, a smart two-funnelled paddler in the livery of Mr David MacBrayne swept past perilously close on the puffer's starboard beam at full stretch, with an imperious and quite unnecessarily prolonged blast on her whistle, and then sped off towards Tighnabruaich pier, laying out as she did so a phosphorescent twin-track, turbulent wake in which gleaming ribbon the hapless *Vital Spark* lurched and dipped with the awkward ungainliness of a floating bathtub.

Sunny Jim, who had been down in the fo'c'sle frying up sausages for the crew's dinner, came scrambling up on deck to find out what was responsible for sending half the contents of the pan skittering across the stove.

"Ye clown," he shouted after the vanishing paddler: "that's the maist o' wir denner on the deck! So mich for conseederation and the rule o' the road!"

"Neffer heed him Jum," said the Captain, "it iss not worth your while getting aal hot and bothered. Yon's Sandy McIver and his precious *Grenadier*, behavin' ass if he owns the river, but I can assure you there wass a time when he wass chust ass angry wi' the *Vital Spark* ass you are wi' him noo. And he's neffer forgotten nor forgiven either, in spite of

what it says in the Good Book, which iss why he dam' near
runs us doon every time he sees the shup.

"Dan or Dougie will tell you aal aboot it."

But Macphail was busy in the engines and Dougie, off
watch, was catnapping in the fo'c'sle so with a little persuasion, once he had his pipe going to his satisfaction, Para
Handy told the tale.

~

"It aal happened twelve years ago chust a matter of a few
weeks after the shup had been launched, and we were on
the very first trup wi' her ootside Ardlamont Point. We'd
had a few teething problems. The cargo hatch wass letting
in watter at the fore end and we'd had to have some of the
deck planks caulked, the steam-winch wass the very duvvle
to get sterted, the shaft wass leakin' oil and the biler wass
apt to prime. But over the piece we got aal this set to rights.

"Worst of aal, though, wass that after less than a week the
steam whustle broke doon and the same day that happened, while we wass laid up wan night in Bowling Harbour,
somebody stole the stern lamp on us while we wass ashore
takin' a refreshment.

"Well, I wassna goin' to risk the vessel in the river without the lamp. We do chust occasionally meet up wi' a shup
wi' a better turn o' speed than the *Vital Spark*, Jum, and
because of that it iss chust a sensible precaution to be
showing a light astern at night. And it would have been
madness to sail without a steam whustle, for how would we
let a slower shup know we wass preparin' to pass her" —
here Para Handy totally ignored the exaggerated snort of
derision emanating from the engine-room at his feet — "or
cope wi' fog on the Firth?

"Ass luck would have it, there wass an old steamer in the
basin at Bowling, waiting' her turn to go into McCulloch's
bone-yerd to be broken up for scrap. Sorley McCulloch
owed me a few favours for aal the bags of coal he had from
me over the years for what the owner doesna see willna
hurt him, and I am a great believer in havin' frien's in effery
port in the river, for you never ken when you might need
them: so Sorley didna tak' mich persuasion to let me have
the stern lamp and the steam whustle off the old shup.

"The lamp wass fine, a wheen bigger than we really needed,
and set on a higher sternpost than wir ain, but she gave oot a

most spendid illumination and there wass no chance of us bein' run doon in the derk if any shup comin' up astern of us should happen to have the pace to overtake the vessel.

"It was the steam whustle that wass the real cracker! Aal solid brass you could see your face in wance the boy had her polished to rights. It wass designed for a shup many times bigger than the *Vital Spark* and when you gi'ed her a blaw, for a stert you dam' near drained oot aal the steam from Macphail's biler tubes and you sure as bleezes put the fear o' daith in whateffer shup you wass passin', or the harbour-master and the longshoremen at whateffer pier it wass that you wass comin' into. We soonded like the *Campania*.

"I tell you we had some high-jinks the next week or two! When Dougie was at the helm, he chust couldna resist blawin' the whustle at any excuse at aal and Dan got real vexed wi' him. It wassna chust playin' havoc wi' his steam pressure, it wass fair dingin' his hearin' wi' the noise o' the blasts. Worse, since he neffer knew from wan moment tae the next chust when Dougie would take it into his heid to let her go, and since he was aye hunkered doon wi' his nose buried in wan o' his penny novelles, he lost coont o' the number o' times that he got sich a fleg when the whustle went aff that he jumped up and banged his heid on the deck beams in the enchine-room.

"If Dougie was here he would tell you himself...

"It wass two weeks efter the new lamp and whustle wass put on the vessel that they really proved their value, but that wass also the occasion when we fell foul o' McIver in the *Grenadier*.

"We wass on the same trup we are today — from the Broomielaw to Tarbert wi' a load o' salt. The dufference wass that, wance we had discharged the cargo, we wass to go up to Lochgilphead for a ferm flittin' that wass to be took over to Otter Ferry on the other side o' Loch Fyne.

"You ken yoursel' what Loch Gilp is like, chust a great spread o' mudflats at onythin' less than half-tide, the toon itself standin' at the heid o' the shallowest stretch o' watter on the river, worse even than the Holy Loch. Of course, that's why Mr MacBrayne's terminal is at Ardrishaig three miles sooth, for there's no right pier at Lochgilphead. A steamer couldna come near it even at high watter. There iss chust a jetty for the likes o' the local fishin' smacks and even the *Vital Spark* couldna get alongside it. We would have to beach offshore at half-tide and the flittin' would be brought alongside on cairts.

"Well, we lay overnight at Tarbert after we'd unloaded the salt, and went ashore to peruse the neebourhood, ass you might say. But we were back on board early. Hurricane Jeck was no' wi' us, ye'll understand. There wass chust me and Dan and Dougie and a young laddie caaled Campbell, the sowl, and him from Fort Wulliam tae. He couldna help that either, the puir duvvle, but they're awful Hielan' roon' aboot Fort Wulliam.

"The thing wass we had to be up sherp in the mornin' to take on some coal for oor ain bunkers — the owner had some sort of an arranchement wi' wan o' the Tarbert merchants. What herm the owner had ever done him I dinna ken, but it really didna bear thinkin' aboot when you saw the quality and quantity o' stanes we wass takin' on. We wanted to be away by eleven at the latest if we were to get to Loch Gilp at the right time o' the tide ready to pick up the flittin'.

"Ass it wass it wass half past eleven afore we nosed oot o' the harbour. The Inveraray Company's *Lord of the Isles* wis chust on the point o' pullin' awa' from the main steamer pier, efter loadin' up an excursion party for Ardrishaig and Inveraray, and it wouldna be long before the MacBrayne steamer frae Gleska was due to arrive on passage to Ardrishaig. Indeed ass we headed north we saw the *Grenadier* comin' thunderin' up the Loch from the sooth, wi' McIver standin' oot on the wing o' the brudge and tryin' to look important. The man neffer had the presence for it, but then when you had wance seen Hurricane Jeck tak' a shup into a pier, onythin' else wass chust a let-doon.

"Though it wass a bright sunny day when we set off, within chust ten minutes we had run into a dark fog-bank that wass that thick, you could have cut it up intae blocks wi' a knife and sold it as briquettes.

"I tell you it wass me wass relieved we had the new stern-light for I knew fine the *Lord of the Isles* wass in our wake, and I didna fancy suddenly findin' her chust a few feet aff oor rudder and lookin' for a right-o'-passage. Dougie lit the lamp and raised it ass high ass he could up the stern-post, I put the laddie up into the bows wi' a bell tae ring to let us ken if he saw or heard onythin' ahead, and we picked oor way up the loch.

"Sure enough, in due course we heard the whoop o' a steamer's whustle dead astern and efter a few meenits we could chust mak' oot the foremast lights and the navigation lights of a shup. It wass the *Lord of the Isles* sure enough. I gave a quick blast on oor ain whustle effery noo and then to mak' sure she knew we wass there, but wi' the illumination o' the new stern lamp there wass no doubt she had seen us. She held her position for a half-an-hour and then we saw her lights swing off to port, and she picked her way in to Ardrishaig pier a mile or so away.

"Ten minutes later, and there came a whustle blast immediately astern again, a kind o' a signal maybe — two shorts, a long and two shorts again.

" 'I canna think who this is,' said I to Dougie, 'but we'd best let him ken we're here.' And I blasted oot the same tattoo on our own new whustle.

"The unseen shup gave the signal back, so we replied again. He whustled. We whustled. I tell you there wass some din on the Loch that mornin', Macphail put his heid oot o' his cubby and said a few un-Chrustian things, but if this unknown shup wass that close astern o' us — despite the bright lamp that he could surely see — then I certainly wass not goin' to risk the vessel by keepin' quiet.

"Occasionally we could mak' oot the masthead light of whatever shup it was that wass followin' us, and at times even the loom o' her bows when the fog lifted for a moment.

" 'I dinna like this at aal, Dougie,' I said. 'She's too close for my likin'.

" 'Neffer mind Peter,' says he. 'We are certainly well into Loch Gilp by now and if we chust swing to starboard and anchor, then she can go where she wants, and we can bide our time till the fog lifts.'

"I put the wheel hard to starboard with a final, long blast on the big whustle, shouted on Dan to stop the enchines, and sent Dougie for'ard to let go the anchor.

"And three things happened aal at wance.

"First, we ran oot of the fog-bank ass suddenly ass we had run into it, and there were the white hooses of Lochgilphead chust a mile ahead.

"Next, from our port quarter came a desperate, furious clang on an enchine-room telegraph ringin' and ringin' ass if somebody's life depended on it.

"Last, from the same direction there wass a most awful grinding sound like steel on stone, and the ear-spluttin' crash of falling objects, breaking glass, and smashing crockery, splintering wud and so on, that seemed to go on and on for effer. When it did stop, their wass such a racket of cries and shouts and screams — and curses too — that you would swear that the day of chudgement had come to Loch Fyneside.

"When I turned to see what the commotion wass, here wass the bow half — no more — of a big shup pokin' oot o' the fog. She had run herself fast aground on the Loch Gilp shallows and I could mak' oot her name quite plain. It wass the *Grenadier*.

"Dougie and me unshipped the punt, and rowed over to see if we could help. But the paddler wass fast aground on an ebbing tide and she'd be where she was for seven or eight hoors till the sea came back.

"McIver was leaning over the brudge-wing chust beside himself and bleck in the face wi' rage.

" 'Macfarlane,' he bellowed wance he recognised us. 'Where the bleezes did you get thon lamp, and thon dam' whustle? Are ye oot o' yer mind completely pittin' gear like that in a steam gabbart?

" 'Ah wis followin' ye because Ah thocht ye wis the *Lord of the Isles* and I thocht ye wis pickin' intae Ardrishaig. No' intae this — this — this *sump*,' he howled as he saw the Loch Gilp mud-flats, which were quickly dryin' oot as the tide went doon.

"The owner heard aal aboot it and made me get rid o' the bonny new lamp and the braw big whustle. But I'd had good value oot o' them. There's no' another skipper on the Clyde can boast o' havin' personally grounded wan o' Mr MacBrayne's most treasured possessions — when he wassna even on board of her!

"In aal fairness Jum, I dinna grudge poor McIver a few sausages cowped on our deck. I cowped mair than that on his!"

FACTNOTE

Lochgilphead indeed never did have a steamer pier, for the head of the shallow loch was quite inaccessible to vessels of any size. The town was served by Ardrishaig, whose commodious pier also marked the staging post for passengers proceeding on to Oban and the Western Highlands by way of the Crinan Canal, this being the eastern point of entry to that waterway.

MacBrayne's *Grenadier* was a handsome, clipper-bowed

ROTHESAY HARBOUR — *The view across the town's outer harbour, as seen from the pier, looks towards a seafront silhouette which has been much altered in relatively recent years. Many of the buildings to the right of the picture have now been demolished, and the landscaped and pedestrianised spaces of Guildford Square have been created in their place.*

paddler launched in 1885. For most of the year she was based at Oban but she became a regular replacement for the *Columba* on the Glasgow to Ardrishaig service during the off-peak months. Her end was dramatic and tragic — destroyed by fire at Oban pier in 1927 in one of the very few incidents involving Clyde or West Highland steamers which resulted in loss of life, in this case her Captain and two of her crew. As far as I know *Grenadier* was never aground, but her predecessor *Mountaineer* stranded in fog on rocks lying off Lismore near the entrance to the Sound of Mull and, though passengers and crew were taken off without any problems, she became a total loss.

The Cunarder *Campania* was built at the Fairfield Yard on the Upper Clyde in 1893. The largest (620' overall) and fastest (23 knots) of her brief generation of Transatlantic liners, she held the Blue Riband for four years from 1893 till 1897, losing it in that year to the Norddeutscher Lloyd liner *Kaiser Wilhelm der Grosse*, fore-runner of the next generation and, again, the world's largest ship. From that date mastery of the lucrative North Atlantic passenger trade rested with the Germans till Cunard in 1906 put into service those two incomparable sisters, *Mauretania* and the doomed *Lusitania*.

In retrospect, in a quite unexpected way, *Campania* exemplified the breathtaking pace of maritime development by breaking new ground both at the beginning and at the very end of her career.

When launched she was the first Cunarder to be fitted with twin screws and the first of that company's ships, therefore, not to have been provided with some form of auxiliary sail-power (an extraordinary anachronism from our standpoint, but the norm in the Victorian era) and thus the first designed to be wholly reliant on her engines.

But just 25 years later, when she was lost at sea following a collision in the Firth of Forth with the Battleship *Renown*, she had passed her last four years of life (after conversion in 1914) *as an aircraft-carrier*, the maritime base and mobile platform for a form of transport so undreamed-of at the time of her launch that even to have put it forward as a possibility would have been to invite the ridicule reserved for dabblers in science fantasy.

28

The Rickshaw and the Pram

The papers had for days been full of nothing but increasing speculation about the impending confrontation between the Russian and Japanese Imperial Fleets in the Far East, and loud and long had been the argument and debate, involving our politicians as readily as our naval strategists, as to the relative strengths (and weaknesses) of the two participants.

Encountering Para Handy seated on a bollard on Princes Pier on a fine evening in late May, I determined to canvass the opinion of a mariner of so many years experience as to the merits or otherwise of the opposing forces.

"What is your opinion of Admiral Rojdestvensky's strength in terms of capital ships, Captain," I enquired. "Do you think he is capable of outgunning Togo's forces sufficiently to overcome their superiority in range?"

"Eh?" asked Para Handy.

"Well, let me put it another way. The humiliation the Russians suffered at Port Arthur last year must weigh heavily upon their commanders at this juncture. Do you see that as a 'plus' — an incentive to greatness: or a 'minus' — a collective millstone round their necks?"

"Pardon?" said Para Handy: "I really do not have the furst idea what you are talking aboot, Mr Munro."

"Good Lord, Captain," I exclaimed, astonished. "Have you not been following the news? Is it possible that you do not realise that — even as we speak — the naval forces of Japan and Russia could well be locked in battle in the greatest confrontation in the history of war at sea: a battle which could well determine future sovereignty and autarchy across the whole Far Eastern political and social theatre, with devastating consequences for the rest of the world? That right now, the first shots could well be bracketing the ships in the van of the two fleets and determining the course of history for decades to come?"

Para Handy twisted on his bollard and squinted up at the blue sky and the golden glow of the evening sun.

"Well," he said, "they're certainly getting a grand day for it!"

~

As we made our way into the railway station and headed towards its convenient Refreshment Rooms I endeavoured, but with scant success, to explain to the Captain just why the eyes of the world were anxiously turned towards the Sea of Japan.

"I have neffer had much time for the Chapanese," he confessed as we carried our glasses to a table set in the fresh air and affording fine views across the Firth to the Gareloch, "running aboot in rickshaws ass if that wass a fit occupation for a chentleman. Or iss that the Chinese? No matter: and ass for the Rooshians, well Macphail wass in among them several times when he was goin' foreign, and he hassna a good word to say for them. Durty duvvles, by aal his accoont of them, livin' on raw fush and potatos, and nothin' to drink but some kind o' fulthy firewater that would rot your boots.

"What iss the hairm in lettin' the pair o' them knock aal seven bells oot of each other, and then step in and pick up the bits and pieces that we want for oorselves?"

Reflecting that British Foreign Policy over several generations had often followed that particular stratagem, I felt it best to change the subject.

"What have you been up to of late," I asked. "And what is the news on the river?"

"Little enough," said he, "though there wass that wee bit of excitement we got involved in at Crinan basin last week, you maybe heard aboot it, when Callum MacAndrew the lock-keeper's wife had the truplets."

I confessed that this was all news to me, and asked for some more details. "Triplets are certainly real cause for celebration," I said. "A rare event indeed!"

"Chust so," said Para Handy: "and the celebrations wass nearly an even rarer event. If it hadna been for Dougie's agility and a bit o' quick thinking from Sunny Jim then there chust wouldna have been ony celebrations at aal. This was the way of it.

"Callum MacAndrew's wife iss a second cousin of my ain, from Strathshira, and of course the news o' her truplets had been trumpeted the length and breadth of the west. We was on oor way to Colonsay wi' coals, and ass soon ass we put into the first of the locks at Ardrishaig, Fergus McKay the lock-keeper wass down to the shup to give me the good news and ask us a favour.

"Callum's brither works as a cooper at Glendarroch Distillery at Ardrishaig, and wheneffer he got word aboot the truplets he had a confabulation wi' wan o the men in the still-room and he promised to divert a wee firkin' o' spurit to help wet the heids of aal the weans. 'Wi' three o' them to be toasted it's a terrible expense for Callum if we dinna make a wee contribution and onyway it's no' really costing the dustillery,' said he firmly, 'but chust the Excisemen. And who cares aboot them at a time like this.'

"The question wass, wance the spurits had been liberated oot o' the warehoose, how wass they to be taken to Callum's hoose at the Crinan Basin up at the ither end o' the Canal? This wass what Fergus hoped that the *Vital Spark* could do for the faimily — and of course I said no bother, no bother at aal."

At that point I felt I simply had to make some comment. "Really Captain," I observed, "I am disappointed in you: I thought that you had foresworn this sort of high-jinks. You have had all too many close calls with the law in the last year or two."

"Blood iss thicker than watter," said Para Handy firmly. "Would you have had me desert my cousin and her man in their hour of need? Forbye, I am firmly of the opeenion that effery Hielan' chentleman is entitled to a dram o' his native spurit withoot the unwanted intervention of Excisemen, for I am sure that the spurits have been around a lot longer than they have.

"So we waited in the basin for Callum's brither to appear wi' the wee firkin.

"Weel, he finally did appear — but empty-handed.

" 'Issn't this the calamity!' he cried. 'You will have to tell Callum that there will be no whusky, the Excisemen spotted us takin' the firkin oot o' the Warehoose and we had to throw it into the Darroch Burn and mak' a run for it! It wass either that or the jyle for us, but I am aawful vexed, for there wull be no spurits to toast the bairns up at the Crinan Basin!'

"It wass Dougie who saved the day. He minded that the Darroch Burn, efter it had passed by the side waall of the dustillery where it provided the power for the watter-wheels that drove the enchines for the paddles in the mash-tubs, ran on doon the glebe and *under* the Crinan Canal by way of a kind of a tunnel before it spult oot into the Loch.

" 'There iss a a sort of an iron grill in the tunnel under the canal,' said he, 'which stops aal the broken bits of bar-rels or whateffer from blockin' the watter channel. If the firkin wass thrown into the Darroch, then that iss where she wull be.'

"And you know, Dougie wass quite right! We went up the Canal as far as the Darroch Burn and he chumped oot onto the towpath and doon the side to the culvert o' the stream and sure enough half way through it, and stuck at the metal grill, wass the firkin o' whusky, chust ass good ass new!

"I can tell you that Callum's brither gave Dougie a real hero's welcome when he got back aboard the vessel wi' the firkin under his oxter!

"We took it on board and hid it well under a loose plate in the hold, chust in case of ony maraudin' Excisemen chumpin' the shup on passage, and off we went.

"It wass when we reached the Crinan Basin that we realised that oor troubles wass chust beginning.

"The Excisemen wass not goin' to give up aal that easy! Pert of the problem of course wass that the Glendarroch wass the only dustillery in that pert o' the country and so they had nothin' else to do wi' their time but poke their long noses into her business. And the rest of it wass that they were dam' sure they knew why the whusky had been taken, and chust exactly where it wass bound for — for they knew fine aboot Callum's truplets by noo, and indeed so did the hauf o' Argyllshire — and they were determined not to lose the firkin withoot a fight.

"When we tied up at the Crinan basin we could see Callum's hoose chust a few hundred yerds along the tow-path and hear the sounds of celebration coming from inside — though they wass aal a bit muted, withoot the whusky necessary to get them properly under way. And between the *Vital Spark* and the hoose there were four or five Excisemen from Glendarroch, aal trying to pretend they wassna there, but keepin' a very close eye on the fowk that went in and oot o' the hoose.

" 'My Chove,' I said to Callum's brither. 'they chust dinna give up, do they? But I cannot see how we can get the firkin past them and up to the hoose for the perty.'

"Then Sunny Jim appeared at the wheelhoose door.

" 'Captain,' says he: 'Am Ah no right in thinkin' that Callum and your kizzin have a wean already?'

" 'Right enough, Jum' I said: 'a laddie of 16 months. But what has that to do wi' it?'

" 'Weel,' said Jim: 'I wis jist thinkin', if wan o' the Aunties or Wives in the hoose wis to tak' that wean oot in its pram for a hurl. And if they wis to come doon here to the shup. And if the pram wis taken on board and — when the Excisemen wisnae lookin' — if the wean wis taken oot for jist a meenit and the wee firkin shoved underneath the mattress on the pram...

" 'Weel,' he concluded. 'I think it wud be a brave Excisemen who wud try to inspect a wean's pram for a wee barrel o' whusky if ye chose the right sort of Auntie or Wife. For if they are onything like some o' the wans Ah've seen in this pert o' the world then I maybe dinna ken what they wud do to the enemy but by the Lord, they frichten me!'

" 'Jum', I said, 'again you are chust sublime. There iss nobody can touch you for cheneral umpidence and sagiocity, unless it iss Hurricane Jeck himself, and he has mony years of advantage over you!'

"And that is chust exactly what we did. Dougie strolled along to the hoose and had a word wi' Callum, and he got his Great Aunt Agnes (her that looks ass if she had fell oot o' the tap of the Ugly Tree and hit aal the brenches on the way doon) to tak' the elder bairn oot for a hurl in his pram, and we put the wee firkin in under him chust like Jum suggested.

"It would have taken the Brigade of Guards to have the courage to interfere with Great Aunt Agnes and the whusky got to the hoose wi' no problem at aal. We waited about 30 meenits chust for the look of the thing afore we made our move, then we got Macphail to dampen doon the furnace, locked up the wheelhoose, sent Sunny Jum to collect hiss melodeon from the fo'c'sle, and set oot along the towpath to the lock-house.

"The Excisemen hung aboot for anither hour or thereby and then admutted defeat and went aff to sulk somewhere else, for wance they heard the soond of singin' comin' from inside the hoose they realised they'd been duped again: but there wassna wan thing they could do aboot it by then because wance whusky is in the gless it disnae have a name tattooed on it and the drams we wis drinkin' could have come from anywhere — even though we aal knew fine what the true facts o' the matter might have been.

"Now admuttedly, Mr Munro, that is aal maybe no' chust as earth shattering as the events in Chapan that you were goin' on aboot earlier, but at least they are closer to home.

"And since it wass us comin' from the East that took the rise oot o' the Excisemen in the West, then maybe that wull give you some thoughts ass to how things wull turn oot for the Emperor and the Tsar at the end o' the day!"

FACTNOTE

There had not been any really significant large-scale naval encounters since the Battle of Trafalgar of 1805 until the 20th century was ushered in with the short-lived Russo-Japanese War of 1904-05. The development of capital ships and their armament had been, largely, a matter of theory and the naval architect's drawing-board rather than close encounters by substantial naval forces in a war zone.

Though there were land battles in the war, notably in Manchuria and North Korea, it is remembered principally for the two naval encounters between the protagonists. In July 1904 the Russian Pacific Fleet put out from Vladivostok and was annihilated by the Japanese. Then in one of the most flambuoyantly tragi-comic episodes in the whole history of war, the Tsar dispatched the Russian *Baltic* fleet to the Pacific to avenge the destruction of their compatriots.

This voyage of more than half-way round the world by way of the Cape of Good Hope took many months but by May 1905 the Russians were in Japanese waters. The two fleets met on May 28th 1905 at Tsushima and the result was another catastrophe for the Russian navy. They deployed 37 ships against the Japanese: Togo's fleet sank 22 of them including six of the eight battleships, largely thanks to the superior speed and fire-power of his own capital ships. That was only surpassed when the first of the British *Dreadnought* class, then on the stocks at Portsmouth, started to enter service the following year.

There was only ever one distillery at Ardrishaig.

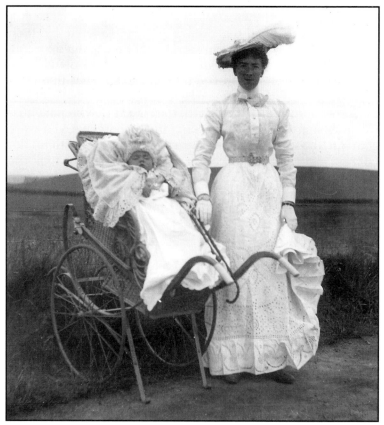

Proud Parent — *The moment I came across this wonderful photograph of proud mother and (presumably) pampered off-spring in the MacGrory collection I knew I simply had to write a story involving a pram to give me an excuse to include the picture in the book! And now you are reading it. It is probably not the case that the child is just about to slide out of the base of the pram, but it certainly looks like it!*

Glendarroch was one of the first of the 'modern' generation of distilleries created after the new Excise Act of 1823 set the industry on its organised, commercial, large-scale (and legal) journey.

Glendarroch opened in 1831 and passed through several hands in the course of its long history. At its peak, the distillery had an output of 80,000 gallons a year but its last owners, the Glenfyne Distillery Co Ltd, finally shut it down in 1937 after more than a century of continuous production. Its buildings were put to a variety of uses in the decades thereafter, though they have now been completely demolished.

And yes, there was a stream: there were in fact *two* streams to serve the plant. One, the Ard Burn, provided the water for the distilling process: the other powered the water wheels.

This second stream, the Darroch, flowed down the glen from the distillery and passed under the Crinan Canal by way of a narrow culvert before finally debouching into Loch Gilp and so to Loch Fyne.

29

Sublime Tobacco

Once breakfast was finished, the Captain felt in his pocket for his pipe, then reached into his overhead locker and pulled out a yellow oilskin tobacco pouch. Opening it, Para Handy stared disbelievingly into its interior, sighed, and shook his head in resignation.

"My chove," he said: "I chust do not know where the tobacco goes and that iss a fact. I could have sworn there wass a good two or three oonces left when I put her away last night, but now here she iss quite ass empty ass Old Mother Hubbard's Cupboard..." And he paused at this point to glance suspiciously across the table at the *Vital Spark*'s Engineer, who was the only other smoker on the vessel.

"You needna look at me like that," said that worthy, quite indignantly, pushing his empty breakfast plate away and picking up his mug of tea. "Ah widna use the rubbish that *you* smoke tae smoke a finnan haddie. Ah've mair respect for ma throat. You call that tobacco? Ye'd be as weel to stick your heid doon the lum o' the shup and tak' a few deep breaths. Ah'm sure that wid be better for ye."

Para Handy ignored him.

"It's you that iss lucky you are not a smoker, Dougie," he said to the Mate somewhat enviously. "You chust wudna believe the expense of it!"

"Oh yes I would," said the Mate gloomily, with thoughts of the large family his wages had to support uppermost in his mind. "I most certainly would: it's only the cost that stops me, otherwise I'd be puffin' awa' wi' the rest of you. It wass only getting married that went and put a stop to my smoking. When I wass younger I had a different kind of a pipe for every day of the week."

"Smokin' wass cheaper then, though," continued the Captain, as he salvaged the last few shreds of tobacco from his pouch, laid them carefully into the bowl of his pipe, and reached for a match. "Folk were more wulling to trate you, or to share if you were oot of the makin's yoursel'" — and here he paused to stare meaningfully at Macphail, who was re-filling his own pipe from a well-stocked pouch, but the Engineer paid no heed — "whereas nooadays it's such a price!

"If you're smokin' your own tobacco, aal you're thinkin' aboot iss the expense of it, and you put scarcely enough in your pipe to get it going. Whiles if you're in company where a baccy tin or a pooch iss passing roond, on the ither hand, and so you're smokin' someone else's, then your pipe iss rammed that tight it wullna draw!"

Sunny Jim, who preferred to spend what surplus he could glean from his wages on more rewarding indulgences such as favours or ice-cream sundaes for his girl-of-the-moment, chuckled quietly and observed: "Weel, you could save a lot o' money by buying your vestas from thon jenny-a'-thing shop at Blairmore where you got them at last week!"

～

The puffer had been bound for Ardentinny for oak-bark from the forestry plantations in Glenfinnart when, just as they were abreast of the pier at Blairmore, the Captain had realised that he was out of matches — and remembered also that there was no shop of any decription at Ardentinny.

It was the work of just a few minutes to put in to the pier and from there Sunny Jim had been dispatched to the general store to purchase a carton containing two dozen large boxes of matches. The transaction completed, the puffer continued on her way and three miles further on put inshore and beached as close to the road as she could, close beside Ardentinny's little church, and waited for the arrival of the first forestry dray with its load of oak-bark.

Captain and Engineer, in a rare moment of camaraderie, had sat themselves side-by-side on the main-hatch in the warm afternoon sun and filled their pipes.

Para Handy passed the newly-bought carton of vestas to Macphail, who took out one of the boxes, carefully extracted a match, and struck it on the side of the box. There was a slight crackle, a momentary spark, but nothing more. He tried again. And again. Exasparated, Macphail threw the dud match away and selected another. The same scenario was repeated. He tried a third. The same again. Cursing, he tried another box, and then another and another, but always with the same negative result.

Para Handy, who had been impatiently waiting to get his own pipe lit, could finally wait no longer and snatched the carton of boxes from the Engineer's hands. "You couldna light a fire wi' a can o' kerosene, Dan," he complained testily: "see the metches here, you chust havna the knack for them at aal."

But the Captain fared no better than the Engineer had done, and in disgust Macphail finally went aft to the engine-room and put a taper into the red-hot coals in the furnace, and from that the two men lit their pipes.

Para Handy studied the carton and its worthless boxes of vestas contemptuously.

"Jum!" he shouted.

Sunny Jim, who was down below peeling potatos, came scrambling up on deck a moment later.

"Jum," said the Captain, "I want you to tak' this dam' carton o' vestas back to Cherlie Paterson's shop at Blairmore. Tell him they wullna strike at aal, I want either my money back or else a new carton wi' boxes in it that work."

Jim's protests at being forced into a six-mile round trip over such a relative triviality were disregarded and the puffer's young hand soon found himself stepping out along the coast road with the worthless carton under his arm. His annoyance at being sent on such a trifling errand soon vanished, for it was a most beautiful afternoon, Loch Long was at its spectacular best, the birds were in full song and the wild flowers bordering the roadside were at their colourful zenith — and he was *not* having to trim oak-bark in a dusty, sweltering hold.

When Sunny Jim presented himself at the store in Blairmore and disclosed the nature of his errand, the proprietor was totally unimpressed.

"There's naething wrang wi' my vestas," he said angrily, "You tell Peter Macfarlane that."

"But they wullna *light*!" protested Jim.

"Willna light?" exploded Paterson. "See me wan o' they

boxes and I'll show you whether they light or not," and he grabbed the carton, took out a box, extracted a match and then, leaning forward slightly as he did so, struck it vigorously on the seat of his trousers.

The match immediately burst into flame.

"See whit I mean?" roared the proprietor.

"Ah see whit you mean," replied Sunny Jim quietly, "but I dinna think either Para Handy or Dan Macphail ha'e ony intention of walking six miles from Ardentinny and back jist to strike a match on the seat of *your* breeks every time they want a smoke."

He got his new carton.

~

The Captain laughed at the memory of that. "Aye, you did weel there, Jum: I wush I'd been wi' you for the sake of seeing the expression on Cherlie Paterson's face!

"And *you'd* have enjoyed seein' the expression on Dan's face yon time we bumped intae thon yat the *Blue Dragon* up at Eisdale. We bumped into her in more ways than wan, in fact, for we came into the wee harbour just efter derk, no' expecting ony ither boats to be there, and towing our own dinghy, for we had a deck cairgo of a flittin'. Here and did we no' clatter the yat wi' the dinghy ass we came in.

"The owner wass on deck in a flash, but when he saw there wass no damage done he couldna have been nicer aboot it, and invited us aal on board for a refreshment."

The Engineer, who had been twisting uncomfortably in his seat, said firmly "Dinna you say anither word, Peter, that wis a lot o' years ago, and it's not a very interestin' baur onyway."

"Oh, I'm no so sure aboot that," replied the Captain. "We will let Jum be the judge!

"Onyway, Jum, efter he'd given us a gless wi' something warmin' in it, the yat skipper passed roond a box o' big Havana cigars for us to try. I said no, thanks, if he didna mind I would stick wi' the pipe — but Dan here, who'd neffer smoked a cigar in his naitural, picked oot the biggest wan in the box and lit it up quite jocco.

"Two meenits and he wass chust ass green in the face ass the gress on midsummer day, and two meenits more and he wass up and oot the cabin like a lamplighter and aal we could hear wass him bein' no weel ower the side o' the yat!

It wass a while before Dougie and me let him forget aboot that, I can tell you: and I had to feenish his dram for him that night, too!"

"Och, he's so smairt," said the Engineer, both embarrassed and petulant at once. "Jist ask him aboot the time we wis cairrying the shows for the Tarbert Fair from Brodick, where they'd been for the week afore that, over to Loch Fyne.

"Wan o' the sideshows for the Fair wis a man that had a kind of a trained monkey, that could sit on a perch and stand on its haun's, and jump through girrs, and put on a wee bit of a cloak and tak' it off again, and go in among the folk on the end of a leash wi' a kind of a silver cup in its haun's tae collect the pennies."

It was now the Captain's turn to look uncomfortable. "What on earth is the point of draggin' up old stories this way," he asked Macphail with some fervour, but the Engineer continued as if there had been no interruption.

"Para Handy wis fairly taken wi' the monkey," he said: "and wis aye gettin' the man that owned it too pit it through its paces as we crossed the tap o' Kilbrannan Soond and headed up Loch Fyne.

"When the monkey wis given a wee tin drum and a stick tae bang it with, Para Handy wis that tickled he stuck his pipe in his mooth so he'd baith haun's free to slap his thighs, for he wis laughin' till he wis sair.

"At that the monkey leapt onto his shouthers, pulled the pipe frae his mooth, and went and sat on the side of the vessel and tried tae smoke it itself! Para Handy very near fell aff of the main-hatch he wis laughing that mich, watching the beast tryin' tae imitate whit he'd been dae'ing.

"He didna laugh long! The monkey near choked on the baccy smoke and it pulled the pipe oot of its mooth quicker than it had put it in, looked at it a moment with whit ye'd hae sworn wis an expression of disgust — and then hurled Para Handy's best and only genuine and original meerschaum ower the side o' the shup and into the Loch. So it wis an expensive joke for the Captain that day!"

"Well," said Jim with conviction, "If I wis ever tempted to stert smokin' I'd jist have to remind masel' aboot the mess you two cloons manage tae get yoursel's intae. It's my considered opinion ye're naethin' but a pair of eejits tae cairry on wi' the pipes at aal. They seem to involve ye in an awful lot of aggravation and expense, and I canna see that it's worth it for the sake of a whiff of tobacco."

"Ah," said Paa Handy dreamily, "but that iss where you are aal wrong, Jum. Tobacco is sublime — chust sublime. If Dougie wass here he would tell you that himself..."

FACTNOTE

A 'jenny-a'-thing' was, of course, a general store which sold just about everything (as the cliché has it) from a needle to an anchor. They were the hub around which very many of the more remote rural communities revolved, and in isolated parts of the Highlands and the rural west they still are today.

The pier at Blairmore, on the Cowal coast at the entrance to Loch Long, is one of the few remaining piers on the firth and sea-lochs of the Clyde which are still serviceable and, more importantly, licensed to serve. Our last surviving paddler, the *Waverley*, calls occasionally at Blairmore to pick up passengers for an evening cruise to Lochgoilhead or Arrochar. Ardentinny never had a pier: Passengers were embarked or disembarked from the steamers (by prior arrangement, or by hailing them as they passed) by flitboat.

The *Blue Dragon* (from 1892 till 1904) and her successor *Blue Dragon II* (1905 till 1913) were owned by a quite remarkable English schoolmaster and yachtsman, C C Lynam.

Blue Dragon was a tiny craft, just 25ft overall, yet from the modest beginnings of day-excursions along the south coast of England Lynam sailed her further and further north and became a regular visitor not just in summer, but during winter holidays as well, to the Hebrides and West Highlands.

In the larger *Blue Dragon II* Lynam undertook voyages not just to Orkney and Shetland, but over to Bergen and then north to the North Cape and the midnight sun. She was a two-masted yawl of 43ft overall with roomy cabin-space and six berths. In 1905 she cost him just £300!

Three volumes describing his voyages (all well-illustrated and comprehensive but highly idiosyncratic, not to say eccentric) were published between 1908 and 1913. Now very scarce they are much prized by bibliophiles as remarkable accounts of Edwardian maritime adventure, and the attitudes and amenities of the age.

An encounter with a puffer, her engineer and one of the yacht's cigars is indeed related in Lynam's chronicles!

Meerschaum pipes, made from a fine white clay (the word itself derives from the German for sea-foam) were then among the most highly regarded of smoking implements and the bowls were almost always carved or moulded into intricate and decorative shapes such as character or caricature heads of men or women, whether historical or imaginary: or of beasts of myth, legend or fact.

Good early meerschaums are sought-after by collectors: and the Captain would certainly not have been happy to lose his!

30

Hurricane Jack, Entrepreneur

Hurricane Jack clattered up the ladder from the fo'c'sle and disappeared out onto the deck of the *Vital Spark*. "Weel," said Macphail sardonically, "that's the last ye'll see of *that* five shullings."

The puffer was lying overnight at the Broomielaw where she had been spotted by the doughty Jack, who was on the last night of a brief but eventful shore leave before taking passage as able seaman on an Australia-bound wool packet: the mariner had a problem, and he had come aboard to share it with Para Handy.

Jack's problem, not unusually, was to do with money, or rather the lack of it: quite simply, his leave had outlasted his funds and his final night of freedom before a 90-day passage promised to be one to forget, rather than one to remember. Para Handy had not hesitated for one second before agreeing to fund that final spree and sent Jack ashore clutching two half-crowns. He had refused, with reluctance, Jack's pressing invitation that he should join him on the grounds that the *Vital Spark* was due to leave on the six a.m. tide. A further, overwhelming reason for refusal was that Jack now had in his pocket the Captain's entire current assets with the exception only of a handful of coppers — something which Para Handy was absolutely determined that his oldest friend should never suspect, and very unwilling that his cynical crew should ever know.

"Five shullings!" he said contemptuously, "ass if that mattered at aal. Five shullings iss nothing to Jeck!"

"It's certainly naethin' to you, noo," continued the engineer implacably, "for that's it gone for good. Yon fella has jist nae idea whatsoever o' the value o' money, nor the

213

prunciples of ownership. It's nae wonder he's never got twa pennies tae rub thegither."

"Jeck iss the sort of man that could quite easily have been a mullionaire, if he had pit his mind to it," said Para Handy with dignity and conviction: "but what you will neffer understand, Macphail, iss that there iss some chentlemen to whom money is only a minor conseederation compared wi' the sheer enchoyment of life. And it iss his life, and ensuring the happiness of his fellow human beings, that matters to Jeck. He doesna give a docken aboot money, but I can assure you that if he ever *had* cared aboot it and put his mind to it then he could have made it hand over fist.

"That wass neffer better shown than wan time when he and I wass workin' the Brodick puffer *Mingulay*. We had come doon to Loch Ryan, wi' a cargo of early Arran Pilots for Stranraer, and when we had unloaded the cairgo late on Friday efternoon, the owner sent a telegram to tell us to stay where we were till Monday as he wass negotiating a return load o' whunstane for us.

"That suited us chust fine, and we spruced up and went ashore, for neither Jeck nor I had ever been in Stranraer before, and Jeck wass always in extra good trum in a new surroundings.

"The engineer we had wi' us wass a soor-faced man — sometimes I think it's wan o' the qualifications for the chob, no offence meant Dan, and he wassna at aal interested in seeing what sort of a toon Stranraer wass, so he stayed aboard.

"The place wass hotching! There wass weekend truppers frae Gleska, folk from the country roond aboot, visiting frien's and relations in the toon, a wheen of towerists over from Ireland, and a few from England ass weel.

"The first thing Jeck noticed wass, there wassna mich provided for them in the way of entertainment. Stranraer iss no' at aal like the Clyde holiday resorts, there iss very little diversion for ony visitors — or the toon's own folk, come to that . There wass hundreds o' ladies and chentlemen and faimilies millin' aboot wi' absolutely nothing to do.

" 'That iss a sight to behold, to be sure' says Jeck: 'chust look you, Peter, at aal these folk wi' money burning a hole in their pockets and not a thing to spend it on. This toon iss no canny at aal. A man of ony sagiocity or mental agility wouldna have a problem makin' a good livin' here for he'd have nothing by way o' competition.

"Where iss the oaring-boats for hire, or the bathing-huts, or the motor-boat trups to the lighthoose, or the donkey-rides, or the day excursions up the Firth — or doon it, mebbe — or the aquariums or menageries or circuses or fairs? This toon needs a shake to itself!'

"The second thing that Jeck noticed wass a smert two-funnelled paddle-steamer tied up at the outer wall o' the harbour, quite deserted. She hadna steam up and there wassna a man to be seen moving aboot her.

" 'Now there iss someone that issna opening his eyes to a golden opportunity,' says Jeck: 'the owner o' that shup needs to tak' a tumble to himself. Here's hundreds of tow-erists and visitors chust desperate to spend their money on *something*, and here's a man wi' chust the very thing they're looking for — but instead o' preparing for an excursion programme, he has her lying here like a stranded whale.

" 'Let us see if there iss onybody at hame, and we'll can mebbe put some business his way to our own advantage, for he is badly in need of some advice and encouragement.'

"When we got to the shup we saw that her port of registration wass Belfast, and her name wass *Pride of Rathlin*. And it wass right enough, there wassna a soul on board. There wass one gangway laid from the top of the paddle-box to the quayside but it had a kind of steel gate across the bottom end of it so you couldna get on board.

" 'Strange and stranger still,' says Jeck, and we walked up past the brudge till we wass at the bow of the shup.

"And there, when we looked back, we saw a kind of a bill stuck up on the foremast, very official looking.

" 'My chove,' said Jeck, 'I've seen a few of those in my time at sea. She's been impounded!'

"I hadna a notion what he wass taalking aboot. Jeck chumped on board the shup, and beckoned on me to follow him.

"The notice wass headed WARRANT: BY ORDER OF THE SHERIFF OF DUMFRIES AND GALLOWAY in big, bleck capitals. Jeck studied the small print underneath. I couldna make heid nor tail of it.

" 'Nae wonder she's chust lying here,' said Jeck, straightening up. 'She's no' paid her Harbour Dues for months, and the port authorities hass had her poinded by the Shuriff's Officers, the owner daurna move her till he pays the dues and the fines. Man, Peter, whatna opportunity!'

" 'Opportunity for what,' I asked him.

" 'Why, to *unpound* her — unoffeecially, of course.'

" 'You canna get awa' wi' that, Jeck,' said I, 'it's against the law!'

" 'Aye we can,' said Jeck, cheerfully, 'it iss the weekend! The law's no here, apart from maybe wan toon polisman — but he iss sittin' wi' his feet up right now, and no' wantin' his Seturday disturbed or his Sabbath interrupted. The Shuriff and his men is awa' hame to their teas and they'll no' be back till Monday.

"Look at the crowds in the toon, Peter, and not a thing for them to do. Now how many tickets d'you think we could sell for a day cruise to the Isle of Man tomorrow? *Hundreds!* Bet your life on it! Now it iss going to tak' some organising, but we can do it if we set oor minds to it.'

"I sterted to protest, but you know what Jeck iss like when he gets cairried awa' wi' wan o' his schemes. He wudna listen to reason at aal. And you couldna but admire the sheer agility of the man when it cam' to gettin' the scheme moving.

"First thing he did, he went back to the *Mingulay* and woke up our Engineer, a man by the name o' MacFadyen, and telt him to go and find a blecksmith to burn aff the iron gate fixed to the gangway of the *Pride of Rathlin* and then go on board to tak' a look at her enchines and work oot how mony men he'd need wi' him to work her.

"His next caall wass at the toon printers. He had them run off a hundred posters advertising a *Grand Excursion to the Isle of Man* leaving at 9 o'clock sherp on Saturday mornin', fares of six shullings for adults, three shullings for weans, ony bairns in prams no cherge. Then he gave two young lads a half-a-crown apiece to go aal roond the toon sticking up the posters, with a special emphasis on hotels and public hooses where the visitors was maist likely to be.

"Then he foond oot which wass the biggest of the toon's bakers and which the biggest butcher, and he went and spoke to them and offered them the chance to run the dining saloons on the shup the next day, wi' chust a smaal percentage for himself as a pert of the bargain. They chumped at the chance, and long into the derkness there was a coming and going of handcarts to the shup ass the provisions wass loaded aboard her.

"Meantime Jeck had got a hold of the Stranraer Cooncil's Toon Crier and togged him up in his gear and sent him aal roond the toon wi' his handbell, bellowing the news aboot the next day's trup to the lieges.

"He even foond a wee brass band that wass playin' to the chentry in wan o' the biggest hotels in the toon, and offered them free meals and passage, and aal they could tak' when they passed the hat roond, if they would come on the trup and provide some musical entertainment for the passengers next day.

"Then he went and had a confabulation wi' the Landlord o' the Harbour Inn, and efter some discussion and a frank exchange of views, they cam' to an agreement by which the man would run the refreshment rooms on the shup wi' the help of some of the ither Stranraer publicans that he knew well enough to trust, and for the pruvilege they would pay Jeck so much for effery bottle of spirits or barrel of beer they sold.

"Last thing, he and MacFadyen the Engineer went into the public bar at the Harbour Inn and recruited the men they needed for the enchine-room and for the deck.

"Jeck and MacFadyen slept on board the steamer that night, but Jeck made me stay on board the puffer.

" 'And I'm sorry, Peter, but I am not going to allow you on the trup tomorrow neither,' he said. 'Pertly this iss for your own good, chust in case onything goes wrang, for you are a skipper and it would a real blot on your sheet if you wass to be taken to court for piracy on the high seas, or whateffer the sheriff and his gang might cry it.

" 'And pertly,' he continued, 'it iss for my own protection ass weel. What I want you to do, ass soon ass we have sailed, is to get a couple o' the longshoremen to gi'e you a hand to shuft the puffer into the berth the steamer wass in, and nail this to the mast of the *Mingulay*' — and he hand-ed me the Warrant that he'd tore doon from the paddler's mast — 'so that if onybody offeecial jalouses that there's something no' quite right and comes to mak' an investiga-tion, then you simply tell them that a frien' o' yours hass borrowed the steamer for the day — and that he wull be bringing her back that night in wan piece, with no ques-tions asked — and in the meantime the puffer iss being left ass a sort of a pledge, like in a pawnshop, for the safe return of the paddler.'

"I didna like ony of it, but you know what Jeck's like, wance he has the bit between his teeth there iss no stop-ping him, so I chust held my tongue.

"Next morning there wass a crowd ten deep on the quayside by half-past-eight, when Jeck opened up the gangway. He stood at the tap of it himsel', wi' a leather satchel that he'd managed to borrow frae a conductor with wan o' the toon's charabancs round his shouthers, and twa rolls of cloakroom tickets in his hand, blue for adults and yellow for weans, and took the money.

"Wance the shup wass full — and she wass that full they couldna have squeezed the matchstick man from Hengler's on board — Jeck headed for the brudge, cast of fore and aft, and conned her out into Loch Ryan and awa'.

"The trup wass the talk of Stranraer for weeks. The refreshment rooms did a roarin' tred, for Jeck had had a word in the ear o' the Landlord o' the Harbour Bar, and the prices wass set very reasonable indeed. 'Better sell 1,000 pints at saxpence than 500 at sevenpence' as Jeck put it, and the result wass there wass a great air of jollity aal the way to the Isle of Man and back.

"Jeck didna daur land her there, of course, for there would be too many questions asked, but she made three or four close passes o' the main pier at Douglas, Jeck oot on the brudge wing wi' his kep on three hairs, a cheery wave for aal the world and the whustle lanyard in his hand, keeping time wi' the baund, which he had playin' *Liberty Bell* in the forepeak.

"On the way back the refreshment rooms and the dining saloons wass busier than ever, and there was dancing on the promenade deck and a great sing-song going in the foresaloon.

"She docked back at Stranraer at seven o'clock that Saturday evening, but I wassna there to see it. By that time someone had gone to the polis aboot it — Jeck was aalways convinced it wass wan o' the publicans who hadna been invited into the act by the Landlord o' the Harbour Inn, and him jealous because noo Jeck had taken aal his Saturday trade awa' to the high seas.

"The local polis came roond and looked at the state of things at the pierhead, and took a good long look at the puffer and me sitting smoking on her main-hatch. He said nothin', chust shook his heid and walked away. But soon afterwards he came back wi' fower big men in dark coats and snap-brim hats, and they read something I couldna understand from a long document that wan of them held up in front of him.

"Then they came aboard the puffer and it wass made clear that if I didna go to the polis station of my own free wull then I would very quickly go the hard way.

"They arrested Jeck the moment the shup docked and the case came up furst thing Monday morning — they dinna haud back doon in Wigtonshire. In the cell Jeck had told me not to worry, he'd tell them I had chust been his dupe — I didna think that wass very flattering of him but I knew fine he meant it for the best so I didna tak' offence. And he'd have no trouble paying the fine, said he. It couldna be more than £50, and he'd taken near on £200.

"The shuriff wass the meanest-lookin chiel I'd ever come across and though I wass discherged ass 'nothing mair nor less than a fool in a rogue's clutches' ass he put it (and thenks for the kind words, I thought at the time) he threw the book at poor Jeck. He gi'ed him hiss ancestry and telt his fortune for the best pert of 30 minutes and then said: 'sentence of the court is a fine of £200 or three months imprisonment.'

"Jeck paid the fine, of course.

"As he said, money iss only money, but to give up your freedom iss to give up your heart, and to give up your heart is to cut yourself off from the happiness and friendship of the world.

"So that's wan o' the mony reasons, Dan, that I neffer begrudge Jeck anything. The man is wan o' life's leprechauns, dispensing nothing but kindness and mirth and wi'oot wan drap o' malice in him. He should be preserved ass a national monument, for he iss a credit to the human race."

FACTNOTE

Stranraer would probably vie with Campbeltown for the title of most isolated Scottish town were it not for its importance as the sea-link to Northern Ireland. Most of the goods coming from or going to that country, which used to trundle in and out of Stranraer by rail, are now transported by juggernauts for which the roads and (more basically still) the rolling landscapes of Wigtonshire and its environs were never designed.

The town stands at the head of Loch Ryan and it was from here, in Para Handy's time, that ships of the Larne and Stranraer Steamboat Company ran their services. Today

THE IRISH DIMENSION — There was, around the turn of the century, an established and comprehensive steamer service around the towns and villages of the Belfast Lough, and the MacGrory brothers visited Northern Ireland on more than one occasion. Here is the paddler Slieve Bearnagh *(Mount Bearnagh) leaving Belfast Docks. She was built on the Clyde at J and G Thomson's yard in 1894.*

there are two major roll-on, roll-off shipping terminals located on the Loch, one at Stranraer, the other at Cairnryan on its eastern shore.

More than 50 years ago the Loch was a vitally important wartime base. Its sheltered waters were home to huge squadrons of flying boats, notably the Catalinas and the larger Sunderlands which patrolled hundreds of miles out into the Atlantic to guard and protect the vast convoys of merchant ships, Britain's lifeline of hope, from the waiting U-boats whose wolf-packs lay in stealthy ambush in the Western Approaches.

Later in the war it was at Cairnryan that component sections of the 'Mulberry' floating harbour, itself crucial to the ultimate success of the D-Day landings, were constructed.

One especially poignant memory of the Stranraer to Larne service was the foundering in heavy weather off the Irish coast of the *Princess Victoria* on January 31st 1953. There was heavy loss of life in this, one of the worst-ever maritime disasters in British waters in peacetime. The ship was the fourth vessel of that name on the service: but she was also, to the time of writing at least, the last.

On the outskirts of Stranraer stands the imposing North West Castle Hotel, a popular destination for golfers and curlers (it has its own ice-rink) but once the home of the

Arctic explorer Sir John Ross. Like Parry before him and Franklin after him he was obsessed with the idea of discovering the fabled North West passage across the top of Canada to the Pacific. So was the Royal Navy, which explains why so many unsuccessful expeditions were funded out of the public purse. Ross's published account of his second voyage recounts in detail how he and his ships put in to Loch Ryan en route to the Arctic, and how he came ashore to visit home before they left.

That particular expedition sailed from Loch Ryan on June 13th 1829: it did not return to this country for more than four years coming into Stromness harbour in Orkney on October 12th 1833.

AND FINALLY — Perhaps the greatest evocation of how the sea around the coasts of Argyll was the life of our Victorian and Edwardian forebears would not be the handsome steamers, which were the investments of the wealthy: nor the more humble steam-lighters and gabbarts which were the bread-and-butter of the employed seamen: but the simple fishing skiffs, numbered in their hundreds, which were owned and crewed by families, their skills and their knowledge (like the boats themselves) handed down from generation to genera-tion. This picture of just one tiny corner of Campbeltown har-bour says that more eloquently than words could ever do.